DEATH

Agatha Ch...
the Queen ...
and books ...translated into every
major language, and her sales are calculated in tens
of millions.

She began writing at the end of the First World
War, when she created Hercule Poirot, the little
Belgian detective with the egg-shaped head and the
passion for order – the most popular sleuth in fiction
since Sherlock Holmes. Poirot, fluffy Miss Marple
and her other detectives have appeared in the films,
radio programmes and stage plays based on her
books.

Agatha Christie also wrote six romantic novels
under the pseudonym Mary Westmacott, several
plays and a book of poems; as well, she assisted her
archaeologist husband Sir Max Mallowan on many
expeditions to the Near East.

Postern of Fate was the last book she wrote before
her death in 1976, but in 1975 William Collins
published *Curtain: Poirot's Last Case*, which she
wrote in the 1940s. The last Miss Marple book (also
written in the 1940s) and her autobiography have
not yet been published.

AGATHA CHRISTIE

Death on the Nile

FONTANA/Collins

First published 1956
First issued in Fontana Books 1960
Nineteenth Impression January 1977

© Agatha Christie Ltd, 1937

Made and printed in Great Britain by
William Collins Sons & Co Ltd Glasgow

To
SYBIL BURNETT
*who also loves wandering
about the world*

Chapter One

I

'Linnet Ridgeway!'

'That's *her*!' said Mr. Burnaby, the landlord of the Three Crowns.

He nudged his companion.

The two men stared with round bucolic eyes and slightly open mouths.

A big scarlet Rolls-Royce had just stopped in front of the local post office.

A girl jumped out, a girl without a hat and wearing a frock that looked (but only *looked*) simple. A girl with golden hair and straight autocratic features—a girl with a lovely shape—a girl such as was seldom seen in Malton-under-Wode.

With a quick imperative step she passed into the post office.

'That's her!' said Mr. Burnaby again. And he went on in a low awed voice: 'Millions she's got . . . Going to spend thousands on the place. Swimming-pools there's going to be, and Italian gardens and a ballroom and half of the house pulled down and rebuilt. . . .'

'She'll bring money into the town,' said his friend. He was a lean, seedy-looking man. His tone was envious and grudging.

Mr. Burnaby agreed.

'Yes, it's a great thing for Malton-under-Wode. A great thing it is.'

Mr. Burnaby was complacent about it.

'Wake us all up proper,' he added.

'Bit of difference from Sir George,' said the other.

'Ah, it was the 'orses did for him,' said Mr. Burnaby indulgently. 'Never 'ad no luck.'

'What did he get for the place?'

'A cool sixty thousand, so I've heard.'

The lean man whistled.

Mr. Burnaby went on triumphantly: 'And they say she'll have spent another sixty thousand before she's finished!'

'Wicked!' said the lean man. 'Where'd she *get* all that money from?'

'America, so I've heard. Her mother was the only daughter of one of those millionaire blokes. Quite like the pictures, isn't it?'

The girl came out of the post office and climbed into the car.

As she drove off, the lean man followed her with his eyes. He muttered:

'It seems all wrong to me—her looking like that. Money *and* looks—it's too much! If a girl's as rich as that she's no right to be a good-looker as well. And she *is* a good-looker . . . Got everything, that girl has. Doesn't seem fair. . . .'

2

Extract from the Social column of the *Daily Blague*.

Among those supping at Chez Ma Tante I noticed beautiful Linnet Ridgeway. She was with the Hon. Joanna Southwood, Lord Windlesham and Mr. Toby Bryce. Miss Ridgeway, as everyone knows, is the daughter of Melhuish Ridgeway who married Anna Hartz. She inherits from her grandfather, Leopold Hartz, an immense fortune. The lovely Linnet is the sensation of the moment and it is rumoured that an engagement may be announced shortly. Certainly Lord Windlesham seemed very épris!!

3

The Hon. Joanna Southwood said:

'Darling, I think it's going to be all perfectly *marvellous*!'

She was sitting in Linnet Ridgeway's bedroom at Wode Hall.

From the window the eye passed over the gardens to open country with blue shadows of woodlands.

'It's rather perfect, isn't it?' said Linnet.

She leaned her arms on the window sill. Her face was eager, alive, dynamic. Beside her, Joanna Southwood seemed, somehow, a little dim—a tall thin young woman of twenty-seven, with a long clever face and freakishly plucked eyebrows.

'And you've done so much in the time! Did you have lots of architects and things?'

'Three.'

'What are architects like? I don't think I've ever seen any.'

'They were all right. I found them rather unpractical sometimes.'

'Darling, you soon put *that* right! You are the *most* practical creature!'

Joanna picked up a string of pearls from the dressing-table.

'I suppose these are real, aren't they, Linnet?'

'Of course.'

'I know it's "of course" to you, my sweet, but it wouldn't be to most people. Heavily cultured or even Woolworth! Darling, they really are *incredible*, so exquisitely matched. They must be worth the *most* fabulous sums!'

'Rather vulgar, you think?'

'No, not at all—just pure beauty. What *are* they worth?'

'About fifty thousand.'

'What a lovely lot of money! Aren't you afraid of having them stolen?'

'No, I always wear them—and anyway they're insured.'

'Let me wear them till dinner-time, will you, darling? It would give me such a thrill.'

Linnet laughed.

'Of course, if you like.'

'You know, Linnet, I really do envy you. You've simply got *everything*. Here you are at twenty, your own mistress, with any amount of money, looks, superb health. You've even got *brains*! When are you twenty-one?'

'Next June. I shall have a grand coming-of-age party in London.'

'And then are you going to marry Charles Windlesham? All the dreadful little gossip writers are getting so excited about it. And he really is frightfully devoted.'

Linnet shrugged her shoulders.

'I don't know. I don't really want to marry anyone yet.'

'Darling, how right you are! It's never quite the same afterwards, is it?'

The telephone shrilled and Linnet went to it.

'Yes? Yes?'

The butler's voice answered her:

'Miss de Bellefort is on the line. Shall I put her through?'

'Bellefort? Oh, of course, yes, put her through.'

A click and a voice, an eager, soft, slightly breathless voice: 'Hullo, is that Miss Ridgeway? *Linnet!*'

'*Jackie darling!* I haven't heard anything of you for ages and *ages*!'

'I know. It's awful. Linnet, I want to see you terribly.'

'Darling, can't you come down here? My new toy. I'd love to show it to you.'

'That's just what I want to do.'

'Well, jump into a train or a car.'

'Right, I will. A frightfully dilapidated two-seater. I bought it for fifteen pounds, and some days it goes beautifully. But it has moods. If I haven't arrived by tea-time you'll know it's had a mood. So long, my sweet.'

Linnet replaced the receiver. She crossed back to Joanna.

'That's my oldest friend, Jacqueline de Bellefort. We were together at a convent in Paris. She's had the most terrible bad luck. Her father was a French Count, her mother was American—a Southerner. The father went off with some woman, and her mother lost all her money in the Wall Street crash. Jackie was left absolutely broke. I don't know how she's managed to get along the last two years.'

Joanna was polishing her deep-blood-coloured nails with her friend's nail pad. She leant back with her head on one side scrutinising the effect.

'Darling,' she drawled, 'won't that be rather *tiresome*? If any misfortunes happen to my friends I always drop them *at once*! It sounds heartless, but it saves such a lot of trouble later! They always want to borrow money off you, or else they start a dressmaking business and you have to get the most terrible clothes from them. Or they paint lampshades, or do batik scarves.'

'So, if I lost all my money, you'd drop me to-morrow?'

'Yes, darling, I would. You can't say I'm not honest about it! I only like successful people. And you'll find that's true of nearly everybody—only most people won't admit it. They just say that really they can't put up with Mary or Emily or Pamela any more! "Her troubles have made her so *bitter* and peculiar, poor dear!"'

'How beastly you are, Joanna!'

'I'm only on the make, like everyone else.'

'*I'm* not on the make!'

'For obvious reasons! You don't have to be sordid when good-looking, middle-aged American trustees pay you over a vast allowance every quarter.'

'And you're wrong about Jacqueline,' said Linnet. 'She's

8

not a sponge. I've wanted to help her, but she won't let me. She's as proud as the devil.'

'What's she in such a hurry to see you for? I'll bet she wants something! You just wait and see.'

'She sounded excited about something,' admitted Linnet. 'Jackie always did get frightfully worked up over things. She once stuck a penknife into someone!'

'Darling, how thrilling!'

'A boy who was teasing a dog. Jackie tried to get him to stop. He wouldn't. She pulled him and shook him, but he was much stronger than she was, and at last she whipped out a penknife and plunged it right into him. There was the *most* awful row!'

'I should think so. It sounds most uncomfortable!'

Linnet's maid entered the room. With a murmured word of apology, she took down a dress from the wardrobe and went out of the room with it.

'What's the matter with Marie?' asked Joanna. 'She's been crying.'

'Poor thing! You know I told you she wanted to marry a man who has a job in Egypt. She didn't know much about him, so I thought I'd better make sure he was all right. It turned out that he had a wife already—and three children.'

'What a lot of enemies you must make, Linnet.'

'Enemies?' Linnet looked surprised.

Joanna nodded and helped herself to a cigarette.

'Enemies, my sweet. You're so devastatingly efficient. And you're so frightfully good at doing the right thing.'

Linnet laughed.

'Why, I haven't got an enemy in the world.'

4

Lord Windlesham sat under the cedar tree. His eyes rested on the graceful proportions of Wode Hall. There was nothing to mar its old-world beauty; the new buildings and additions were out of sight round the corner. It was a fair and peaceful sight bathed in the autumn sunshine. Nevertheless, as he gazed, it was no longer Wode Hall that Charles Windlesham saw. Instead, he seemed to see a more imposing Elizabethan mansion, a long sweep of park, a more bleak background. . . . It was his own family seat, Charltonbury, and in the foreground stood a figure—a girl's figure, with bright golden hair and an eager confident face . . . Linnet as mistress of Charltonbury!

He felt very hopeful. That refusal of hers had not been at all a definite refusal. It had been little more than a plea for time. Well, he could afford to wait a little. . . .

How amazingly suitable the whole thing was! It was certainly advisable that he should marry money, but not such a matter of necessity that he could regard himself as forced to put his own feelings on one side. And he loved Linnet. He would have wanted to marry her even if she had been practically penniless, instead of one of the richest girls in England. Only, fortunately, she *was* one of the richest girls in England. . . .

His mind played with attractive plans for the future. The Mastership of the Roxdale perhaps, the restoration of the west wing, no need to let the Scotch shooting. . . .

Charles Windlesham dreamed in the sun.

5

It was four o'clock when the dilapidated little two-seater stopped with a sound of crunching gravel. A girl got out of it—a small slender creature with a mop of dark hair. She ran up the steps and tugged at the bell.

A few minutes later she was being ushered into the long stately drawing-room, and an ecclesiastical butler was saying with the proper mournful intonation: 'Miss de Bellefort.'

'Linnet!'

'Jackie!'

Windlesham stood a little aside, watching sympathetically as this fiery little creature flung herself open-armed upon Linnet.

'Lord Windlesham—Miss de Bellefort—my best friend.'

A pretty child, he thought—not really pretty but decidedly attractive, with her dark curly hair and her enormous eyes. He murmured a few tactful nothings and then managed unobtrusively to leave the two friends together.

Jacqueline pounced—in a fashion that Linnet remembered as being characteristic of her.

'Windlesham? Windlesham? *That's* the man the papers always say you're going to marry! Are you, Linnet? *Are* you?'

Linnet murmured: 'Perhaps.'

'Darling—I'm so glad! He looks nice.'

'Oh, don't make up your mind about it—I haven't made up my own mind yet.'

'Of course not! Queens always proceed with due deliberation to the choosing of a consort!'

'Don't be ridiculous, Jackie.'

'But you *are* a queen, Linnet! You always were. *Sa Majesté, la reine Linette. Linette la blonde!* And I—I'm the Queen's confidante! The trusted Maid of Honour.'

'What nonsense you talk, Jackie darling! Where have you been all this time? You just disappear. And you never write.'

'I hate writing letters. Where have I been? Oh, about three parts submerged, darling. In JOBS, you know. Grim jobs with grim women!'

'Darling, I wish you'd——'

'Take the Queen's bounty? Well, frankly, darling, that's what I'm here for. No, not to borrow money. It's not got to that yet! But I've come to ask a great big important favour!'

'Go on.'

'If you're going to marry the Windlesham man, you'll understand, perhaps.'

Linnet looked puzzled for a minute; then her face cleared.

'Jackie, do you mean——?'

'Yes, darling, *I'm engaged*!'

'So that's it! I thought you were looking particularly alive somehow. You always do, of course, but even more than usual.'

'That's just what I feel like.'

'Tell me all about him.'

'His name's Simon Doyle. He's big and square and incredibly simple and boyish and utterly adorable! He's poor—got no money. He's what you call "county" all right—but very impoverished county—a younger son and all that. His people come from Devonshire. He loves country and country things. And for the last five years he's been in the City in a stuffy office. And now they're cutting down and he's out of a job. Linnet, I shall *die* if I can't marry him! I shall die! I shall die! I shall *die*. . . .'

'Don't be ridiculous, Jackie.'

'I shall die, I tell you! I'm crazy about him. He's crazy about me. We can't live without each other.'

'Darling, you *have* got it badly!'

'I know. It's awful, isn't it? This love business gets hold of you and you can't do anything about it.'

She paused for a minute. Her dark eyes dilated, looked suddenly tragic. She gave a little shiver.

'It's—even frightening sometimes! Simon and I were made for each other. I shall never care for anyone else. And *you've* got to help us, Linnet. I heard you'd bought this place and it put an idea into my head. Listen, you'll have to have a land agent—perhaps two. I want you to give the job to Simon.'

'Oh!' Linnet was startled.

Jacqueline rushed on: 'He's got all that sort of thing at his fingertips. He knows all about estates—was brought up on one. And he's got his business training too. Oh, Linnet, you will give him a job, won't you, for love of me? If he doesn't make good, sack him. But he will. And we can live in a little house, and I shall see lots of you, and everything in the garden will be too, too divine.'

She got up.

'Say you will, Linnet. Say you will. Beautiful Linnet! Tall golden Linnet! My own very special Linnet! Say you will!'

'Jackie——'

'You will?'

Linnet burst out laughing.

'Ridiculous Jackie! Bring along your young man and let me have a look at him and we'll talk it over.'

Jackie darted at her, kissing her exuberantly.

'*Darling Linnet*—you're a real friend! I knew you were. You wouldn't let me down—ever. You're just the loveliest thing in the world. Good-bye.'

'But, Jackie, you're *staying*.'

'Me? No, I'm not. I'm going back to London, and to-morrow I'll come back and bring Simon and we'll settle it all up. You'll adore him. He really is a *pet*.'

'But can't you wait and just have tea?'

'No, I can't wait, Linnet. I'm too excited. I must get back and tell Simon. I know I'm mad, darling, but I can't help it. Marriage will cure me, I expect. It always seems to have a very sobering effect on people.'

She turned at the door, stood a moment, then rushed back for a last quick birdlike embrace.

'Dear Linnet—there's no one like you.'

M. Gaston Blondin, the proprietor of that modish little restaurant Chez Ma Tante, was not a man who delighted to honour many of his clientèle. The rich, the beautiful, the notorious, and the well-born might wait in vain to be singled out and paid special attention. Only in the rarest cases did M. Blondin, with gracious condescension, greet a guest, accompany him to a privileged table, and exchange with him suitable and apposite remarks.

On this particular night, M. Blondin had exercised his royal prerogative three times—once for a Duchess, once for a famous racing peer, and once for a little man of comical appearance with immense black moustaches, who, a casual onlooker would have thought, could bestow no favour on Chez Ma Tante by his presence there.

M. Blondin, however, was positively fulsome in his attentions. Though clients had been told for the last half hour that a table was not to be had, one now mysteriously appeared, placed in a most favourable position. M. Blondin conducted the client to it with every appearance of *empressement*.

'But naturally, for *you* there is *always* a table, Monsieur Poirot! How I wish that you would honour us oftener!'

Hercule Poirot smiled, remembering that past incident wherein a dead body, a waiter, M. Blondin, and a very lovely lady had played a part.

'You are too amiable, Monsieur Blondin,' he said.

'And you are alone, Monsieur Poirot?'

'Yes, I am alone.'

'Oh, well, Jules here will compose for you a little meal that will be a poem—positively a poem! Women, however charming, have this disadvantage: they distract the mind from food! You will enjoy your dinner, Monsieur Poirot; I promise you that. Now as to wine——'

A technical conversation ensued, Jules, the *maître d'hôtel*, assisting.

Before departing, M. Blondin lingered a moment, lowering his voice confidentially.

'You have grave affairs on hand?'

Poirot shook his head.

'I am, alas, a man of leisure,' he said softly. 'I have made the economies in my time and I have now the means to enjoy a life of idleness.'

'I envy you.'

'No, no, you would be unwise to do so. I can assure you, it is not so gay as it sounds.' He sighed. 'How true is the saying that man was forced to invent work in order to escape the strain of having to think.'

M. Blondin threw up his hands.

'But there is so much! There is travel!'

'Yes, there is travel. Already I have not done so badly. This winter I shall visit Egypt, I think. The climate, they say, is superb! One will escape from the fogs, the greyness, the monotony of the constantly falling rain.'

'Ah! Egypt,' breathed M. Blondin.

'One can even voyage there now, I believe, by train, escaping all sea travel except the Channel.'

'Ah, the sea, it does not agree with you?'

Hercule Poirot shook his head and shuddered slightly.

'I, too,' said M. Blondin with sympathy. 'Curious the effect it has upon the stomach.'

'But only upon certain stomachs! There are people on whom the motion makes no impression whatever. They actually *enjoy* it!'

'An unfairness of the good God,' said M. Blondin.

He shook his head sadly, and, brooding on the impious thought, withdrew.

Smooth-footed, deft-handed waiters ministered to the table. Toast Melba, butter, an ice pail, all the adjuncts to a meal of quality.

The Negro orchestra broke into an ecstasy of strange discordant noises. London danced.

Hercule Poirot looked on, registered impressions in his neat orderly mind.

How bored and weary most of the faces were! Some of those stout men, however, were enjoying themselves . . . whereas a patient endurance seemed to be the sentiment exhibited on their partners' faces. The fat woman in purple was looking radiant. . . . Undoubtedly the fat had certain compensations in life . . . a zest—a gusto—denied to those of more fashionable contours.

A good sprinkling of young people—some vacant-looking —some bored—some definitely unhappy. How absurd to call youth the time of happiness—youth, the time of greatest vulnerability!

His glance softened as it rested on one particular couple. A well-matched pair—tall broad-shouldered man, slender delicate girl. Two bodies that moved in a perfect rhythm of happiness. Happiness in the place, the hour, and in each other.

The dance stopped abruptly. Hands clapped and it started again. After a second *encore* the couple returned to their table close by Poirot. The girl was flushed, laughing. As she sat, he could study her face, lifted laughing to her companion.

There was something else beside laughter in her eyes. Hercule Poirot shook his head doubtfully.

'She cares too much, that little one,' he said to himself. 'It is not safe. No, it is not safe.'

And then a word caught his ear, 'Egypt.'

Their voices came to him clearly—the girl's young, fresh, arrogant, with just a trace of soft-sounding foreign R's, and the man's pleasant, low-toned, well-bred English.

'I'm *not* counting my chickens before they're hatched, Simon. I tell you Linnet won't let us down!'

'*I* might let *her* down.'

'Nonsense—it's just the right job for you.'

'As a matter of fact I think it is. . . . I haven't really any doubts as to my capability. And I mean to make good—for *your* sake!'

The girl laughed softly, a laugh of pure happiness.

'We'll wait three months—to make sure you don't get the sack—and then——'

'And then I'll endow thee with my worldly goods—that's the hang of it, isn't it?'

'And, as I say, we'll go to Egypt for our honeymoon. Damn the expense! I've always wanted to go to Egypt all my life. The Nile and the Pyramids and the sand . . .'

He said, his voice slightly indistinct: 'We'll see it together, Jackie . . . together. Won't it be marvellous?'

'I wonder. Will it be as marvellous to you as it is to me? Do you really care—as much as I do?'

Her voice was suddenly sharp—her eyes dilated—almost with fear.

The man's answer came quickly crisp: 'Don't be absurd, Jackie.'

But the girl repeated: 'I wonder . . .'

Then she shrugged her shoulders. 'Let's dance.'

Hercule Poirot murmured to himself:

'*Une qui aime et un qui se laisse aimer.* Yes, I wonder too.'

Joanna Southwood said: 'And suppose he's a terrible tough?'

Linnet shook her head. 'Oh, he won't be. I can trust Jacqueline's taste.'

Joanna murmured: 'Ah, but people don't run true to form in love affairs.'

Linnet shook her head impatiently. Then she changed the subject.

'I must go and see Mr. Pierce about those plans.'

'Plans?'

'Yes, some dreadful insanitary old cottages. I'm having them pulled down and the people moved.'

'How sanitary and public-spirited of you, darling!'

'They'd have had to go anyway. Those cottages would have overlooked my new swimming pool.'

'Do the people who live in them like going?'

'Most of them are delighted. One or two are being rather stupid about it—really tiresome in fact. They don't seem to realise how vastly improved their living conditions will be!'

'But you're being quite high-handed about it, I presume.'

'My dear Joanna, it's to their advantage really.'

'Yes, dear. I'm sure it is. Compulsory benefit.'

Linnet frowned. Joanna laughed.

'Come now, you *are* a tyrant, admit it. A beneficent tyrant if you like!'

'I'm not the least bit of a tyrant.'

'But you like your own way!'

'Not especially.'

'Linnet Ridgeway, can you look me in the face and tell me of *any one occasion* on which you've failed to do exactly as you wanted?'

'Heaps of times.'

'Oh, yes, "heaps of times"—just like that—but no concrete example. And you simply can't think up one, darling, however hard you try! The triumphal progress of Linnet Ridgeway in her golden car.'

Linnet said sharply: 'You think I'm selfish?'

'No—just irresistible. The combined effect of money and charm. Everything goes down before you. What you can't buy with cash you buy with a smile. Result: Linnet Ridge-way, the Girl Who Has Everything.'

'Don't be ridiculous, Joanna!'

'Well, haven't you got everything?'

'I suppose I have. . . . It sounds rather disgusting, some-how!'

'Of course it's disgusting, darling! You'll probably get terribly bored and blasé by and by. In the meantime, enjoy the triumphal progress in the golden car. Only I wonder, I really do wonder, what will happen when you want to go down a street which has a board up saying "No Thorough-fare".'

'Don't be idiotic, Joanna.' As Lord Windlesham joined them, Linnet said, turning to him: 'Joanna is saying the nastiest things to me.'

'All spite, darling, all spite,' said Joanna vaguely as she got up from her seat.

She made no apology for leaving them. She had caught the glint in Windlesham's eye.

He was silent for a minute or two. Then he went straight to the point.

'Have you come to a decision, Linnet?'

Linnet said slowly: 'Am I being a brute? I suppose, if I'm not sure, I ought to say "No"——'

He interrupted her:

'Don't say it. You shall have time—as much time as you want. But I think, you know, we should be happy together.'

'You see,' Linnet's tone was apologetic, almost childish, 'I'm enjoying myself so much—especially with all this.' She waved a hand. 'I wanted to make Wode Hall into my real ideal of a country house, and I do think I've got it nice, don't you?'

'It's beautiful. Beautifully planned. Everything perfect. You're very clever, Linnet.'

He paused a minute and went on: 'And you like Charlton-bury, don't you? Of course it wants modernising and all that—but you're so clever at that sort of thing. You enjoy it.'

'Why, of course, Charltonbury's divine.'

She spoke with ready enthusiasm, but inwardly she was conscious of a sudden chill. An alien note had sounded, dis-turbing her complete satisfaction with life. She did not analyse the feeling at the moment, but later, when Windlesham had left her, she tried to probe the recesses of her mind.

Charltonbury—yes, that was it—she had resented the mention of Charltonbury. But why? Charltonbury was modestly famous. Windlesham's ancestors had held it since the time of Elizabeth. To be mistress of Charltonbury was a position unsurpassed in society. Windlesham was one of the most desirable peers in England.

Naturally he couldn't take Wode seriously. . . . It was not in any way to be compared with Charltonbury.

Ah, but Wode was *hers*! She had seen it, acquired it, rebuilt and re-dressed it, lavished money on it. It was her own possession—her kingdom.

But in a sense it wouldn't count if she married Windlesham. What would they want with two country places? And of the two, naturally Wode Hall would be the one to be given up.

She, Linnet Ridgeway, wouldn't exist any longer. She would be Countess of Windlesham, bringing a fine dowry to Charltonbury and its master. She would be queen consort, not queen any longer.

'I'm being ridiculous,' said Linnet to herself.

But it was curious how she did hate the idea of abandoning Wode. . . .

And wasn't there something else nagging at her?

Jackie's voice with that queer blurred note in it saying: 'I shall *die* if I can't marry him! I shall die. I shall die . . .'

So positive, so earnest. Did she, Linnet, feel like that about Windlesham? Assuredly she didn't. Perhaps she could never feel like that about anyone. It must be—rather wonderful—to feel like that. . . .

The sound of a car came through the open window.

Linnet shook herself impatiently. That must be Jackie and her young man. She'd go out and meet them.

She was standing in the open doorway as Jacqueline and Simon Doyle got out of the car.

'Linnet!' Jackie ran to her. 'This is Simon. Simon, here's Linnet. She's just the most wonderful person in the world.'

Linnet saw a tall, broad-shouldered young man, with very dark blue eyes, crisply curling brown hair, a square chin, and a boyish, appealing, simple smile. . . .

She stretched out a hand. The hand that clasped hers was firm and warm. . . . She liked the way he looked at her, the naïve genuine admiration.

Jackie had told him she was wonderful, and he clearly thought that she was wonderful. . . .

A warm sweet feeling of intoxication ran through her veins.

'Isn't this all lovely?' she said. 'Come in, Simon, and let me welcome my new land agent properly.'

And as she turned to lead the way she thought: 'I'm frightfully—frightfully happy. I like Jackie's young man . . . I like him enormously. . . .'

And then with a sudden pang: 'Lucky Jackie. . . .'

8

Tim Allerton leant back in his wicker chair and yawned as he looked out over the sea. He shot a quick sidelong glance at his mother.

Mrs. Allerton was a good-looking, white-haired woman of fifty. By imparting an expression of pinched severity to her mouth every time she looked at her son, she sought to disguise the fact of her intense affection for him. Even total strangers were seldom deceived by this device and Tim himself saw through it perfectly.

He said: 'Do you really like Majorca, Mother?'

'Well,' Mrs. Allerton considered, 'it's cheap.'

'And cold,' said Tim with a slight shiver.

He was a tall, thin young man, with dark hair and a rather narrow chest. His mouth had a very sweet expression: his eyes were sad and his chin was indecisive. He had long delicate hands.

Threatened by consumption some years ago, he had never displayed a really robust physique. He was popularly supposed 'to write,' but it was understood among his friends that inquiries as to literary output were not encouraged.

'What are you thinking of, Tim?'

Mrs. Allerton was alert. Her bright, dark-brown eyes looked suspicious.

Tim Allerton grinned at her:

'I was thinking of Egypt.'

'Egypt?' Mrs. Allerton sounded doubtful.

'Real warmth, darling. Lazy golden sands. The Nile. I'd like to go up the Nile, wouldn't you?'

'Oh, I'd *like* it.' Her tone was dry. 'But Egypt's expensive, my dear. Not for those who have to count the pennies.'

Tim laughed. He rose, stretched himself. Suddenly he looked alive and eager. There was an excited note in his voice.

'The expense will be my affair. Yes, darling. A little flutter on the Stock Exchange. With thoroughly satisfactory results. I heard this morning.'

'This morning?' said Mrs. Allerton sharply. 'You only had one letter and that——'

She stopped and bit her lip.

Tim looked momentarily undecided whether to be amused or annoyed. Amusement gained the day.

'And that was from Joanna,' he finished coolly. 'Quite right, Mother. What a queen of detectives you'd make! The famous Hercule Poirot would have to look to his laurels if you were about.'

Mrs. Allerton looked rather cross.

'I just happened to see the handwriting——'

'And knew it wasn't that of a stockbroker? Quite right. As a matter of fact it was yesterday I heard from them. Poor Joanna's handwriting *is* rather noticeable—sprawls about all over the envelope like an inebriated spider.'

'What does Joanna say? Any news?'

Mrs. Allerton strove to make her voice sound casual and ordinary. The friendship between her son and his second cousin, Joanna Southwood, always irritated her. Not, as she put it to herself, that there was 'anything in it.' She was quite sure there wasn't. Tim had never manifested a sentimental interest in Joanna, nor she in him. Their mutual attraction seemed to be founded on gossip and the possession of a large number of friends and acquaintances in common. They both liked people and discussing people. Joanna had an amusing if caustic tongue.

It was not because Mrs. Allerton feared that Tim might fall in love with Joanna that she found herself always becoming a little stiff in manner if Joanna were present or when letters from her arrived.

It was some other feeling hard to define—perhaps an unacknowledged jealousy in the unfeigned pleasure Tim always seemed to take in Joanna's society. He and his mother were such perfect companions that the sight of him absorbed and interested in another woman always startled Mrs. Allerton slightly. She fancied, too, that her own presence on these occasions set some barrier between the two members of the younger generation. Often she had come upon them eagerly absorbed in some conversation and, at sight of her, their talk had wavered, had seemed to include her rather too purposefully and as if duty bound. Quite definitely, Mrs. Allerton did not like Joanna Southwood. She thought her insincere, affected, and essentially superficial. She found it very hard to prevent herself saying so in unmeasured tones.

In answer to her question, Tim pulled the letter out of his pocket and glanced through it. It was quite a long letter, his mother noted.

'Nothing much,' he said. 'The Devenishes are getting a divorce. Old Monty's been had up for being drunk in charge of a car. Windlesham's gone to Canada. Seems he was pretty badly hit when Linnet Ridgeway turned him down. She's definitely going to marry this land agent person.'

'How extraordinary! Is he very dreadful?'

'No, no, not at all. He's one of the Devonshire Doyles. No money, of course—and he was actually engaged to one of Linnet's best friends. Pretty thick, that.'

'I don't think it's at all nice,' said Mrs. Allerton, flushing.

Tim flashed her a quick affectionate glance.

'I know, darling. You don't approve of snaffling other people's husbands and all that sort of thing.'

'In my day we had our standards,' said Mrs. Allerton. 'And a very good thing too! Nowadays young people seem to think they can just go about doing anything they choose.'

Tim smiled. 'They don't only think it. They do it. *Vide* Linnet Ridgeway!'

'Well, I think it's horrid!'

Tim twinkled at her.

'Cheer up, you old die-hard! Perhaps I agree with you. Anyway, *I* haven't helped myself to anyone's wife or fiancée yet.'

'I'm sure you'd never do such a thing,' said Mrs. Allerton. She added with spirit, 'I've brought you up properly.'

'So the credit is yours, not mine.'

He smiled teasingly at her as he folded the letter and put it away again. Mrs. Allerton let the thought just flash across her mind: 'Most letters he shows to me. He only reads me snippets from Joanna's.'

But she put the unworthy thought away from her, and decided, as ever, to behave like a gentlewoman.

'Is Joanna enjoying life?' she asked.

'So so. Says she thinks of opening a delicatessen shop in Mayfair.'

'She always talks about being hard up,' said Mrs. Allerton with a tinge of spite, 'but she goes about everywhere and her clothes must cost her a lot. She's always beautifully dressed.'

'Ah, well,' said Tim, 'she probably doesn't pay for them. No, Mother, I don't mean what your Edwardian mind suggests to you. I just mean quite literally that she leaves her bills unpaid.'

Mrs. Allerton sighed.

'I never know how people manage to do that.'

'It's a kind of special gift,' said Tim. 'If only you have sufficient extravagant tastes, and absolutely no sense of money values, people will give you any amount of credit.'

'Yes, but you come to the Bankruptcy Court in the end like poor Sir George Wode.'

'You have a soft spot for that old horse coper—probably because he called you a rosebud in eighteen seventy-nine at a dance.'

'I wasn't born in eighteen seventy-nine,' Mrs. Allerton retorted with spirit. 'Sir George has charming manners, and I won't have you calling him a horse coper.'

'I've heard funny stories about him from people that know.'

'You and Joanna don't mind what you say about people; anything will do so long as it's sufficiently ill-natured.'

Tim raised his eyebrows.

'My dear, you're quite heated. I didn't know old Wode was such a favourite of yours.'

'You don't realise how hard it was for him, having to sell Wode Hall. He cared terribly about that place.'

Tim suppressed the easy retort. After all, who was he to judge? Instead he said thoughtfully:

'You know, I think you're not far wrong there. Linnet asked him to come down and see what she'd done to the place, and he refused quite rudely.'

'Of course. She ought to have known better than to ask him.'

'And I believe he's quite venomous about her—mutters things under his breath whenever he sees her. Can't forgive her for having given him an absolutely top price for the worm-eaten family estate.'

'And you can't understand that?' Mrs. Allerton spoke sharply.

'Frankly,' said Tim calmly, 'I can't. Why live in the past? Why cling on to things that have been?'

'What are you going to put in their place?'

He shrugged his shoulders. 'Excitement, perhaps. Novelty. The joy of never knowing what may turn up from day to day. Instead of inheriting a useless tract of land, the pleasure of making money for yourself—by your own brains and skill.'

'A successful deal on the Stock Exchange, in fact!'

He laughed. 'Why not?'

'And what about an equal *loss* on the Stock Exchange?'

'That, dear, is rather tactless. And quite inappropriate to-day. . . . What about this Egypt plan?'

'Well——'

He cut in, smiling at her: 'That's settled. We've both always wanted to see Egypt.'

'When do you suggest?'

'Oh, next month. January's about the best time there. We'll enjoy the delightful society in this hotel a few weeks longer.'

'Tim,' said Mrs Allerton reproachfully. Then she added guiltily: 'I'm afraid I promised Mrs. Leech that you'd go with her to the police station. She doesn't understand any Spanish.'

Tim made a grimace.

'About her ring? The blood-red ruby of the horse-leech's daughter? Does she still persist in thinking it's been stolen? I'll go if you like, but it's a waste of time. She'll only get some wretched chambermaid into trouble. I distinctly saw it on her finger when she went into the sea that day. It came off in the water and she never noticed.'

'She says she is quite sure she took it off and left it on her dressing-table.'

'Well, she didn't. I saw it with my own eyes. The woman's a fool. Any woman's a fool who goes prancing into the sea in December, pretending the water's quite warm just because the sun happens to be shining rather brightly at the moment. Stout women oughtn't to be allowed to bathe anyway; they look so revolting in bathing dresses.'

Mrs. Allerton murmured, 'I really feel I ought to give up bathing.'

Tim gave a shout of laughter.

'You? You can give most of the young things points and to spare.'

Mrs. Allerton sighed and said, 'I wish there were a few more young people for you here.'

Tim Allerton shook his head decidedly.

'I don't. You and I get along rather comfortably without outside distractions.'

'You'd like it if Joanna were here.'

'I wouldn't.' His tone was unexpectedly resolute. 'You're all wrong there. Joanna amuses me, but I don't really like her, and to have her around much gets on my nerves. I'm thankful she isn't here. I should be quite resigned if I were never to see Joanna again.'

He added, almost below his breath, 'There's only one woman in the world I've got a real respect and admiration for, and I think, Mrs. Allerton, you know very well who that woman is.'

His mother blushed and looked quite confused.

Tim said gravely: 'There aren't very many really nice women in the world. You happen to be one of them.'

9

In an apartment overlooking Central Park in New York, Mrs. Robson exclaimed: 'If that isn't just too lovely! You really are the luckiest girl, Cornelia.'

Cornelia Robson flushed responsively. She was a big clumsy-looking girl with brown doglike eyes.

'Oh, it will be wonderful!' she gasped.

Old Miss Van Schuyler inclined her head in a satisfied fashion at this correct attitude on the part of poor relations. 'I've always dreamed of a trip to Europe,' sighed Cornelia, 'but I just didn't feel I'd ever get there.'

'Miss Bowers will come with me as usual, of course,' said Miss Van Schuyler, 'but as a social companion I find her limited—very limited. There are many little things that Cornelia can do for me.'

'I'd just love to, Cousin Marie,' said Cornelia eagerly.

'Well, well, then that's settled,' said Miss Van Schuyler. 'Just run and find Miss Bowers, my dear. It's time for my egg-nog.'

Cornelia departed. Her mother said: 'My dear Marie, I'm really *most* grateful to you! You know I think Cornelia suffers a lot from not being a social success. It makes her feel kind of mortified. If I could afford to take her to places —but you know how it's been since Ned died.'

'I'm very glad to take her,' said Miss Van Schuyler. 'Cornelia has always been a nice handy girl, willing to run errands, and not so selfish as some of these young people nowadays.'

Mrs. Robson rose and kissed her rich relative's wrinkled and slightly yellow face.

'I'm just ever so grateful,' she declared.

On the stairs she met a tall capable-looking woman who was carrying a glass containing a yellow foamy liquid.

'Well, Miss Bowers, so you're off to Europe?'

'Why, yes, Mrs. Robson.'

'What a lovely trip!'

'Why, yes, I should think it would be very enjoyable.'

'But you've been abroad before?'

'Oh, yes, Mrs. Robson. I went over to Paris with Miss Van Schuyler last fall. But I've never been to Egypt before.'

Mrs. Robson hesitated.

'I do hope—there won't be any—trouble.'

She had lowered her voice. Miss Bowers, however, replied in her usual tone:

'Oh, *no*, Mrs. Robson; I shall take good care of *that*. I keep a very sharp look-out always.'

But there was still a faint shadow on Mrs. Robson's face as she slowly continued down the stairs.

10

In his office down town Mr. Andrew Pennington was opening his personal mail. Suddenly his fist clenched itself and came down on his desk with a bang; his face crimsoned and two big veins stood out on his forehead. He pressed a buzzer on his desk and a smart-looking stenographer appeared with commendable promptitude.

'Tell Mr. Rockford to step in here?'

'Yes, Mr. Pennington.'

A few minutes later, Sterndale Rockford, Pennington's partner, entered the office. The two men were not unlike—both tall, spare, with greying hair and clean-shaven, clever faces.

'What's up, Pennington?'

Pennington looked up from the letter he was re-reading. He said. 'Linnet's married . . .'

'*What?*'

'You heard what I said! Linnet Ridgeway's *married*!'

'How? When? Why didn't we hear about it?'

Pennington glanced at the calendar on his desk.

'She wasn't married when she wrote this letter, but she's married now. Morning of the fourth. That's to-day.'

Rockford dropped into a chair.

'Whew! No warning! Nothing? Who's the man?'

Pennington referred again to the letter.

'Doyle. Simon Doyle.'

'What sort of a fellow is he? Ever heard of him?'

'No. She doesn't say much. . . .' He scanned the lines of clear, upright handwriting. 'Got an idea there's something hole-and-corner about the business . . . That doesn't matter. The whole point is, she's married.'

The eyes of the two men met. Rockford nodded.

'This needs a bit of thinking out,' he said quietly.

'What are we going to do about it?'

'I'm asking you.'

The two men sat silent. Then Rockford asked. 'Got any plan?'

Pennington said slowly: 'The *Normandie* sails to-day. One of us could just make it.'

'You're crazy! What's the big idea?'

Pennington began: 'Those British lawyers——' and stopped.

'What about 'em. Surely you're not going over to tackle 'em? You're mad!'

'I'm not suggesting that you—or I—should go to England.'

'What's the big idea, then?'

Pennington smoothed out the letter on the table.

'Linnet's going to Egypt for her honeymoon. Expects to be there a month or more. . . .'

'Egypt—eh?'

Rockford considered. Then he looked up and met the other's glance.

'Egypt,' he said; '*that's* your idea!'

'Yes—a chance meeting. Over on a trip. Linnet and her husband—honeymoon atmosphere. It might be done.'

Rockford said doubtfully: 'She's sharp, Linnet is . . . but ——'

Pennington went on softly: 'I think there might be ways of—managing it.'

Again their eyes met. Rockford nodded.

'All right, big boy.'

Pennington looked at the clock.

'We'll have to hustle—whichever of us is going.'

'You go,' said Rockford promptly. 'You always made a hit with Linnet. "Uncle Andrew." That's the ticket!'

Pennington's face had hardened. He said: 'I hope I can pull it off.'

'You've got to pull it off,' his partner said. 'The situation's critical. . . .'

II

William Carmichael said to the thin, weedy youth who opened the door inquiringly: 'Send Mr. Jim to me, please.'

Jim Fanthorp entered the room and looked inquiringly at his uncle. The older man looked up with a nod and a grunt.

'Humph, there you are.'

'You asked for me?'

'Just cast an eye over this.'

The young man sat down and drew the sheaf of papers towards him. The elder man watched him.

'Well?'

The answer came promptly. 'Looks fishy to me, sir.'

Again the senior partner of Carmichael, Grant & Carmichael uttered his characteristic grunt.

Jim Fanthorp re-read the letter which had just arrived by air mail from Egypt:

. . . It seems wicked to be writing business letters on such a day. We have spent a week at Mena House and made an expedition to the Fayum. The day after tomorrow we are going up the Nile to Luxor and Assuan by steamer, and perhaps on to Khartoum. When we went into Cook's this morning to see about our tickets who do you think was the first person I saw?—my American trustee, Andrew Pennington. I think you met him two years ago when he was over. I had no idea he was in Egypt and he had no idea that I was! Nor that I was married! My letter, telling him of my marriage, must just have missed him. He is actually going up the Nile on the same trip that we are. Isn't it a coincidence? Thank you so much for all you have done in this busy time. I——

As the young man was about to turn the page, Mr. Carmichael took the letter from him.

'That's all,' he said. 'The rest doesn't matter. Well, what do you think?'

His nephew considered for a moment—then he said:

27

'Well—I think—not a coincidence. . . .'

The other nodded approval.

'Like a trip to Egypt?' he barked out.

'You think that's advisable?'

'I think there's no time to lose.'

'But, why me?'

'Use your brains, boy; use your brains. Linnet Ridgeway has never met you; no more has Pennington. If you go by air you may get there in time.'

'I—I don't like it, sir. What am I to do?'

'Use your eyes. Use your ears. Use your brains—if you've got any. And, if necessary—act.'

'I—I don't like it.'

'Perhaps not—but you've got to do it.'

'It's—necessary?'

'In my opinion,' said Mr. Carmichael, 'it's absolutely vital.'

12

Mrs. Otterbourne, readjusting the turban of native material that she wore draped round her head, said fretfully:

'I really don't see why we shouldn't go on to Egypt. I'm sick and tired of Jerusalem.'

As her daughter made no reply, she said, 'You might at least answer when you're spoken to.'

Rosalie Otterbourne was looking at a newspaper reproduction of a face. Below it was printed:

Mrs. Simon Doyle, who before her marriage was the well-known society beauty, Miss Linnet Ridgeway. Mr. and Mrs. Doyle are spending their holiday in Egypt.

Rosalie said, 'You'd like to move on to Egypt, Mother?'

'Yes, I would,' Mrs. Otterbourne snapped. 'I consider they've treated us in a most cavalier fashion here. My being here is an advertisement—I ought to get a special reduction in terms. When I hinted as much, I consider they were most impertinent—*most* impertinent. I told them exactly what I thought of them.'

The girl sighed. She said: 'One place is very like another. I wish we could get right away.'

'And this morning,' went on Mrs. Otterbourne, 'the manager actually had the impertinence to tell me that all the rooms had been booked in advance and that he would require ours in two days' time.'

'So we've got to go somewhere.'

'Not at all. I'm quite prepared to fight for my rights.'

Rosalie murmured: 'I suppose we might as well go on to Egypt. It doesn't make any difference.'

'It's certainly not a matter of life or death,' agreed Mrs. Otterbourne.

But there she was quite wrong—for a matter of life and death was exactly what it was.

Chapter Two

'That's Hercule Poirot, the detective,' said Mrs. Allerton.

She and her son were sitting in brightly painted scarlet basket chairs outside the Cataract Hotel at Assuan. They were watching the retreating figures of two people—a short man dressed in a white silk suit and a tall slim girl.

Tim Allerton sat up in an unusually alert fashion.

'That funny little man?' he asked incredulously.

'That funny little man!'

'What on earth's he doing out here?' Tim asked.

His mother laughed. 'Darling, you sound quite excited. Why do men enjoy crime so much? I hate detective stories and never read them. But I don't think Monsieur Poirot is here with any ulterior motive. He's made a good deal of money and he's seeing life, I fancy.'

'Seems to have an eye for the best-looking girl in the place.'

Mrs. Allerton tilted her head a little on one side as she considered the retreating backs of M. Poirot and his companion.

The girl by his side overtopped him by some three inches. She walked well, neither stiffly nor slouchingly.

'I suppose she *is* quite good-looking,' said Mrs. Allerton. She shot a little glance sideways at Tim. Somewhat to her amusement the fish rose at once.

'She's more than quite. Pity she looks so bad-tempered and sulky.'

'Perhaps that's just expression, dear.'

'Unpleasant young devil, I think. But she's pretty enough.'

The subject of these remarks was walking slowly by Poirot's side. Rosalie Otterbourne was twirling an unopened parasol, and

29

her expression certainly bore out what Tim had just said. She looked both sulky and bad-tempered. Her eyebrows were drawn together in a frown, and the scarlet line of her mouth was drawn downward.

They turned to the left out of the hotel gate and entered the cool shade of the public gardens.

Hercule Poirot was prattling gently, his expression that of beatific good humour. He wore a white silk suit, carefully pressed, and a panama hat, and carried a highly ornamental fly whisk with a sham amber handle.

'——it enchants me,' he was saying. 'The black rocks of Elephantine, and the sun, and the little boats on the river. Yes, it is good to be alive.'

He paused and then added: 'You do not find it so, Mademoiselle?'

Rosalie Otterbourne said shortly: 'It's all right, I suppose. I think Assuan's a gloomy sort of place. The hotel's half empty, and everyone's about a hundred——'

She stopped—biting her lip.

Hercule Poirot's eyes twinkled.

'It is true, yes, I have one leg in the grave.'

'I—I wasn't thinking of you,' said the girl. 'I'm sorry. That sounded rude.'

'Not at all. It is natural you should wish for companions of your own age. Ah, well, there is one young man, at least.'

'The one who sits with his mother all the time? I like her— but I think he looks dreadful—so conceited!'

Poirot smiled.

'And I—am I conceited?'

'Oh, I don't think so.'

She was obviously uninterested—but the fact did not seem to annoy Poirot. He merely remarked with placid satisfaction: 'My best friend says that I am very conceited.'

'Oh, well,' said Rosalie vaguely, 'I suppose you have something to be conceited about. Unfortunately crime doesn't interest me in the least.'

Poirot said solemnly, 'I am delighted to learn that you have no guilty secret to hide.'

Just for a moment the sulky mask of her face was transformed as she shot him a swift questioning glance. Poirot did not seem to notice it as he went on:

'Madame, your mother, was not at lunch to-day. She is not indisposed, I trust?'

'This place doesn't suit her,' said Rosalie briefly. 'I shall be glad when we leave.'

'We are fellow passengers, are we not? We both make the excursion up to Wâdi Halfa and the Second Cataract?'

'Yes.'

They came out from the shade of the gardens on to a dusty stretch of road bordered by the river. Five watchful bead-sellers, two vendors of postcards, three sellers of plaster scarabs, a couple of donkey boys and some detached but hopeful infantile riff-raff closed in upon them.

'You want beads, sir? Very good, sir. Very cheap. . . .'

'Lady, you want scarab? Look—great queen—very lucky. . . .'

'You look, sir—real lapis. Very good, very cheap. . . .'

'You want ride donkey, sir? This very good donkey. This donkey Whisky and Soda, sir . . .'

'You want to go granite quarries, sir? This very good donkey. Other donkey very bad, sir, that donkey fall down. . . .'

'You want postcard—very cheap—very nice. . . .'

'Look, lady. . . . Only ten piastres—very cheap—lapis—this ivory. . . .'

'This very good fly whisk—this all-amber. . . .'

'You go out in boat, sir? I got very good boat, sir. . . .'

'You go back to hotel, lady? This first-class donkey. . . .'

Hercule Poirot made vague gestures to rid himself of this human cluster of flies. Rosalie stalked through them like a sleep-walker.

'It's best to pretend to be deaf and blind,' she remarked.

The infantile riff-raff ran alongside murmuring plaintively: 'Bakshish? Bakshish? Hip hip hurrah—very good, very nice. . . .'

Their gaily coloured rags trailed picturesquely, and the flies lay in clusters on their eyelids. They were the most persistent. The others fell back and launched a fresh attack on the next comer.

Now Poirot and Rosalie only ran the gauntlet of the shops —suave, persuasive accents here. . . .

'You visit my shop to-day, sir?' 'You want that ivory crocodile, sir?' 'You not been in my shop yet, sir? I show you very beautiful things.'

They turned into the fifth shop and Rosalie handed over several rolls of film—the object of the walk.

Then they came out again and walked towards the river's edge.

One of the Nile steamers was just mooring. Poirot and Rosalie looked interestedly at the passengers.

'Quite a lot, aren't there?' commented Rosalie.

She turned her head as Tim Allerton came up and joined them. He was a little out of breath as though he had been walking fast.

They stood there for a moment or two, and then Tim spoke.

'An awful crowd as usual, I suppose,' he remarked disparagingly, indicating the disembarking passengers.

'They're usually quite terrible,' agreed Rosalie.

All three wore the air of superiority assumed by people who are already in a place when studying new arrivals.

'Hullo!' exclaimed Tim, his voice suddenly excited. 'I'm damned if that isn't Linnet Ridgeway.'

If the information left Poirot unmoved, it stirred Rosalie's interest. She leaned forward and her sulkiness quite dropped from her as she asked: 'Where? That one in white?'

'Yes, there with the tall man. They're coming ashore now. He's the new husband, I suppose. Can't remember his name now.'

'Doyle,' said Rosalie. 'Simon Doyle. It was in all the newspapers. She's simply rolling, isn't she?'

'Only about the richest girl in England,' replied Tim cheerfully.

The three lookers-on were silent watching the passengers come ashore. Poirot gazed with interest at the subject of the remarks of his companions. He murmured: 'She is beautiful.'

'Some people have got everything,' said Rosalie bitterly.

There was a queer grudging expression on her face as she watched the other girl come up the gangplank.

Linnet Doyle was looking as perfectly turned out as if she were stepping on to the centre of the stage of a revue. She had something too of the assurance of a famous actress. She was used to being looked at, to being admired, to being the centre of the stage wherever she went.

She was aware of the keen glances bent upon her—and at the same time almost unaware of them; such tributes were part of her life.

She came ashore playing a rôle, even though she played it unconsciously. The rich beautiful society bride on her honeymoon. She turned, with a little smile and a light remark, to the tall man by her side. He answered, and the sound of his voice seemed to interest Hercule Poirot. His eyes lit up and he drew his brows together.

The couple passed close to him. He heard Simon Doyle say:

'We'll try and make time for it, darling. We can easily stay a week or two if you like it here.'

His face was turned towards her, eager, adoring, a little humble.

Poirot's eyes ran over him thoughtfully—the square shoulders, the bronzed face, the dark blue eyes, the rather childlike simplicity of the smile.

'Lucky devil,' said Tim after they had passed. 'Fancy finding an heiress who hasn't got adenoids and flat feet!'

'They look frightfully happy,' said Rosalie with a note of envy in her voice. She added suddenly, but so low that Tim did not catch the words, 'It isn't fair.'

Poirot heard, however. He had been frowning somewhat perplexedly, but now he flashed a quick glance towards her.

Tim said: 'I must collect some stuff for my mother now.'

He raised his hat and moved off. Poirot and Rosalie retraced their steps slowly in the direction of the hotel, waving aside fresh proffers of donkeys.

'So it is not fair, Mademoiselle?' asked Poirot gently.

The girl flushed angrily.

'I don't know what you mean.'

'I am repeating what you said just now under your breath. Oh, yes, you did.'

Rosalie Otterbourne shrugged her shoulders.

'It really seems a little too much for one person. Money, good looks, marvellous figure and——'

She paused and Poirot said:

'And love? Eh? And love? But you do not know—she may have been married for her money!'

'Didn't you see the way he looked at her?'

'Oh, yes, Mademoiselle. I saw all there was to see—indeed I saw something that you did not.'

'What was that?'

Poirot said slowly: 'I saw, Mademoiselle, dark lines below a woman's eyes. I saw a hand that clutched a sun-shade so tight that the knuckles were white. . . .'

Rosalie was staring at him.

'What do you mean?'

'I mean that all is not the gold that glitters. I mean that, though this lady is rich and beautiful and beloved, there is all the same *something* that is not right. And I know something else.'

'Yes?'

'I know,' said Poirot, frowning, 'that somewhere, at some time, I have heard that voice before—the voice of Monsieur Doyle—and I wish I could remember where.'

But Rosalie was not listening. She had stopped dead. With the point of her sunshade she was tracing patterns in the loose sand. Suddenly she broke out fiercely:

'I'm odious. I'm quite odious. I'm just a beast through and through. I'd like to tear the clothes off her back and stamp on her lovely, arrogant, self-confident face. I'm just a jealous cat—but that's what I feel like. She's so horribly successful and poised and assured.'

Hercule Poirot looked a little astonished by the outburst. He took her by the arm and gave her a friendly little shake.

'*Tenez*—you will feel better for having said that!'

'I just hate her! I've never hated anyone so much at first sight.'

'Magnificent!'

Rosalie looked at him doubtfully. Then her mouth twitched and she laughed.

'*Bien*,' said Poirot, and laughed too.

They proceeded amicably back to the hotel.

'I must find Mother,' said Rosalie, as they came into the cool dim hall.

Poirot passed out on the other side on to the terrace overlooking the Nile. Here were little tables set for tea, but it was early still. He stood for a few moments looking at the river, then strolled down through the garden.

Some people were playing tennis in the hot sun. He paused to watch them for a while, then went on down the steep path. It was here, sitting on a bench overlooking the Nile, that he came upon the girl of Chez Ma Tante. He recognised her at once. Her face, as he had seen it that night, was securely etched upon his memory. The expression on it now was very different. She was paler, thinner, and there were lines that told of a great weariness and misery of spirit.

He drew back a little. She had not seen him, and he watched her for a while without her suspecting his presence. Her small foot tapped impatiently on the ground. Her eyes, dark with a kind of smouldering fire, had a queer kind of suffering dark triumph in them. She was looking out across

34

the Nile where the white-sailed boats glided up and down the river.

A face—and a voice. He remembered them both. This girl's face and the voice he had heard just now, the voice of a newly made bridegroom. . . .

And even as he stood there considering the unconscious girl, the next scene in the drama was played.

Voices sounded above. The girl on the seat started to her feet. Linnet Doyle and her husband came down the path. Linnet's voice was happy and confident. The look of strain and tenseness of muscle had quite disappeared, Linnet was happy.

The girl who was standing there took a step or two forward. The other two stopped dead.

'Hullo, Linnet,' said Jacqueline de Bellefort. 'So here you are! We never seem to stop running into each other. Hullo, Simon, how are you?'

Linnet Doyle had shrunk back against the rock with a little cry. Simon Doyle's good-looking face was suddenly convulsed with rage. He moved forward as though he would have liked to strike the slim girlish figure.

With a quick birdlike turn of her head she signalled her realisation of a stranger's presence. Simon turned his head and noticed Poirot. He said awkwardly: 'Hullo, Jacqueline; we didn't expect to see you here.'

The words were unconvincing in the extreme.

The girl flashed white teeth at them.

'Quite a surprise?' she asked. Then, with a little nod, she walked up the path.

Poirot moved delicately in the opposite direction. As he went, he heard Linnet Doyle say:

'Simon—for God's sake! Simon—what can we do?'

Chapter Three

Dinner was over. The terrace outside the Cataract Hotel was softly lit. Most of the guests staying at the hotel were there sitting at little tables.

Simon and Linnet Doyle came out, a tall, distinguished-looking grey-haired man, with a keen, clean-shaven American face, beside them. As the little group hesitated for a moment in the doorway, Tim Allerton rose from his chair near by and came forward.

'You don't remember me, I'm sure,' he said pleasantly to Linnet, 'but I'm Joanna Southwood's cousin.'

'Of course—how stupid of me! You're Tim Allerton. This is my husband'—a faint tremor in the voice, pride, shyness?—'and this is my American trustee, Mr. Pennington.'

Tim said: 'You must meet my mother.'

A few minutes later they were sitting together in a party —Linnet in the corner, Tim and Pennington each side of her, both talking to her, vying for her attention. Mrs. Allerton talked to Simon Doyle.

The swing doors revolved. A sudden tension came into the beautiful upright figure sitting in the corner between the two men. Then it relaxed as a small man came out and walked across the terrace.

Mrs. Allerton said: 'You're not the only celebrity here, my dear. That funny little man is Hercule Poirot.'

She had spoken lightly, just out of instinctive social tact to bridge an awkward pause, but Linnet seemed struck by the information.

'Hercule Poirot? Of course—I've heard of him. . . .'

She seemed to sink into a fit of abstraction. The two men on either side of her were momentarily at a loss.

Poirot had strolled across to the edge of the terrace, but his attention was immediately solicited.

'Sit down, Monsieur Poirot. What a lovely night!'

He obeyed.

'*Mais oui, Madame,* it is indeed beautiful.'

He smiled politely at Mrs. Otterbourne. What draperies of black ninon and that ridiculous turban effect! Mrs. Otterbourne went on in her high complaining voice:

'Quite a lot of notabilities here now, aren't there? I expect we shall see a paragraph about it in the papers soon. Society beauties, famous novelists——'

She paused with a slight mock-modest laugh.

Poirot felt, rather than saw, the sulky frowning girl opposite him flinch and set her mouth in a sulkier line than before.

'You have a novel on the way at present, Madame?' he inquired.

Mrs. Otterbourne gave her little self-conscious laugh again.

'I'm being dreadfully lazy. I really must set to. My public is getting terribly impatient—and my publisher, poor man! Appeals by every post! Even cables!'

Again he felt the girl shift in the darkness.

'I don't mind telling you, Monsieur Poirot, I am partly

here for local colour. *Snow on the desert's Face*—that is the title of my new book. Powerful—suggestive. Snow—on the desert—melted in the first flaming breath of passion.'

Rosalie got up, muttering something, and moved away down into the dark garden.

'One must be strong,' went on Mrs. Otterbourne, wagging the turban emphatically. 'Strong meat—that is what my books are—all important. Libraries banned—no matter! I speak the truth. Sex—ah! Monsieur Poirot—why is everyone so afraid of sex? The pivot of the universe! You have read my books?'

'Alas, Madame! You comprehend, I do not read many novels. My work——'

Mrs. Otterbourne said firmly: 'I must give you a copy of *Under the Fig Tree*. I think you will find it significant. It is outspoken—but it is *real*!'

'That is most kind of you, Madame. I will read it with pleasure.'

Mrs. Otterbourne was silent a minute or two. She fidgeted with a long chain of beads that was wound twice round her neck. She looked swiftly from side to side.

'Perhaps—I'll just slip up and get it for you now.'

'Oh, Madame, pray do not trouble yourself. Later——'

'No, no. It's no trouble.' She rose. 'I'd like to show you——'

'What is it, Mother?'

Rosalie was suddenly at her side.

'Nothing, dear. I was just going up to get a book for Monsieur Poirot.'

'The *Fig Tree*? I'll get it.'

'You don't know where it is, dear. I'll go.'

'Yes, I do.'

The girl went swiftly across the terrace and into the hotel.

'Let me congratulate you, Madame, on a very lovely daughter,' said Poirot, with a bow.

'Rosalie? Yes, yes—she is good-looking. But she's very *hard*, Monsieur Poirot. And no sympathy with illness. She always thinks she knows best. She imagines she knows more about my health than I do myself——'

Poirot signalled to a passing waiter.

'A liqueur, Madame? A chartreuse? A crème de menthe?'

Mrs. Otterbourne shook her head vigorously.

'No, no. I am practically a teetotaller. You may have noticed I never drink anything but water—or perhaps lemonade. I cannot bear the taste of spirits.'

'Then may I order you a lemon squash, Madame?'

37

He gave the order—one lemon squash and one benedictine.

The swing door revolved. Rosalie passed through and came towards them, a book in her hand.

'Here you are,' she said. Her voice was quite expressionless —almost remarkably so.

'Monsieur Poirot has just ordered me a lemon squash,' said her mother.

'And you, Mademoiselle, what will you take?'

'Nothing.' She added, suddenly conscious of the curtness: 'Nothing, thank you.'

Poirot took the volume which Mrs. Otterbourne held out to him. It still bore its original jacket, a gaily coloured affair representing a lady, with smartly shingled hair and scarlet fingernails, sitting on a tiger skin, in the traditional costume of Eve. Above her was a tree with the leaves of an oak, bearing large and improbably coloured apples.

It was entitled *Under the Fig Tree*, by Salome Otterbourne. On the inside was a publisher's blurb. It spoke enthusiastically of the superb courage and realism of this study of a modern woman's love life. 'Fearless, unconventional, realistic,' were the adjectives used.

Poirot bowed and murmured: 'I am honoured, Madame.'

As he raised his head, his eyes met those of the authoress's daughter. Almost involuntarily he made a little movement. He was astonished and grieved at the eloquent pain they revealed.

It was at that moment that the drinks arrived and created a welcome diversion.

Poirot lifted his glass gallantly.

'*A votre santé, Madame—Mademoiselle.*'

Mrs. Otterbourne, sipping her lemonade, murmured, 'So refreshing—delicious!'

Silence fell on the three of them. They looked down to the shining black rocks in the Nile. There was something fantastic about them in the moonlight. They were like vast prehistoric monsters lying half out of the water. A little breeze came up suddenly and as suddenly died away. There was a feeling in the air of hush—of expectancy.

Hercule Poirot brought his gaze back to the terrace and its occupants. Was he wrong, or was there the same hush of expectancy there? It was like a moment on the stage when one is waiting for the entrance of the leading lady.

And just at that moment the swing doors began to revolve once more. This time it seemed as though they did so with a special air of importance. Everyone had stopped talking and was looking towards them.

A dark slender girl in a wine-coloured evening frock came through. She paused for a minute, then walked deliberately across the terrace and sat down at an empty table. There was nothing flaunting, nothing out of the way about her demeanour, and yet it had somehow the studied effect of a stage entrance.

'Well,' said Mrs. Otterbourne. She tossed her turbaned head. 'She seems to think she is somebody, that girl!'

Poirot did not answer. He was watching. The girl had sat down in a place where she could look deliberately across at Linnet Doyle. Presently, Poirot noticed, Linnet Doyle leant forward and said something and a moment later got up and changed her seat. She was now sitting facing in the opposite direction.

Poirot nodded thoughtfully to himself.

It was about five minutes later that the other girl changed her seat to the opposite side of the terrace. She sat smoking and smiling quietly, the picture of contented ease. But always, as though unconsciously, her meditative gaze was on Simon Doyle's wife.

After a quarter of an hour Linnet Doyle got up abruptly and went into the hotel. Her husband followed her almost immediately.

Jacqueline de Bellefort smiled and twisted her chair round. She lit a cigarette and stared out over the Nile. She went on smiling to herself.

Chapter Four

'Monsieur Poirot.'

Poirot got hastily to his feet. He had remained sitting out on the terrace alone after everyone else had left. Lost in meditation he had been staring at the smooth shiny black rocks when the sound of his name recalled him to himself.

It was a well-bred, assured voice, a charming voice, although perhaps a trifle arrogant.

Hercule Poirot, rising quickly, looked into the commanding eyes of Linnet Doyle. She wore a wrap of rich purple velvet over her white satin gown and she looked more lovely and more regal than Poirot had imagined possible.

'You are Monsieur Hercule Poirot?' said Linnet.

It was hardly a question.

'At your service, Madame.'

'You know who I am, perhaps?'

'Yes, Madame. I have heard your name. I know exactly who you are.'

Linnet nodded. That was only what she had expected. She went on, in her charming autocratic manner: 'Will you come with me into the card room, Monsieur Poirot? I am very anxious to speak to you.'

'Certainly, Madame.'

She led the way into the hotel. He followed. She led him into the deserted card room and motioned him to close the door. Then she sank down on a chair at one of the tables and he sat down opposite her.

She plunged straightaway into what she wanted to say. There were no hesitations. Her speech came flowingly.

'I have heard a great deal about you, Monsieur Poirot, and I know that you are a very clever man. It happens that I am urgently in need of someone to help me—and I think very possibly that you are the man who would do it.'

Poirot inclined his head.

'You are very amiable, Madame, but you see, I am on holiday, and when I am on holiday I do not take cases.'

'That could be arranged.'

It was not offensively said—only with the quiet confidence of a young woman who had always been able to arrange matters to her satisfaction.

Linnet Doyle went on: 'I am the subject, Monsieur Poirot, of an intolerable persecution. That persecution has got to stop! My own idea was to go to the police about it, but my—my husband seems to think that the police would be powerless to do anything.'

'Perhaps—if you would explain a little further?' murmured Poirot politely.

'Oh, yes, I will do so. The matter is perfectly simple.'

There was still no hesitation—no faltering. Linnet Doyle had a clear-cut businesslike mind. She only paused a minute so as to present the facts as concisely as possible.

'Before I met my husband, he was engaged to a Miss de Bellefort. She was also a friend of mine. My husband broke off his engagement to her—they were not suited in any way. She, I am sorry to say, took it rather hard. . . . I—am very sorry about that—but these things cannot be helped. She

40

made certain—well, threats—to which I paid very little attention, and which, I may say, she has not attempted to carry out. But instead she has adopted the extraordinary course of—of following us about wherever we go.'

Poirot raised his eyebrows.

'Ah—rather an unusual—er—revenge.'

'Very unusual—and very ridiculous! But also—annoying.' She bit her lip.

Poirot nodded.

'Yes, I can imagine that. You are, I understand, on your honeymoon?'

'Yes. It happened—the first time—at Venice. She was there —at Danielli's. I thought it was just coincidence. Rather embarrassing, but that was all. Then we found her on board the boat at Brindisi. We—we understood that she was going on to Palestine. We left her, as we thought, on the boat. But —but when we got to Mena House she was there—waiting for us.'

Poirot nodded.

'And now?'

'We came up the Nile by boat. I—I was half expecting to find her on board. When she wasn't there I thought she had stopped being so—so childish. But when we got here— she—she was here—waiting.'

Poirot eyed her keenly for a moment. She was still perfectly composed, but the knuckles of the hand that was gripping the table were white with the force of her grip.

He said: 'And you are afraid this state of things may continue?'

'Yes.' She paused. 'Of course the whole thing is idiotic! Jacqueline is making herself utterly ridiculous. I am surprised she hasn't got more pride—more dignity.'

Poirot made a slight gesture.

'There are times, Madame, when pride and dignity—they go by the board! There are other—stronger emotions.'

'Yes, possibly.' Linnet spoke impatiently. 'But what on earth can she hope to *gain* by all this?'

'It is not always a question of gain, Madame.'

Something in his tone struck Linnet disagreeably. She flushed and said quickly: 'You are right. A discussion of motives is beside the point. The crux of the matter is that this has got to be stopped.'

'And how do you propose that that should be accomplished, Madame?' Poirot asked.

'Well—naturally—my husband and I cannot continue being subjected to this annoyance. There must be some kind of legal redress against such a thing.'

She spoke impatiently. Poirot looked at her thoughtfully as he asked: 'Has she threatened you in actual words in public? Used insulting language? Attempted any bodily harm?'

'No.'

'Then, frankly, Madame, I do not see what you can do. If it is a young lady's pleasure to travel in certain places, and those places are the same where you and your husband find themselves—*eh bien*—what of it? The air is free to all! There is no question of her forcing herself upon your privacy? It is always in public that these encounters take place?'

'You mean there is nothing that I can do about it?'

Linnet sounded incredulous.

Poirot said placidly: 'Nothing at all, as far as I can see. Mademoiselle de Bellefort is within her rights.'

'But—but it is maddening! It is *intolerable* that I should have to put up with this!'

Poirot said dryly: 'I sympathise with you, Madame—especially as I imagine that you have not often had to put up with things.'

Linnet was frowning.

'There *must* be some way of stopping it,' she murmured.

Poirot shrugged his shoulders.

'You can always leave—move on somewhere else,' he suggested.

'Then she will follow!'

'Very possibly—yes.'

'It's absurd!'

'Precisely.'

'Anyway, why should I—we—run away? As though—as though——'

She stopped.

'Exactly, Madame. As though——! It is all there, is it not?'

Linnet lifted her head and stared at him.

'What do you mean?'

Poirot altered his tone. He leant forward; his voice was confidential, appealing. He said very gently: 'Why do you mind so much, Madame?'

'Why? But it's maddening! Irritating to the last degree! I've told you why!'

Poirot shook his head.

'Not altogether.'

'What do you mean?' Linnet asked again.

Poirot leant back, folded his arms and spoke in a detached impersonal manner.

'*Ecoutez*, Madame. I will recount to you a little history. It is that one day, a month or two ago, I am dining in a restaurant in London. At the table next to me are two people, a man and a girl. They are very happy, so it seems, very much in love. They talk with confidence of the future. It is not that I listen to what is not meant for me; they are quite oblivious of who hears them and who does not. The man's back is to me, but I can watch the girl's face. It is very intense. She is in love—heart, soul, and body—and she is not of those who love lightly and often. With her it is clearly the life and the death. They are engaged to be married, these two; that is what I gather; and they talk of where they shall pass the days of their honeymoon. They plan to go to Egypt.'

He paused. Linnet said sharply: 'Well?'

Poirot went on: 'That is a month or two ago, but the girl's face—I do not forget it. I know that I shall remember if I see it again. And I remember too the man's voice. And I think you can guess, Madame, when it is I see the one and hear the other again. It is here in Egypt. The man is on his honeymoon, yes—but he is on his honeymoon with another woman.'

Linnet said sharply: 'What of it? I had already mentioned the facts.'

'The facts—yes.'

'Well then?'

Poirot said slowly: 'The girl in the restaurant mentioned a friend—a friend who, she was very positive, would not let her down. That friend, I think, was you, Madame.'

'Yes. I told you we had been friends.'

Linnet flushed.

'And she trusted you?'

'Yes.'

She hesitated for a moment, biting her lip impatiently; then, as Poirot did not seem disposed to speak, she broke out:

'Of course the whole thing was very unfortunate. But these things happen, Monsieur Poirot.'

'Ah! yes, they happen, Madame.' He paused. 'You are of the Church of England, I presume?'

'Yes.' Linnet looked slightly bewildered.

'Then you have heard portions of the Bible read aloud in church. You have heard of King David and of the rich man who had many flocks and herds and the poor man who had one ewe lamb—and of how the rich man took the poor man's one ewe lamb. That was something that happened, Madame.'

Linnet sat up. Her eyes flashed angrily.

'I see perfectly what you are driving at, Monsieur Poirot! You think, to put it vulgarly, that I stole my friend's young man. Looking at the matter sentimentally—which is, I suppose, the way people of your generation cannot help looking at things—that is possibly true. But the real hard truth is different. I don't deny that Jackie was passionately in love with Simon, but I don't think you take into account that he may not have been equally devoted to her. He was very fond of her, but I think that even before he met me he was beginning to feel that he had made a mistake. Look at it clearly, Monsieur Poirot. Simon discovers that it is I he loves, not Jackie. What is he to do? Be heroically noble and marry a woman he does not care for—and thereby probably ruin three lives—for it is doubtful whether he could make Jackie happy under those circumstances? If he were actually married to her when he met me I agree that it *might* be his duty to stick to her—though I'm not really sure of that. If one person is unhappy the other suffers too. But an engagement is not really binding. If a mistake has been made, then surely it is better to face the fact before it is too late. I admit that it was very hard on Jackie, and I'm terribly sorry about it— but there it is. It was inevitable.'

'I wonder.'

She stared at him.

'What do you mean?'

'It is very sensible, very logical—all that you say! But it does not explain one thing.'

'What is that?'

'Your own attitude, Madame. See you, this pursuit of you, you might take it in two ways. It might cause you annoyance—yes, or it might stir your pity—that your friend should have been so deeply hurt as to throw all regard for the conventions aside. But that is not the way you react. No, to you this persecution is *intolerable*—and why? It can be for one reason only—that you feel a sense of guilt.'

Linnet sprang to her feet.

'How dare you? Really, Monsieur Poirot, this is going too far.'

44

'But I do dare, Madame! I am going to speak to you quite frankly. I suggest to you that, although you may have endeavoured to gloss over the fact to yourself, you did deliberately set about taking your husband from your friend. I suggest that you felt strongly attracted to him at once. But I suggest that there was a moment when you hesitated, when you realised that there was a *choice*—that you could refrain or go on. I suggest that the initiative rested with *you*—not with Monsieur Doyle. You are beautiful, Madame; you are rich; you are clever, intelligent—and you have charm. You could have exercised that charm or you could have restrained it. You had everything, Madame, that life can offer. Your friend's life was bound up in one person. You knew that, but, though you hesitated, you did not hold your hand. You stretched it out and, like the rich man in the Bible, you took the poor man's one ewe lamb.'

There was a silence. Linnet controlled herself with an effort and said in a cold voice: 'All this is quite beside the point!'

'No, it is not beside the point. I am explaining to you just why the unexpected appearances of Mademoiselle de Bellefort have upset you so much. It is because though she may be unwomanly and undignified in what she is doing, you have the inner conviction that she has right on her side.'

'That's not true.'

Poirot shrugged his shoulders.

'You refuse to be honest with yourself.'

'Not at all.'

Poirot said gently: 'I should say, Madame, that you have had a happy life, that you have been generous and kindly in your attitude towards others.'

'I have tried to be,' said Linnet. The impatient anger died out of her face. She spoke simply—almost forlornly.

'And that is why the feeling that you have deliberately caused injury to someone upsets you so much, and why you are so reluctant to admit the fact. Pardon me if I have been impertinent, but the psychology, it is the most important fact in a case.'

Linnet said slowly: 'Even supposing what you say were true—and I don't admit it, mind—what can be done about it now? One can't alter the past; one must deal with things as they are.'

Poirot nodded.

'You have the clear brain. Yes, one cannot go back over the past. One must accept things as they are. And sometimes, Madame, that is all one can do—accept the consequences of one's past deeds.'

'You mean,' asked Linnet incredulously, 'that I can do nothing—*nothing*?'

'You must have courage, Madame; that is what it seems like to me.'

Linnet said slowly:

'Couldn't you—talk to Jackie—to Miss de Bellefort? Reason with her?'

'Yes, I could do that. I will do that if you would like me to do so. But do not expect much result. I fancy that Mademoiselle de Bellefort is so much in the grip of a fixed idea that nothing will turn her from it.'

'But surely we can do *something* to extricate ourselves?'

'You could, of course, return to England and establish yourself in your own house.'

'Even then, I suppose, Jacqueline is capable of planting herself in the village, so that I should see her every time I went out of the grounds.'

'True.'

'Besides,' said Linnet slowly, 'I don't think that Simon would agree to run away.'

'What is his attitude in this?'

'He's furious—simply furious.'

Poirot nodded thoughtfully.

Linnet said appealingly, 'You will—talk to her?'

'Yes, I will do that. But it is my opinion that I shall not be able to accomplish anything.'

Linnet said violently: 'Jackie is extraordinary! One can't tell what she will do!'

'You spoke just now of certain threats she had made. Would you tell me what those threats were?'

Linnet shrugged her shoulders.

'She threatened to—well—kill us both. Jackie can be rather —Latin sometimes.'

'I see.' Poirot's tone was grave.

Linnet turned to him appealingly.

'You will act for me?'

'No, Madame.' His tone was firm. 'I will not accept a commission from you. I will do what I can in the interests of humanity. That, yes. There is here a situation that is full of

46

difficulty and danger. I will do what I can to clear it up—but I am not very sanguine as to my chance of success.'

Linnet Doyle said slowly: 'But you will not act for *me*?'

'No, Madame,' said Hercule Poirot.

Chapter Five

Hercule Poirot found Jacqueline de Bellefort sitting on the rocks directly overlooking the Nile. He had felt fairly certain that she had not retired for the night and that he would find her somewhere about the grounds of the hotel.

She was sitting with her chin cupped in the palms of her hands, and she did not turn her head or look around at the sound of his approach.

'Mademoiselle de Bellefort?' asked Poirot. 'You permit that I speak to you for a little moment?'

Jacqueline turned her head slightly. A faint smile played round her lips.

'Certainly,' she said. 'You are Monsieur Hercule Poirot, I think? Shall I make a guess? You are acting for Mrs. Doyle, who has promised you a large fee if you succeed in your mission.'

Poirot sat down on the bench near her.

'Your assumption is partially correct,' he said, smiling. 'I have just come from Madame Doyle, but I am not accepting any fee from her and, strictly speaking, I am not acting for her.'

'Oh!'

Jacqueline studied him attentively.

'Then why have you come?' she asked abruptly.

Hercule Poirot's reply was in the form of another question.

'Have you ever seen me before, Mademoiselle?'

She shook her head.

'No, I do not think so.'

'Yet I have seen you. I sat next to you once at Chez Ma Tante. You were there with Monsieur Simon Doyle.'

A strange masklike expression came over the girl's face. She said, 'I remember that evening. . . .'

'Since then,' said Poirot, 'many things have occurred.'

'As you say, many things have occurred.'

Her voice was hard with an undertone of desperate bitterness.

47

'Mademoiselle, I speak as a friend. Bury your dead!'

She looked startled.

'What do you mean?'

'Give up the past! Turn to the future! What is done is done. Bitterness will not undo it.'

'I'm sure that that would suit dear Linnet admirably.'

Poirot made a gesture.

'I am not thinking of her at this moment! I am thinking of *you*. You have suffered—yes—but what you are doing now will only prolong that suffering.'

She shook her head.

'You're wrong. There are times when I almost enjoy myself.'

'And that, Mademoiselle, is the worst of all.'

She looked up swiftly.

'You're not stupid,' she said. She added slowly, 'I believe you mean to be kind.'

'Go home, Mademoiselle. You are young; you have brains, the world is before you.'

Jacqueline shook her head slowly.

'You don't understand—or you won't. Simon is my world.'

'Love is not everything, Mademoiselle,' Poirot said gently. 'It is only when we are young that we think it is.'

But the girl still shook her head.

'You don't understand.' She shot him a quick look. 'You know all about it, of course? You've talked to Linnet? And you were in the restaurant that night . . . Simon and I loved each other.'

'I know that you loved him.'

She was quick to perceive the inflection of his words. She repeated with emphasis:

'*We loved each other*. And I loved Linnet. . . . I trusted her. She was my best friend. All her life Linnet has been able to buy everything she wanted. She's never denied herself anything. When she saw Simon she wanted him—and she just took him.'

'And he allowed himself to be—bought?'

Jacqueline shook her dark head slowly.

'No, it's not quite like that. If it were, I shouldn't be here now. . . . You're suggesting that Simon isn't worth caring for. . . . If he'd married Linnet for her money, that would be true. But he didn't marry her for her money. It's more complicated than that. There's such a thing as *glamour*,

Monsieur Poirot. And money helps that. Linnet had an "atmosphere," you see. She was the queen of a kingdom—the young princess—luxurious to her fingertips. It was like a stage setting. She had the world at her feet, one of the richest and most sought-after peers in England wanting to marry her. And she stoops instead to the obscure Simon Doyle. . . . Do you wonder it went to his head?' She made a sudden gesture. 'Look at the moon up there. You see her very plainly, don't you? She's very real. But if the sun were to shine you wouldn't be able to see her at all. It was rather like that. I was the moon. . . . When the sun came out, Simon couldn't see me any more. . . . He was dazzled. He couldn't see anything but the sun—Linnet.'

She paused and then went on: 'So you see it was—glamour. She went to his head. And then there's her complete assurance—her habit of command. She's so sure of herself that she makes other people sure. Simon was weak, perhaps, but then he's a very simple person. He would have loved me and me only if Linnet hadn't come along and snatched him up in her golden chariot. And I know—I know perfectly —that he wouldn't ever have fallen in love with her if she hadn't made him.'

'That is what you think—yes.'

'I *know* it. He loved me—he will always love me.'

Poirot said: 'Even now?'

A quick answer seemed to rise to her lips, then be stifled. She looked at Poirot and a deep burning colour spread over her face. She looked away; her head dropped down. She said in a low stifled voice: 'Yes, I know. He hates me now. Yes, hates me. . . . He'd better be careful!'

With a quick gesture she fumbled in a little silk bag that lay on the seat. Then she held out her hand. On the palm of it was a small pearl-handled pistol—a dainty toy it looked.

'Nice little thing, isn't it?' she said. 'Looks too foolish to be real, but it is real! One of those bullets would kill a man or a woman. And I'm a good shot.' She smiled a faraway, reminiscent smile.

'When I went home as a child with my mother, to South Carolina, my grandfather taught me to shoot. He was the old-fashioned kind that believes in shooting—especially where honour is concerned. My father, too, he fought several duels as a young man. He was a good swordsman. He killed a man once. That was over a woman. So you see, Monsieur Poirot'—she met his eyes squarely—'I've hot blood in me! I bought this when it first happened. I meant to kill one or other of them—the trouble was I couldn't decide which. Both of them would have been unsatisfactory. If I'd thought Linnet would have looked afraid—but she's got plenty of physical courage. She can stand up to physical action. And then I thought I'd—wait! That appealed to me more and more. After all, I could do it any time; it would be more fun to wait and—think about it! And then this idea came to my mind—to follow them! Whenever they arrived at some faraway spot and were together and happy, they should see *Me*! And it worked. It got Linnet badly—in a way nothing else could have done! It got right under her skin. . . . That was when I began to enjoy myself. . . . And there's nothing she can do about it! I'm always perfectly pleasant and polite! There's not a word they can take hold of! It's poisoning everything—everything—for them.' Her laugh rang out, clear and silvery.

Poirot grasped her arm.

'Be quiet. Quiet, I tell you.'

Jacqueline looked at him.

'Well?' she asked. Her smile was definitely challenging.

'Mademoiselle, I beseech you, do not do what you are doing.'

'Leave dear Linnet alone, you mean!'

'It is deeper than that. Do not open your heart to evil.'

Her lips fell apart; a look of bewilderment came into her eyes.

Poirot went on gravely: 'Because—if you do—evil will come. . . . Yes, very surely evil will come. . . . It will enter in and make its home within you, and after a little while it will no longer be possible to drive it out.'

Jacqueline stared at him. Her glance seemed to waver, to flicker uncertainly.

She said: 'I—don't know——' Then she cried out definitely, 'You can't stop me.'

'No,' said Hercule Poirot. 'I cannot stop you.' His voice was sad.

'Even if I were to—kill her, you couldn't stop me.'

'No—not if you were willing to pay the price.'

Jacqueline de Bellefort laughed.

'Oh, I'm not afraid of death! What have I got to live for, after all? I suppose you believe it's very wrong to kill a person who has injured you—even if they've taken away everything you had in the world?'

Poirot said steadily: 'Yes, Mademoiselle. I believe it is the unforgivable offence—to kill.'

Jacqueline laughed again.

'Then you ought to approve of my present scheme of revenge; because, you see, as long as it works, I shan't use that pistol. . . . But I'm afraid—yes, afraid sometimes—it all goes red—I want to hurt her—to stick a knife into her, to put my dear little pistol close against her head and then—just press with my finger—*Oh!*'

The exclamation startled him.

'What is it, Mademoiselle?'

She had turned her head and was staring into the shadows. 'Someone—standing over there. He's gone now.'

Hercule Poirot looked round sharply.

The place seemed quite deserted.

'There seems no one here but ourselves, Mademoiselle.' He got up. 'In any case I have said all I came to say. I wish you good-night.'

Jacqueline got up too. She said almost pleadingly, 'You do understand—that I can't do what you ask me to do?'

Poirot shook his head.

'No—for you could do it! There is always a moment! Your friend Linnet—there was a moment, too, in which she could have held her hand. . . . She let it pass by. And if one does that, then one is committed to the enterprise and there comes no second chance.'

'No second chance . . .' said Jacqueline de Bellefort.

She stood brooding for a moment; then she lifted her head defiantly.

'Good-night, Monsieur Poirot.'

He shook his head sadly and followed her up the path to the hotel.

Chapter Six

On the following morning Simon Doyle joined Hercule Poirot as the latter was leaving the hotel to walk down to the town.

'Good-morning, Monsieur Poirot.'

'Good-morning, Monsieur Doyle.'

'You going to the town? Mind if I stroll along with you?'

'But certainly. I shall be delighted.'

The two men walked side by side, passed out through the gateway and turned into the cool shade of the gardens. Then Simon removed his pipe from his mouth and said, 'I understand, Monsieur Poirot, that my wife had a talk with you last night?'

'That is so.'

Simon Doyle was frowning a little. He belonged to that type of men of action who find it difficult to put thoughts into words and who have trouble in expressing themselves clearly.

'I'm glad of one thing,' he said. 'You've made her realise that we're more or less powerless in the matter.'

'There is clearly no legal redress,' agreed Poirot.

'Exactly. Linnet didn't seem to understand that.' He gave a faint smile. 'Linnet's been brought up to believe that every annoyance can automatically be referred to the police.'

'It would be pleasant if such were the case,' said Poirot.

There was a pause. Then Simon said suddenly, his face going very red as he spoke:

'It's—it's infamous that she should be victimised like this! She's done nothing! If anyone likes to say I behaved like a cad, they're welcome to say so! I suppose I did. But I won't have the whole thing visited on Linnet. She had nothing whatever to do with it.'

Poirot bowed his head gravely but said nothing.

'Did you—er—have you—talked to Jackie—Miss de Bellefort?'

'Yes, I have spoken with her.'

'Did you get her to see sense?'

'I'm afraid not.'

Simon broke out irritably: 'Can't she see what an ass she's making of herself? Doesn't she realise that no decent woman would behave as she is doing? Hasn't she got any pride or self-respect?'

Poirot shrugged his shoulders.

'She has only a sense of—injury, shall we say?' he replied.

'Yes, but damn it all, man, decent girls don't behave like this! I admit I was entirely to blame. I treated her damned badly and all that. I should quite understand her being thoroughly fed up with me and never wishing to see me again. But this following me round—it's—it's *indecent*! Making a show of herself! What the devil does she hope to get out of it?'

'Perhaps—revenge!'

'Idiotic! I'd really understand better if she'd tried to do something melodramatic—like taking a pot shot at me.'

'You think that would be more like her—yes?'

'Frankly I do. She's hot-blooded—and she's got an ungovernable temper. I shouldn't be surprised at her doing anything while she was in a white-hot rage. But this spying business——'

He shook his head.

'It is more subtle—yes! It is intelligent!'

Doyle stared at him.

'You don't understand. It's playing hell with Linnet's nerves.'

'And yours?'

Simon looked at him with momentary surprise.

'Me? I'd like to wring the little devil's neck.'

'There is nothing, then, of the old feeling left?'

'My dear Monsieur Poirot—how can I put it? It's like the moon when the sun comes out. You don't know it's there any more. When once I'd met Linnet—Jackie didn't exist.'

'*Tiens, c'est drôle, ça!*' muttered Poirot.

'I beg your pardon.'

'Your simile interested me, that is all.'

Again flushing, Simon said: 'I suppose Jackie told you that I'd only married Linnet for her money? Well, that's a damned lie! I wouldn't marry any woman for money! What Jackie doesn't understand is that it's difficult for a fellow when—when—a woman cares for him as she cared for me.'

'Ah?'

Poirot looked up sharply.

Simon blundered on: 'It—it—sounds a caddish thing to say, but Jackie was *too* fond of me!'

'*Une qui aime et un qui se laisse aimer*,' murmured Poirot.

'Eh? What's that you say? You see, a man doesn't want to feel that a woman cares more for him than he does for her.' His voice grew warm as he went on. 'He doesn't want to feel *owned*, body and soul. It's that damned *possessive* attitude! This man is *mine*—he *belongs* to me! That's the sort of thing I can't stick—no man could stick! He wants to get away—to get free. He wants to own his woman; he doesn't want *her* to own *him*.'

He broke off, and with fingers that trembled slightly he lit a cigarette.

Poirot said: 'And it is like that that you felt with Mademoiselle Jacqueline?'

'Eh?' Simon stared and then admitted: 'Er—yes—well, yes, as a matter of fact I did. She doesn't realise that, of course. And it's not the sort of thing I could ever tell her. But I *was* feeling restless—and then I met Linnet, and she just swept me off my feet! I'd never seen anything so lovely. It was all so amazing. Everyone kowtowing to her—and then her singling out a poor chump like me.'

His tone held boyish awe and astonishment.

'I see,' said Poirot. He nodded thoughtfully. 'Yes—I see.'

'Why can't Jackie take it like a man?' demanded Simon resentfully.

A very faint smile twitched Poirot's upper lip.

'Well, you see, Monsieur Doyle, to begin with she is *not* a man.'

'No, no—but I meant take it like a good sport! After all, you've got to take your medicine when it comes to you. The fault's mine, I admit. But there it is! If you no longer care for a girl, it's simply madness to marry her. And, now that I see what Jackie's really like and the lengths she is likely to go to, I feel I've had rather a lucky escape.'

'The lengths she is likely to go to,' Poirot repeated thoughtfully. 'Have you an idea, Monsieur Doyle, what those lengths are?'

Simon looked at him, rather startled.

'No—at least, what do you mean?'

'You know she carries a pistol about with her?'

Simon frowned, then shook his head.

'I don't believe she'll use that—now. She might have done so earlier. But I believe it's got past that. She's just spiteful now—trying to take it out of us both.'

Poirot shrugged his shoulders.

'It may be so,' he said doubtfully.

'It's Linnet I'm worrying about,' declared Simon, somewhat unnecessarily.

'I quite realise that,' said Poirot.

'I'm not really afraid of Jackie doing any melodramatic shooting stuff, but this spying and following business has absolutely got Linnet on the raw. I'll tell you the plan I've made, and perhaps you can suggest improvements on it. To begin with, I've announced fairly openly that we're going to stay here ten days. But to-morrow the steamer *Karnak* starts from Shellâl to Wâdi Halfa. I propose to book passages on that under an assumed name. To-morrow we'll go on an excursion to Philae. Linnet's maid can take the luggage. We'll join the *Karnak* at Shellâl. When Jackie finds we don't come back, it will be too late—we shall be well on our way. She'll assume we have given her the slip and gone back to Cairo. In fact I might even bribe the porter to say so. Inquiry at the tourist offices won't help her, because our names won't appear. How does that strike you?'

'It is well imagined, yes. And suppose she waits here till you return?'

'We may not return. We would go on to Khartoum and then perhaps by air to Kenya. She can't follow us all over the globe.'

'No; there must come a time when financial reasons forbid. She has very little money, I understand.'

Simon looked at him with admiration.

'That's clever of you. Do you know, I hadn't thought of that. Jackie's as poor as they make them.'

'And yet she has managed to follow you so far?'

Simon said doubtfully:

'She's got a small income, of course. Something under two hundred a year, I imagine. I suppose—yes, I suppose she must have sold out the capital to do what she's doing.'

'So that the time will come when she has exhausted her resources and is quite penniless?'

'Yes. . . .'

Simon wriggled uneasily. The thought seemed to make him uncomfortable. Poirot watched him attentively.

'No,' he remarked. 'No, it is not a pretty thought. . . .'

Simon said rather angrily, 'Well, *I* can't help it!' Then he added, 'What do you think of my plan?'

'I think it may work, yes. But it is, of course, a *retreat*.'

Simon flushed.

'You mean, we're running away? Yes, that's true. . . . But Linnet——'

Poirot watched him, then gave a short nod.

'As you say, it may be the best way. But remember, Mademoiselle de Bellefort has brains.'

Simon said sombrely: 'Some day, I feel, we've got to make a stand and fight it out. Her attitude isn't reasonable.'

'Reasonable, *mon Dieu*!' cried Poirot.

'There's no reason why women shouldn't behave like rational beings,' Simon asserted stolidly.

Poirot said dryly: 'Quite frequently they do. That is even

more upsetting!' He added, 'I, too, shall be on the *Karnak*. It is part of my itinerary.'

'Oh!' Simon hesitated, then said, choosing his words with some embarrassment: 'That isn't—isn't—er—on our account in any way? I mean I wouldn't like to think——'

Poirot disabused him quickly:

'Not at all. It was all arranged before I left London. I always make my plans well in advance.'

'You don't just move on from place to place as the fancy takes you? Isn't the latter really pleasanter?'

'Perhaps. But to succeed in life every detail should be arranged well beforehand.'

Simon laughed and said: 'That is how the more skilful murderer behaves, I suppose.'

'Yes—though I must admit that the most brilliant crime I remember and one of the most difficult to solve was committed on the spur of the moment.'

Simon said boyishly: 'You must tell us something about your cases on board the *Karnak*.'

'No, no; that would be 'to talk—what do you call it?—the shop.'

'Yes, but your kind of shop is rather thrilling. Mrs. Allerton thinks so. She's longing to get a chance to cross-question you.'

'Mrs. Allerton? That is the charming grey-haired woman who has such a devoted son?'

'Yes. She'll be on the *Karnak* too.'

'Does she know that you——?'

'Certainly not,' said Simon with emphasis. 'Nobody knows. I've gone on the principle that it's better not to trust anybody.'

'An admirable sentiment—and one which I always adopt. By the way, the third member of your party, the tall grey-haired man——'

'Pennington?'

'Yes. He is travelling with you?'

Simon said grimly: 'Not very usual on a honeymoon, you were thinking? Pennington is Linnet's American trustee. We ran across him by chance in Cairo.'

'*Ah, vraiment!* You permit a question? She is of age, Madame your wife?'

Simon looked amused.

'She isn't actually twenty-one yet—but she hadn't got to ask anyone's consent before marrying me. It was the greatest surprise to Pennington. He left New York on the *Carmanic* two days before Linnet's letter got there telling him of our marriage, so he knew nothing about it.'

'The *Carmanic*——' murmured Poirot.

'It was the greatest surprise to him when we ran into him at Shepheard's in Cairo.'

'That was indeed the coincident!'

'Yes, and we found that he was coming on this Nile trip —so naturally we foregathered; couldn't have done anything else decently. Besides that, it's been—well, a relief in some ways.' He looked embarrassed again. 'You see, Linnet's been all strung up—expecting Jackie to turn up anywhere and everywhere. While we were alone together, the subject kept coming up. Andrew Pennington's a help that way, we have to talk of outside matters.'

'Your wife has not confided in Mr. Pennington?'

'No.' Simon's jaw looked aggressive. 'It's nothing to do with anyone else. Besides, when we started on this Nile trip we thought we'd seen the end of the business.'

Poirot shook his head.

'You have not seen the end of it yet. No—the end is not yet at hand. I am very sure of that.'

'I say, Monsieur Poirot, you're not very encouraging.'

Poirot looked at him with a slight feeling of irritation. He thought to himself: 'The Anglo-Saxon, he takes nothing seriously but playing games! He does not grow up.'

Linnet Doyle—Jacqueline de Bellefort—both of them took the business seriously enough. But in Simon's attitude he could find nothing but male impatience and annoyance. He said: 'You will permit me an impertinent question? Was it your idea to come to Egypt for your honeymoon?'

Simon flushed.

'No, of course not. As a matter of fact I'd rather have gone anywhere else, but Linnet was absolutely set upon it. And so—and so——'

He stopped rather lamely.

'Naturally,' said Poirot gravely.

He appreciated the fact that, if Linnet Doyle was set upon anything, that thing had to happen.

He thought to himself: 'I have now heard three separate accounts of the affair—Linnet Doyle's, Jacqueline de Bellefort's, Simon Doyle's. Which of them is nearest to the truth?'

Chapter Seven

Simon and Linnet Doyle set off on their expedition to Philae about eleven o'clock the following morning. Jacqueline de Bellefort, sitting on the hotel balcony, watched them set off in the picturesque sailing-boat. What she did not see was the departure of a car—laden with luggage, and in which sat a demure-looking maid—from the front door of the hotel. It turned to the right in the direction of Shellâl.

Hercule Poirot decided to pass the remaining two hours before lunch on the island of Elephantine, immediately opposite the hotel.

He went down to the landing-stage. There were two men just stepping into one of the hotel boats, and Poirot joined them. The men were obviously strangers to each other. The younger of them had arrived by train the day before. He was a tall, dark-haired young man, with a thin face and a pugnacious chin. He was wearing an extremely dirty pair of grey flannel trousers and a high-necked polo jumper singularly unsuited to the climate. The other was a slightly podgy middle-aged man who lost no time in entering into conversation with Poirot in idiomatic but slightly broken English. Far from taking part in the conversation, the younger man merely scowled at them both and then deliberately turned his back on them and proceeded to admire the agility with which the Nubian boatman steered the boat with his toes as he manipulated the sail with his hands.

It was very peaceful on the water, the great smooth slippery black rocks gliding by and the soft breeze fanning their faces. Elephantine was reached very quickly and on going ashore Poirot and his loquacious acquaintance made straight for the Museum. By this time the latter had produced a card which he handed to Poirot with a little bow. It bore the inscription: 'Signor Guido Richetti, Archeologo.'

Not to be outdone, Poirot returned the bow and extracted his own card. These formalities completed, the two men stepped into the Museum together, the Italian pouring forth a stream of erudite information. They were by now conversing in French.

The young man in the flannel trousers strolled listlessly

round the Museum, yawning from time to time, and then escaped to the outer air.

Poirot and Signor Richetti at last followed him. The Italian was energetic in examining the ruins, but presently Poirot, espying a green-lined sunshade which he recognised on the rocks down by the river, escaped in that direction.

Mrs. Allerton was sitting on a large rock, a sketch-book by her side and a book on her lap.

Poirot removed his hat politely and Mrs. Allerton at once entered into conversation.

'Good-morning,' she said. 'I suppose it would be quite impossible to get rid of some of these awful children.'

A group of small black figures surrounded her, all grinning and posturing and holding out imploring hands as they lisped 'Bakshish' at intervals, hopefully.

'I thought they'd get tired of me,' said Mrs. Allerton sadly. 'They've been watching me for over two hours now—and they close in on me little by little; and then I yell "Imshi" and brandish my sunshade at them and they scatter for a minute or two. And then they come back and stare and stare, and their eyes are simply disgusting, and so are their noses, and I don't believe I really like children—not unless they're more or less washed and have the rudiments of manners.'

She laughed ruefully.

Poirot gallantly attempted to disperse the mob for her, but without avail. They scattered and then reappeared, closing in once more.

'If there were only any peace in Egypt, I should like it better,' said Mrs. Allerton. 'But you can never be alone anywhere. Someone is always pestering you for money, or offering you donkeys, or beads, or expeditions to native villages, or duck shooting.'

'It is the great disadvantage, that is true,' agreed Poirot.

He spread his handkerchief cautiously on the rock and sat somewhat gingerly upon it.

'Your son is not with you this morning?' he went on.

'No, Tim had some letters to get off before we leave. We're doing the trip to the Second Cataract, you know.'

'I, too.'

'I'm so glad. I want to tell you that I'm quite thrilled to meet you. When we were in Majorca, there was a Mrs. Leech there, and she was telling us the most wonderful things about you. She'd lost a ruby ring bathing, and she was just lamenting that you weren't there to find it for her.'

'Ah, *parbleu*, but I am not the diving seal!'

They both laughed.

Mrs. Allerton went on:

'I saw you from my window walking down the drive with Simon Doyle this morning. Do tell me what you make of him! We're all so excited about him.'

'Ah? Truly?'

'Yes. You know his marriage to Linnet Ridgeway was the greatest surprise. She was supposed to be going to marry Lord Windlesham and then suddenly she gets engaged to this man no one had ever heard of!'

'You know her well, Madame?'

'No, but a cousin of mine, Joanna Southwood, is one of her best friends.'

'Ah, yes, I have read that name in the papers.' He was silent a moment and then went on, 'She is a young lady very much in the news, Mademoiselle Joanna Southwood.'

'Oh, she knows how to advertise herself all right,' snapped Mrs. Allerton.

'You do not like her, Madame?'

'That was a nasty remark of mine.' Mrs. Allerton looked penitent. 'You see I'm old-fashioned. I don't like her much. Tim and she are the greatest friends, though.'

'I see,' said Poirot.

His companion shot a quick look at him. She changed the subject.

'How very few young people there are out here! That pretty girl with the chestnut hair and the appalling mother in the turban is almost the only young creature in the place. You have talked to her a good deal, I notice. She interests me, that child.'

'Why is that, Madame?'

'I feel sorry for her. You can suffer so much when you are young and sensitive. I think she is suffering.'

'Yes, she is not happy, poor little one.'

'Tim and I call her the "sulky girl." I've tried to talk to her once or twice, but she's snubbed me on each occasion. However, I believe she's going on this Nile trip too, and I expect we'll have to be more or less all matey together, shan't we?'

'It is a possible contingency, Madame.'

'I'm very matey really—people interest me enormously. All the different types.' She paused, then said: 'Tim tells me that that dark girl—her name is de Bellefort—is the girl who

60

was engaged to Simon Doyle. It's rather awkward for them—meeting like this.'

'It is awkward—yes,' agreed Poirot.

Mrs. Allerton shot a quick glance at him.

'You know, it may sound foolish, but she almost frightened me. She looked so—intense.'

Poirot nodded his head slowly.

'You were not far wrong, Madame. A great force of emotion is always frightening.'

'Do people interest you too, Monsieur Poirot? Or do you reserve your interest for potential criminals?'

'Madame—that category would not leave many people outside it.'

Mrs. Allerton looked a trifle startled.

'Do you really mean that?'

'Given the particular incentive, that is to say,' Poirot added.

'Which would differ?'

'Naturally.'

Mrs. Allerton hesitated—a little smile on her lips.

'Even I perhaps?'

'Mothers, Madame, are particularly ruthless when their children are in danger.'

She said gravely, 'I think that's true—yes, you're quite right.'

She was silent a minute or two, then she said, smiling: 'I'm trying to imagine motives for crime suitable for everyone in the hotel. It's quite entertaining. Simon Doyle, for instance?'

Poirot said, smiling: 'A very simple crime—a direct short-cut to his objective. No subtlety about it.'

'And therefore very easily detected?'

'Yes; he would not be ingenious.'

'And Linnet?'

'That would be like the Queen in your *Alice in Wonderland*, "Off with her head." '

'Of course. The divine right of monarchy! Just a little bit of the Naboth's vineyard touch. And the dangerous girl—Jacqueline de Bellefort—could *she* do a murder?'

Poirot hesitated for a minute or two, then he said doubtfully, 'Yes, I think she could.'

'But you're not sure?'

'No. She puzzles me, that little one.'

'I don't think Mr. Pennington could do one, do you? He looks so desiccated and dyspeptic—with no red blood in him.'

'But possibly a strong sense of self-preservation.'

'Yes, I suppose so. And poor Mrs. Otterbourne in her turban?'

'There is always vanity.'

'As a motive for murder?' Mrs. Allerton asked doubtfully.

'Motives for murder are sometimes very trivial, Madame.'

'What are the most usual motives, Monsieur Poirot?'

'Most frequent—money. That is to say, gain in its various ramifications. Then there is revenge—and love, and fear, and pure hate, and beneficence——'

'Monsieur Poirot!'

'Oh, yes, Madame. I have known of—shall we say A?—being removed by B solely in order to benefit C. Political murders often come under that heading. Someone is considered to be harmful to civilisation and is removed on that account. Such people forget that life and death are the affair of the good God.'

He spoke gravely.

Mrs. Allerton said quietly: 'I am glad to hear you say that. All the same, God chooses his instruments.'

'There is danger in thinking like that, Madame.'

She adopted a lighter tone.

'After this conversation, Monsieur Poirot, I shall wonder that there is anyone left alive!'

She got up.

'We must be getting back. We have to start immediately after lunch.'

When they reached the landing-stage they found the young man in the polo jumper just taking his place in the boat. The Italian was already waiting. As the Nubian boatman cast the sail loose and they started, Poirot addressed a polite remark to the stranger.

'There are very wonderful things to be seen in Egypt, are there not?'

The young man was now smoking a somewhat noisome pipe. He removed it from his mouth and remarked briefly and very emphatically, in astonishingly well-bred accents: 'They make me sick.'

Mrs. Allerton put on her pince-nez and surveyed him with pleasurable interest.

'Indeed? And why is that?' Poirot asked.

'Take the Pyramids. Great blocks of useless masonry, put up to minister to the egoism of a despotic bloated king. Think of the sweated masses who toiled to build them and died doing it. It makes me sick to think of the suffering and torture they represent.'

Mrs. Allerton said cheerfully: 'You'd rather have no Pyramids, no Parthenon, no beautiful tombs or temples—just the solid satisfaction of knowing that people got three meals a day and died in their beds.'

The young man directed his scowl in her direction.

'I think human beings matter more than stones.'

'But they do not endure as well,' remarked Hercule Poirot.

'I'd rather see a well-fed worker than any so-called work of art. What matters is the future—not the past.'

This was too much for Signor Richetti, who burst into a torrent of impassioned speech not too easy to follow.

The young man retorted by telling everybody exactly what he thought of the capitalist system. He spoke with the utmost venom.

When the tirade was over they had arrived at the hotel landing-stage.

Mrs. Allerton murmured cheerfully: 'Well, well,' and stepped ashore. The young man directed a baleful glance after her.

In the hall of the hotel Poirot encountered Jacqueline de Bellefort. She was dressed in riding clothes. She gave him an ironical little bow.

'I'm going donkey-riding. Do you recommend the native villages, Monsieur Poirot?'

'Is that your excursion to-day, Mademoiselle? *Eh bien,* they are picturesque—but do not spend large sums on native curios.'

'Which are shipped here from Europe? No, I am not so easy to deceive as that.'

With a little nod she passed out into the brilliant sunshine.

Poirot completed his packing—a very simple affair, since his possessions were always in the most meticulous order. Then he repaired to the dining-room and ate an early lunch.

After lunch the hotel bus took the passengers for the Second Cataract to the station where they were to catch the daily express from Cairo on to Shellâl—a ten-minute run.

The Allertons, Poirot, the young man in the dirty flannel trousers and the Italian were the passengers. Mrs. Otterbourne and her daughter had made the expedition to the Dam and to Philae and would join the steamer at Shellâl.

The train from Cairo and Luxor was about twenty minutes late. However, it arrived at last, and the usual scenes of wild activity occurred. Native porters taking suitcases out of the train collided with other porters putting them in.

Finally, somewhat breathless, Poirot found himself, with an assortment of his own, the Allertons', and some totally unknown luggage, in one compartment, while Tim and his mother were elsewhere with the remains of the assorted baggage.

The compartment in which Poirot found himself was occupied by an elderly lady with a very wrinkled face, a stiff white stock, a good many diamonds and an expression of reptilian contempt for the majority of mankind.

She treated Poirot to an aristocratic glare and retired behind the pages of an American magazine. A big, rather clumsy young woman of under thirty was sitting opposite her. She had eager brown eyes, rather like a dog's, untidy hair, and a terrific air of willingness to please. At intervals the old lady looked over the top of her magazine and snapped an order at her.

'Cornelia, collect the rugs.' 'When we arrive look after my dressing-case. On no account let anyone else handle it.' 'Don't forget my paper-cutter.'

The train run was brief. In ten minutes' time they came to rest on the jetty where the S.S. *Karnak* was awaiting them. The Otterbournes were already on board.

The *Karnak* was a smaller steamer than the *Papyrus* and the *Lotus*, the First Cataract steamers, which are too large to pass through the locks of the Assuan dam. The passengers went on board and were shown their accommodation. Since the boat was not full, most of the passengers had accommodation on the promenade deck. The entire forward part of this deck was occupied by an observation saloon, all glass-enclosed, where the passengers could sit and watch the river unfold before them. On the deck below were a smoking-room and a small drawing-room and on the deck below that, the dining-saloon.

Having seen his possessions disposed in his cabin, Poirot came out on the deck again to watch the process of departure. He joined Rosalie Otterbourne, who was leaning over the side.

'So now we journey into Nubia. You are pleased, Mademoiselle?'

The girl drew a deep breath.

'Yes. I feel that one's really getting away from things at last.'

She made a gesture with her hand. There was a savage aspect about the sheet of water in front of them, the masses of rock without vegetation that came down to the water's edge—here and there a trace of houses, abandoned and ruined as a result of the damming up of the waters. The whole scene had a melancholy, almost sinister charm.

'Away from *people*,' said Rosalie Otterbourne.

'Except those of our own number, Mademoiselle?'

She shrugged her shoulders. Then she said: 'There's something about this country that makes me feel—wicked. It brings to the surface all the things that are boiling inside one. Everything's so unfair—so unjust.'

'I wonder. You cannot judge by material evidence.'

Rosalie muttered: 'Look at—at some people's mothers—and look at mine. There is no God but Sex, and Salome Otterbourne is its Prophet.' She stopped. 'I shouldn't have said that, I suppose.'

Poirot made a gesture with his hands.

'Why not say it—to me? I am one of those who hear many things. If, as you say, you boil inside—like the jam—*eh bien,* let the scum come to the surface, and then one can take it off with a spoon, so.'

He made the gesture of dropping something into the Nile.

'Then, it has gone.'

'What an extraordinary man you are!' Rosalie said. Her sulky mouth twisted into a smile. Then she suddenly stiffened as she exclaimed: 'Well, here are Mrs. Doyle and her husband! I'd no idea *they* were coming on this trip!'

Linnet had just emerged from a cabin half-way down the deck. Simon was behind her. Poirot was almost startled by the look of her—so radiant, so assured. She looked positively arrogant with happiness. Simon Doyle, too, was a transformed being. He was grinning from ear to ear and looking like a happy schoolboy.

'This is grand,' he said as he too leaned on the rail. 'I'm really looking forward to this trip, aren't you, Linnet? It feels, somehow, so much less touristy—as though we were really going into the heart of Egypt.'

His wife responded quickly: 'I know. It's so much—wilder, somehow.'

Her hand slipped through his arm. He pressed it close to his side.

'We're off, Lin,' he murmured.

The steamer was drawing away from the jetty. They had started on their seven-day journey to the Second Cataract and back.

Behind them a light silvery laugh rang out. Linnet whipped round.

Jacqueline de Bellefort was standing there. She seemed amused.

'Hullo, Linnet! I didn't expect to find *you* here. I thought you said you were staying at Assuan another ten days. This is a surprise!'

'You—you didn't——' Linnet's tongue stammered. She forced a ghastly conventional smile. 'I—I didn't expect to see you either.'

'No?'

Jacqueline moved away to the other side of the boat. Linnet's grasp on her husband's arm tightened.

'Simon—Simon——'

All Doyle's good-natured pleasure had gone. He looked furious. His hands clenched themselves in spite of his effort at self-control.

The two of them moved a little away. Without turning his head Poirot caught scraps of disjointed words:

'. . . turn back . . . impossible . . . we could . . .' and then, slightly louder, Doyle's voice, despairing but grim: 'We can't run away for ever, Lin. We've got to go through with it now. . . .'

It was some hours later. Daylight was just fading. Poirot stood in the glass-enclosed saloon looking straight ahead. The *Karnak* was going through a narrow gorge. The rocks came down with a kind of sheer ferocity to the river flowing deep and swift between them. They were in Nubia now.

He heard a movement and Linnet Doyle stood by his side. Her fingers twisted and untwisted themselves; she looked as he had never yet seen her look. There was about her the air of a bewildered child. She said:

'Monsieur Poirot, I'm afraid—I'm afraid of everything. I've never felt like this before. All these wild rocks and the awful grimness and starkness. Where are we going? What's going to happen? I'm afraid, I tell you. Everyone hates me. I've never felt like that before. I've always been nice to people —I've done things for them—and they hate me—lots of people hate me. Except for Simon, I'm surrounded by enemies. . . . It's terrible to feel—that there are people who hate you. . . .'

'But what is all this, Madame?'

She shook her head.

'I suppose—it's nerves. . . . I just feel that—everything's unsafe all round me.'

She cast a quick nervous glance over her shoulder. Then she said abruptly: 'How will all this end? We're caught here. Trapped! There's no way out. We've got to go on. I —I don't know where I am.'

She slipped down on to a seat. Poirot looked down on her gravely; his glance was not untinged with compassion.

'How did she know we were coming on this boat?' she said. 'How could she have known?'

Poirot shook his head as he answered: 'She has brains, you know.'

'I feel as though I shall never escape from her.'

Poirot said: 'There is one plan you might have adopted. In fact I am surprised that it did not occur to you. After all, with you, Madame, money is no object. Why did you not engage your own private dahabiyeh?'

Linnet shook her head rather helplessly.

'If we'd known about all this—but you see we didn't— then. And it was difficult. . . .' She flashed out with sudden impatience: 'Oh! you don't understand half my difficulties. I've got to be careful with Simon. . . . He's—he's absurdly sensitive—about money. About my having so much! He wanted me to go to some little place in Spain with him—he— he wanted to pay all our honeymoon expenses himself. As if it *mattered*! Men are stupid! He's got to get used to—to— living comfortably. The mere idea of a dahabiyeh upset him —the—the needless expense. I've got to educate him—gradually.'

She looked up, bit her lip vexedly, as though feeling that she had been led into discussing her difficulties rather too unguardedly.

She got up.

'I must change. I'm sorry, Monsieur Poirot. I'm afraid I've been talking a lot of foolish nonsense.'

Chapter Eight

Mrs. Allerton, looking quiet and distinguished in her simple black lace evening gown, descended two decks to the dining-room. At the door of it her son caught her up.

'Sorry, darling. I thought I was going to be late.'

'I wonder where we sit.' The saloon was dotted with little tables. Mrs. Allerton paused till the steward, who was busy seating a party of people, could attend to them.

'By the way,' she added, 'I asked little Hercule Poirot to sit at our table.'

'Mother, you didn't!' Tim sounded really taken aback and annoyed.

His mother stared at him in surprise. Tim was usually so easy-going.

'My dear, do you mind?'

'Yes, I do. He's an unmitigated little bounder!'

'Oh, no, Tim! I don't agree with you.'

'Anyway, what do we want to get mixed up with an outsider for? Cooped up like this on a small boat, that sort of thing is always a bore. He'll be with us morning, noon and night.'

'I'm sorry, dear.' Mrs. Allerton looked distressed. 'I thought really it would amuse you. After all, he must have had a varied experience. And you love detective stories.'

Tim grunted.

'I wish you wouldn't have these bright ideas, Mother. We can't get out of it now, I suppose?'

'Really, Tim, I don't see how we can.'

'Oh, well, we shall have to put up with it, I suppose.'

The steward came to them at this minute and led them to a table. Mrs. Allerton's face wore rather a puzzled expression as she followed him. Tim was usually so easy-going and good-tempered. This outburst was quite unlike him. It wasn't as though he had the ordinary Britisher's dislike—and mistrust—of foreigners. Tim was very cosmopolitan. Oh, well—she sighed. Men were incomprehensible! Even one's nearest and dearest had unsuspected reactions and feelings.

As they took their places, Hercule Poirot came quickly and silently into the dining-saloon. He paused with his hand on the back of the third chair.

'You really permit, Madame, that I avail myself of your kind suggestion?'

'Of course. Sit down, Monsieur Poirot.'

'You are most amiable.'

She was uneasily conscious that, as he seated himself, he shot a swift glance at Tim, and that Tim had not quite succeeded in masking a somewhat sullen expression.

Mrs. Allerton set herself to produce a pleasant atmosphere. As they drank their soup, she picked up the passenger list which had been placed beside her plate.

'Let's try and identify everybody,' she suggested cheerfully. 'I always think that's rather fun.'

She began reading: 'Mrs. Allerton, Mr. T. Allerton. That's easy enough! Miss de Bellefort. They've put her at the same table as the Otterbournes, I see. I wonder what she and Rosalie will make of each other. Who comes next? Dr. Bessner. Dr. Bessner? Who can identify Dr. Bessner?'

She bent her glance on a table at which four men sat together.

'I think he must be the fat one with the closely shaved head and the moustache. A German, I should imagine. He seems to be enjoying his soup very much.' Certain succulent noises floated across to them.

Mrs. Allerton continued: 'Miss Bowers? Can we make a guess at Miss Bowers? There are three or four women—no, we'll leave her for the present. Mr. and Mrs. Doyle. Yes, indeed, the lions of this trip. She really is very beautiful, and what a perfectly lovely frock she is wearing.'

Tim turned round in his chair. Linnet and her husband and Andrew Pennington had been given a table in the corner. Linnet was wearing a white dress and pearls.

'It looks frightfully simple to me,' said Tim. 'Just a length of stuff with a kind of cord round the middle.'

'Yes, darling,' said his mother. 'A very nice manly description of an eighty-guinea model.'

'I can't think why women pay so much for their clothes,' Tim said. 'It seems absurd to me.'

Mrs. Allerton proceeded with her study of her fellow passengers.

'Mr. Fanthorp must be one of the four at that table. The intensely quiet young man who never speaks. Rather a nice face, cautious but intelligent.'

Poirot agreed.

'He is intelligent—yes. He does not talk, but he listens

very attentively, and he also watches. Yes, he makes good use of his eyes. Not quite the type you would expect to find travelling for pleasure in this part of the world. I wonder what he is doing here.'

'Mr. Ferguson,' read Mrs. Allerton. 'I feel that Ferguson must be our anti-capitalist friend. Mrs. Otterbourne, Miss Otterbourne. We know all about them. Mr. Pennington? Alias Uncle Andrew. He's a good-looking man, I think——'

'Now, Mother,' said Tim.

'I think he's very good-looking in a dry sort of way,' said Mrs. Allerton. 'Rather a ruthless jaw. Probably the kind of man one reads about in the paper, who operates on Wall Street—or is it *in* Wall Street? I'm sure he must be extremely rich. Next—Monsieur Hercule Poirot—whose talents are really being wasted. Can't you get up a crime for Monsieur Poirot, Tim?'

But her well-meant banter only seemed to annoy her son anew. He scowled and Mrs. Allerton hurried on: 'Mr. Richetti. Our Italian archæological friend. Then Miss Robson and last of all Miss Van Schuyler. The last's easy. The very ugly old American lady who obviously feels herself the queen of the boat and who is clearly going to be very exclusive and speak to nobody who doesn't come up to the most exacting standards! She's rather marvellous, isn't she, really? A kind of period piece. The two women with her must be Miss Bowers and Miss Robson—perhaps a secretary, the thin one with pince-nez, and a poor relation, the rather pathetic young woman who is obviously enjoying herself in spite of being treated like a black slave. I think Robson's the secretary woman and Bowers is the poor relation.'

'Wrong, Mother,' said Tim, grinning. He had suddenly recovered his good humour.

'How do you know?'

'Because I was in the lounge before dinner and the old bean said to the companion woman: "Where's Miss Bowers? Fetch her at once, Cornelia." And away trotted Cornelia like an obedient dog.'

'I shall have to talk to Miss Van Schuyler,' mused Mrs. Allerton.

Tim grinned again.

'She'll snub you, Mother.'

'Not at all. I shall pave the way by sitting near her and conversing, in low (but penetrating), well-bred tones, about any titled relations and friends I can remember. I think a casual mention of your second cousin, once removed, the Duke of Glasgow, would probably do the trick.'

'How unscrupulous you are, Mother!'

Events after dinner were not without their amusing side to a student of human nature.

The socialistic young man (who turned out to be Mr. Ferguson as deduced) retired to the smoking-room, scorning the assemblage of passengers in the observation saloon on the top deck.

Miss Van Schuyler duly secured the best and most undraughty position there by advancing firmly on a table at which Mrs. Otterbourne was sitting and saying, 'You'll excuse me, I am sure, but I *think* my knitting was left here!'

Fixed by a hypnotic eye, the turban rose and gave ground. Miss Van Schuyler established herself and her suite. Mrs. Otterbourne sat down near by and hazarded various remarks, which were met with such chilling politeness that she soon gave up. Miss Van Schuyler then sat in glorious isolation. The Doyles sat with the Allertons. Dr. Bessner retained the quiet Mr. Fanthorp as a companion. Jacqueline de Bellefort sat by herself with a book. Rosalie Otterbourne was restless. Mrs. Allerton spoke to her once or twice and tried to draw her into their group, but the girl responded ungraciously.

M. Hercule Poirot spent his evening listening to an account of Mrs. Otterbourne's mission as a writer.

On his way to his cabin that night he encountered Jacqueline de Bellefort. She was leaning over the rail and, as she turned her head, he was struck by the look of acute misery on her face. There was now no insouciance, no malicious defiance, no dark flaming triumph.

'Good-night, Mademoiselle.'

'Good-night, Monsieur Poirot.' She hesitated, then said: 'You were surprised to find me here?'

'I was not so much surprised as sorry—very sorry. . . .' He spoke gravely.

'You mean sorry—for *me*?'

'That is what I meant. You have chosen, Mademoiselle, the dangerous course. . . . As we here in this boat have embarked on a journey, so you too have embarked on your own private journey—a journey on a swift-moving river, between dangerous rocks, and heading for who knows what currents of disaster. . . .'

'Why do you say this?'

'Because it is true. . . . You have cut the bonds that

moored you to safety. I doubt now if you could turn back if you would.'

She said very slowly: 'That is true. . . .'

Then she flung her head back.

'Ah, well—one must follow one's star, wherever it leads.'

'Beware, Mademoiselle, that it is not a false star. . . .'

She laughed and mimicked the parrot cry of the donkey boys: 'That very bad star, sir! That star fall down. . . .'

He was just dropping off to sleep when the murmur of voices awoke him. It was Simon Doyle's voice he heard, repeating the same words he had used when the steamer left Shellâl.

'We've got to go through with it now. . . .'

'Yes,' thought Hercule Poirot to himself, 'we have got to go through with it now. . . .'

He was not happy.

Chapter Nine

The steamer arrived early next morning at Ez-Sebûa.

Cornelia Robson, her face beaming, a large flapping hat on her head, was one of the first to hurry on shore. Cornelia was not good at snubbing people. She was of an amiable disposition and disposed to like all her fellow creatures.

The sight of Hercule Poirot, in a white suit, pink shirt, large black bow tie and a white topee, did not make her wince as the aristocratic Miss Van Schuyler would assuredly have winced. As they walked together up an avenue of sphinxes, she responded readily to his conventional opening, 'Your companions are not coming ashore to view the temple?'

'Well, you see, Cousin Marie—that's Miss Van Schuyler —never gets up very early. She has to be very, very careful of her health. And of course she wanted Miss Bowers, that's her hospital nurse, to do things for her. And she said, too, that this isn't one of the best temples—but she was frightfully kind and said it would be quite all right for me to come.'

'That was very gracious of her,' said Poirot dryly.

The ingenuous Cornelia agreed unsuspectingly.

'Oh, she's very kind. It's simply wonderful of her to bring me on this trip. I do feel I'm a lucky girl. I just could hardly believe it when she suggested to Mother that I should come too.'

'And you have enjoyed it—yes?'

'Oh, it's been wonderful! I've seen Italy—Venice and Padua and Pisa—and then Cairo—only Cousin Marie wasn't very well in Cairo, so I couldn't get round much, and now this wonderful trip up to Wâdi Halfa and back.'

Poirot said, smiling, 'You have the happy nature, Mademoiselle.'

He looked thoughtfully from her to silent, frowning Rosalie, who was walking ahead by herself.

'She's very nice-looking, isn't she?' said Cornelia, following his glance. 'Only kind of scornful-looking. She's very English, of course. She's not as lovely as Mrs. Doyle. I think Mrs. Doyle's the loveliest, the most elegant woman I've ever seen! And her husband just worships the ground she walks on, doesn't he? I think that grey-haired lady is kind of distinguished-looking, don't you? She's a cousin to a Duke, I believe. She was talking about him right near us last night. But she isn't actually titled herself, is she?'

She prattled on until the dragoman in charge called a halt and began to intone: 'This temple was dedicated to Egyptian God Amun and the Sun God Re-Harakhte—whose symbol was hawk's head. . . .'

It droned on. Dr. Bessner, Baedeker in hand, mumbled to himself in German. He preferred the written word.

Tim Allerton had not joined the party. His mother was breaking the ice with the reserved Mr. Fanthorp. Andrew Pennington, his arm through Linnet Doyle's, was listening attentively, seemingly most interested in the measurements as recited by the guide.

'Sixty-five feet high, is that so? Looks a little less to me. Great fellow, this Rameses. An Egyptian live wire.'

'A big business man, Uncle Andrew.'

Andrew Pennington looked at her appreciatively.

'You look fine this morning, Linnet. I've been a mite worried about you lately. You've looked kind of peaky.'

Chatting together, the party returned to the boat. Once more the *Karnak* glided up the river. The scenery was less stern now. There were palms, cultivation.

It was as though the change in the scenery had relieved some secret oppression that had brooded over the passengers. Tim Allerton had got over his fit of moodiness. Rosalie looked less sulky. Linnet seemed almost light-hearted.

Pennington said to her: 'It's tactless to talk business to a bride on her honeymoon, but there are just one or two things ——'

'Why, of course, Uncle Andrew.' Linnet at once became businesslike. 'My marriage has made a difference, of course.'

'That's just it. Some time or other I want your signature to several documents.'

'Why not now?'

Andrew Pennington glanced round. Their corner of the observation saloon was quite untenanted. Most of the people were outside on the deck space between the observation saloon and the cabin. The only occupants of the saloon were Mr. Ferguson—who was drinking beer at a small table in the middle, his legs, encased in their dirty flannel trousers, stuck out in front of him, whilst he whistled to himself in the intervals of drinking—M. Hercule Poirot, who was sitting close up to the front glass, intent on the panorama unfolding before him, and Miss Van Schuyler, who was sitting in a corner reading a book on Egypt.

'That's fine,' said Andrew Pennington. He left the saloon.

Linnet and Simon smiled at each other—a slow smile that took a few minutes to come to full fruition.

'All right, sweet?' he asked.

'Yes, still all right. . . . Funny how I'm not rattled any more.'

Simon said with deep conviction in his tone: 'You're marvellous.'

Pennington came back. He brought with him a sheaf of closely written documents.

'Mercy!' cried Linnet. 'Have I got to sign all these?'

Andrew Pennington was apologetic.

'It's tough on you, I know, but I'd just like to get your affairs put in proper shape. First of all there's the lease of the Fifth Avenue property . . . then there are the Western Land Concessions . . .' He talked on, rustling and sorting the papers. Simon yawned.

The door to the deck swung open and Mr. Fanthorp came in. He gazed aimlessly round, then strolled forward and stood by Poirot looking out at the pale blue water and the yellow enveloping sands. . . .

'——you sign just there,' concluded Pennington, spreading a paper before Linnet and indicating a space.

Linnet picked up the document and glanced through it. She turned back once to the first page, then, taking up the fountain pen Pennington had laid beside her, she signed her name *Linnet Doyle*. . . .

Pennington took away the paper and spread out another.

Fanthorp wandered over in their direction. He peered out through the side window at something that seemed to interest him on the bank they were passing.

'That's just the transfer,' said Pennington. 'You needn't read it.'

But Linnet took a brief glance through it. Pennington laid down a third paper. Again Linnet perused it carefully.

'They're all quite straightforward,' said Andrew. 'Nothing of interest. Only legal phraseology.'

Simon yawned again.

'My dear girl, you're not going to read the whole lot through, are you? You'll be at it till lunch-time and longer.'

'I always read everything through,' said Linnet. 'Father taught me to do that. He said there might be some clerical error.'

Pennington laughed rather harshly.

'You're a grand woman of business, Linnet.'

'She's much more conscientious than I'd be,' said Simon, laughing. 'I've never read a legal document in my life. I sign where they tell me to sign on the dotted line—and that's that.'

'That's frightfully slipshod,' said Linnet disapprovingly.

'I've no business head,' declared Simon cheerfully. 'Never had. A fellow tells me to sign—I sign. It's much the simplest way.'

Andrew Pennington was looking at him thoughtfully. He said dryly, stroking his upper lip, 'A little risky sometimes, Doyle?'

'Nonsense,' replied Simon. 'I'm not one of those people who believe the whole world is out to do one down. I'm a trusting kind of fellow—and it pays, you know. I've hardly ever been let down.'

Suddenly, to everyone's surprise, the silent Mr. Fanthorp swung around and addressed Linnet.

'I hope I'm not butting in, but you must let me say how much I admire your businesslike capacity. In my profession —er—I am a lawyer—I find ladies sadly unbusinesslike. Never to sign a document unless you read it through is admirable—altogether admirable.'

He gave a little bow. Then, rather red in the face, he turned once more to contemplate the banks of the Nile.

Linnet said rather uncertainly: 'Er—thank you. . . .' She bit her lip to repress a giggle. The young man had looked so preternaturally solemn.

Andrew Pennington looked seriously annoyed.

Simon Doyle looked uncertain whether to be annoyed or amused.

The backs of Mr. Fanthorp's ears were bright crimson.

'Next, please,' said Linnet, smiling up at Pennington.

But Pennington was looking decidedly ruffled.

'I think perhaps some other time would be better,' he said stiffly. 'As—er—Doyle says, if you have to read through all these we shall be here till lunch-time. We mustn't miss enjoying the scenery. Anyway those first two papers were the only urgent ones. We'll settle down to business later.'

'It's frightfully hot in here,' Linnet said. 'Let's go outside.'

The three of them passed through the swing door. Hercule Poirot turned his head. His gaze rested thoughtfully on Mr. Fanthorp's back; then it shifted to the lounging figure of Mr. Ferguson who had his head thrown back and was still whistling softly to himself.

Finally Poirot looked over at the upright figure of Miss Van Schuyler in her corner. Miss Van Schuyler was glaring at Mr. Ferguson.

The swing door on the port side opened and Cornelia Robson hurried in.

'You've been a long time,' snapped the old lady. 'Where've you been?'

'I'm so sorry, Cousin Marie. The wool wasn't where you said it was. It was in another case altogether——'

'My dear child, you are perfectly hopeless at finding anything! You are willing, I know, my dear, but you must try to be a little cleverer and quicker. It only needs *concentration*.'

'I'm so sorry, Cousin Marie. I'm afraid I am very stupid.'

'Nobody need be stupid if they *try*, my dear. I have brought you on this trip, and I expect a little attention in return.'

Cornelia flushed.

'I'm very sorry, Cousin Marie.'

'And where is Miss Bowers? It was time for my drops ten minutes ago. Please go and find her at once. The doctor said it was most important——'

But at this stage Miss Bowers entered, carrying a small medicine glass.

'Your drops, Miss Van Schuyler.'

'I should have had them at eleven,' snapped the old lady. 'If there's one thing I detest it's unpunctuality.'

'Quite,' said Miss Bowers. She glanced at her wristwatch. 'It's exactly half a minute to eleven.'

'By my watch it's ten past.'

'I think you'll find my watch is right. It's a perfect time-keeper. It never loses or gains.' Miss Bowers was quite imperturbable.

Miss Van Schuyler swallowed the contents of the medicine glass.

'I feel definitely worse,' she snapped.

'I'm sorry to hear that, Miss Van Schuyler.'

Miss Bowers did not sound sorry. She sounded completely uninterested. She was obviously making the correct reply mechanically.

'It's too hot in here,' snapped Miss Van Schuyler. 'Find me a chair on the deck, Miss Bowers. Cornelia, bring my knitting. Don't be clumsy or drop it. And then I shall want you to wind some wool.'

The procession passed out.

Mr. Ferguson sighed, stirred his legs and remarked to the world at large, 'Gosh, I'd like to scrag that dame.'

Poirot asked interestedly: 'She is a type you dislike, eh?'

'Dislike? I should say so. What good has that woman ever been to anyone or anything? She's never worked or lifted a finger. She's just battened on other people. She's a parasite—and a damned unpleasant parasite. There are a lot of people on this boat I'd say the world could do without.'

'Really?'

'Yes. That girl in here just now, signing share transfers and throwing her weight about. Hundreds and thousands of wretched workers slaving for a mere pittance to keep her in silk stockings and useless luxuries. One of the richest women in England, so someone told me—and never done a hand's turn in her life.'

'Who told you she was one of the richest women in England?'

Mr. Ferguson cast a belligerent eye at him.

'A man you wouldn't be seen speaking to! A man who works with his hands and isn't ashamed of it! Not one of your dressed-up, foppish good-for-nothings.'

His eye rested unfavourably on the bow tie and pink shirt.

'Me, I work with my brains and am not ashamed of it,' said Poirot, answering the glance.

Mr. Ferguson merely snorted.

'Ought to be shot—the lot of them!' he asserted.

'My dear young man,' said Poirot, 'what a passion you have for violence!'

'Can you tell me of any good that can be done without

it? You've got to break down and destroy before you can build up.'

'It is certainly much easier and much noisier and much more spectacular.'

'What do *you* do for a living? Nothing at all, I bet. Probably call yourself a middle man.'

'I am not a middle man. I am a top man,' declared Hercule Poirot with a slight arrogance.

'What *are* you?'

'I am a detective,' said Hercule Poirot with the modest air of one who says 'I am a king.'

'Good God!' The young man seemed seriously taken aback. 'Do you mean that girl actually totes about a dumb dick? Is she as careful of her precious skin as *that*?'

'I have no connection whatever with Monsieur and Madame Doyle,' said Poirot stiffly. 'I am on a holiday.'

'Enjoying a vacation—eh?'

'And you? Is it not that you are on a holiday also?'

'Holiday!' Mr. Ferguson snorted. Then he added cryptically: 'I'm studying conditions.'

'Very interesting,' murmured Poirot and moved gently out on to the deck.

Miss Van Schuyler was established in the best corner. Cornelia knelt in front of her, her arms outstretched with a skein of grey wool upon them. Miss Bowers was sitting very upright reading the *Saturday Evening Post*.

Poirot wandered gently onward down the starboard deck. As he passed round the stern of the boat he almost ran into a woman who turned a startled face towards him—a dark, piquant, Latin face. She was neatly dressed in black and had been standing talking to a big burly man in uniform—one of the engineers, by the look of him. There was a queer expression on both their faces—guilt and alarm. Poirot wondered what they had been talking about.

He rounded the stern and continued his walk along the port side. A cabin door opened and Mrs. Otterbourne emerged and nearly fell into his arms. She was wearing a scarlet satin dressing-gown.

'So sorry,' she apologised. 'Dear Mr. Poirot—so very sorry. The motion—just the motion, you know. Never did have any sea legs. If the boat would only keep still. . . .' She clutched at his arm. 'It's the pitching I can't stand. . . . Never really happy at sea. . . . And left all alone here hour after hour. That girl of mine—no sympathy—no understanding of her poor old mother who's done everything for her. . . .' Mrs. Otterbourne began to weep. 'Slaved for her I have—worn myself to the bone—to the bone. A *grande amoureuse*—that's what I might have been—a *grande amoureuse*—sacrificed everything—everything. . . . And nobody cares! But I'll tell everyone —I'll tell them now—how she neglects me—how hard she is— making me come on this journey—bored to death. . . . I'll go and tell them now——'

She surged forward. Poirot gently repressed the action.

'I will send her to you, Madame. Re-enter your cabin. It is best that way——'

'No. I want to tell everyone—everyone on the boat——'

'It is too dangerous, Madame. The sea is too rough. You might be swept overboard.'

Mrs. Otterbourne looked at him doubtfully.

'You think so. You really think so?'

'I do.'

He was successful. Mrs. Otterbourne wavered, faltered and re-entered her cabin.

Poirot's nostrils twitched once or twice. Then he nodded and walked on to where Rosalie Otterbourne was sitting between Mrs. Allerton and Tim.

'Your mother wants you, Mademoiselle.'

She had been laughing quite happily. Now her face clouded over. She shot a quick suspicious look at him and hurried along the deck.

'I can't make that child out,' said Mrs. Allerton. 'She varies so. One day she's friendly; the next day, she's positively rude.'

'Thoroughly spoilt and bad-tempered,' said Tim.

Mrs. Allerton shook her head.

'No. I don't think it's that. I think she's unhappy.'

Tim shrugged his shoulders.

'Oh, well, I suppose we've all got our private troubles.' His voice sounded hard and curt.

A booming noise was heard.

'Lunch,' cried Mrs. Allerton delightedly. 'I'm starving.'

That evening, Poirot noticed that Mrs. Allerton was sitting talking to Miss Van Schuyler. As he passed, Mrs. Allerton closed one eye and opened it again. She was saying, 'Of course at Calfries Castle—the dear Duke——'

Cornelia, released from attendance, was out on the deck. She was listening to Dr. Bessner, who was instructing her somewhat ponderously in Egyptology as culled from the pages of Baedeker. Cornelia listened with rapt attention.

Leaning over the rail Tim Allerton was saying: 'Anyhow, it's a rotten world. . . .'

Rosalie Otterbourne answered: 'It's unfair; some people have everything.'

Poirot sighed. He was glad that he was no longer young.

Chapter Ten

On the Monday morning various expressions of delight and appreciation were heard on the deck of the *Karnak*. The steamer was moored to the bank and a few hundred yards away, the morning sun just striking it, was a great temple carved out of the face of the rock. Four colossal figures, hewn out of the cliff, look out eternally over the Nile and face the rising sun.

Cornelia Robson said incoherently: 'Oh, Monsieur Poirot, isn't it wonderful? I mean they're so big and peaceful—and looking at them makes one feel that one's so small and—and rather like an insect—and that nothing matters very much really, does it?'

Mr. Fanthorp, who was standing near by, murmured, 'Very —er—impressive.'

'Grand, isn't it?' said Simon Doyle, strolling up. He went on confidentially to Poirot: 'You know, I'm not much of a fellow for temples and sight-seeing and all that, but a place like this sort of gets you, if you know what I mean. Those old Pharaohs must have been wonderful fellows.'

The other had drifted away. Simon lowered his voice.

'I'm no end glad we came on this trip. It's—well, it's cleared things up. Amazing why it should—but there it is. Linnet's got her nerve back. She says it's because she's actually *faced* the business at last.'

'I think that is very probable,' said Poirot.

'She says that when she actually saw Jackie on the boat she felt terrible—and then, suddenly, it didn't matter any more. We're both agreed that we won't try to dodge her any more. We'll just meet her on her own ground and show her that this ridiculous stunt of hers doesn't worry us a bit. It's just damned bad form—that's all. She thought she'd got us badly rattled, but now, well, we just aren't rattled any more. That ought to show her.'

'Yes,' said Poirot thoughtfully.

'So that's splendid, isn't it?'

'Oh, yes, yes.'

Linnet came along the deck. She was dressed in a soft shade of apricot linen. She was smiling. She greeted Poirot with no particular enthusiasm, just gave him a cool nod and then drew her husband away.

Poirot realised with a momentary flicker of amusement that he had not made himself popular by his critical attitude. Linnet was used to unqualified admiration of all she was or did. Hercule Poirot had sinned noticeably against this creed.

Mrs. Allerton, joining him, murmured:

'What a difference in that girl! She looked worried and not very happy at Assuan. To-day she looks so happy that one might almost be afraid she was fey.'

Before Poirot could respond as he meant, the party was called to order. The official dragoman took charge and the party was led ashore to visit Abu Simbel.

Poirot himself fell into step with Andrew Pennington.

'It is your first visit to Egypt—yes?' he asked.

'Why, no, I was here in nineteen twenty-three. That is to say, I was in Cairo. I've never been this trip up the Nile before.'

'You came over on the *Carmanic*, I believe—at least so Madame Doyle was telling me.'

Pennington shot a shrewd glance in his direction.

'Why, yes, that is so,' he admitted.

'I wondered if you had happened to come across some friends of mine who were aboard—the Rushington Smiths.'

'I can't recall anyone of that name. The boat was full and we had bad weather. A lot of passengers hardly appeared, and in any case the voyage is so short one doesn't get to know who is on board and who isn't.'

'Yes, that is very true. What a pleasant surprise your running into Madame Doyle and her husband. You had no idea they were married?'

'No. Mrs. Doyle had written me, but the letter was forwarded on and I only received it some days after our unexpected meeting in Cairo.'

'You have known her for very many years, I understand?'

'Why, I should say I have, Monsieur Poirot. I've known

Linnet Ridgeway since she was just a cute little thing so high——' He made an illustrating gesture. 'Her father and I were lifelong friends. A very remarkable man, Melhuish Ridgeway—and a very successful one.'

'His daughter comes into a considerable fortune, I understand. . . . Ah, *pardon*—perhaps it is not delicate what I say there.'

Andrew Pennington seemed slightly amused.

'Oh, that's pretty common knowledge. Yes, Linnet's a wealthy woman.'

'I suppose, though, that the recent slump is bound to affect any stocks, however sound they may be?'

Pennington took a moment or two to answer. He said at last: 'That, of course, is true to a certain extent. The position is very difficult in these days.'

Poirot murmured: 'I should imagine, however, that Madame Doyle has a keen business head.'

'That is so. Yes, that is so. Linnet is a clever practical girl.'

They came to a halt. The guide proceeded to instruct them on the subject of the temple built by the great Rameses. The four colossi of Rameses himself, one pair on each side of the entrance, hewn out of the living rock, looked down on the little straggling party of tourists.

Signor Richetti, disdaining the remarks of the dragoman, was busy examining the reliefs of Negro and Syrian captives on the bases of the colossi on either side of the entrance.

When the party entered the temple, a sense of dimness and peace came over them. The still vividly coloured reliefs on some of the inner walls were pointed out, but the party tended to break up into groups.

Dr. Bessner read sonorously in German from a Baedeker, pausing every now and then to translate for the benefit of Cornelia, who walked in a docile manner beside him. This was not to continue, however. Miss Van Schuyler, entering on the arms of the phlegmatic Miss Bowers, uttered a commanding: 'Cornelia, come here,' and the instruction had perforce to cease. Dr. Bessner beamed after her vaguely through his thick lenses.

'A very nice maiden, that,' he announced to Poirot. 'She does not look so starved as some of these young women. No, she has the nice curves. She listens too very intelligently; it is a pleasure to instruct her.'

It fleeted across Poirot's mind that it seemed to be Cornelia's fate either to be bullied or instructed. In any case she was always the listener, never the talker.

Miss Bowers, momentarily released by the peremptory summons of Cornelia, was standing in the middle of the temple, looking about her with her cool, incurious gaze. Her reaction to the wonders of the past was succinct.

'The guide says the name of one of these gods or goddesses was Mut. Can you beat it?'

There was an inner sanctuary where sat four figures eternally presiding, strangely dignified in their dim aloofness.

Before them stood Linnet and her husband. Her arm was in his, her face lifted—a typical face of the new civilisation, intelligent, curious, untouched by the past.

Simon said suddenly: 'Let's get out of here. I don't like these four fellows—especially the one in the high hat.'

'That's Amon, I suppose. And that one is Rameses. Why don't you like them? I think they're very impressive.'

'They're a damned sight too impressive; there's something uncanny about them. Come out into the sunlight.'

Linnet laughed but yielded.

They came out of the temple into the sunshine with the sand yellow and warm about their feet. Linnet began to laugh. At their feet in a row, presenting a momentarily gruesome appearance as though sawn from their bodies, were the heads of half a dozen Nubian boys. The eyes rolled, the heads moved rhythmically from side to side, the lips chanted a new invocation:

'Hip, hip *hurray*! Hip, hip *hurray*! Very good, very nice. Thank you very much.'

'How absurd! How do they do it? Are they really buried very deep?'

Simon produced some small change.

'Very good, very nice, very expensive,' he mimicked.

Two small boys in charge of the 'show' picked up the coins neatly.

Linnet and Simon passed on. They had no wish to return to the boat, and they were weary of sight-seeing. They settled themselves with their backs to the cliff and let the warm sun bake them through.

'How lovely the sun is,' thought Linnet. 'How warm—how safe. . . . How lovely it is to be happy. . . . How lovely to be me—me . . . me . . . Linnet . . .'

Her eyes closed. She was half asleep, half awake, drifting in the midst of thought that was like the sand drifting and blowing.

Simon's eyes were open. They too held contentment. What a fool he'd been to be rattled that first night. . . . There was nothing to be rattled about. . . . Everything was all right. . . . After all, one could trust Jackie——

There was a shout—people running towards him waving their arms—shouting. . . .

Simon stared stupidly for a moment. Then he sprang to his feet and dragged Linnet with him.

Not a minute too soon. A big boulder hurtling down the cliff crashed past them. If Linnet had remained where she was she would have been crushed to atoms.

White-faced they clung together. Hercule Poirot and Tim Allerton ran up to them.

'*Ma foi*, Madame, that was a near thing.'

All four instinctively looked up at the cliff. There was nothing to be seen. But there was a path along the top. Poirot remembered seeing some natives walking along there when they had first come ashore.

He looked at the husband and wife. Linnet looked dazed still—bewildered. Simon, however, was inarticulate with rage.

'God damn her!' he ejaculated.

He checked himself with a quick glance at Tim Allerton.

The latter said: 'Phew, that was near! Did some fool bowl that thing over, or did it get detached on its own?'

Linnet was very pale. She said with difficulty: 'I think—some fool must have done it.'

'Might have crushed you like an eggshell. Sure you haven't got an enemy, Linnet?'

Linnet swallowed twice and found a difficulty in answering the light-hearted raillery.

'Come back to the boat, Madame,' Poirot said quickly. 'You must have a restorative.'

They walked there quickly, Simon still full of pent-up rage, Tim trying to talk cheerfully and distract Linnet's mind from the danger she had run, Poirot with a grave face.

And then, just as they reached the gangplank, Simon stopped dead. A look of amazement spread over his face.

Jacqueline de Bellefort was just coming ashore. Dressed in blue gingham, she looked childish this morning.

'Good God!' said Simon under his breath. 'So it *was* an accident, after all.'

The anger went out of his face. An overwhelming relief showed so plainly that Jacqueline noticed something amiss.

'Good-morning,' she said. 'I'm afraid I'm a little on the late side.'

She gave them all a nod and stepped ashore and proceeded in the direction of the temple.

Simon clutched Poirot's arm. The other two had gone on.

'My God, that's a relief. I thought—I thought——'

Poirot nodded. 'Yes, yes, I know what you thought.' But he himself still looked grave and preoccupied. He turned his head and noted carefully what had become of the rest of the party from the ship.

Miss Van Schuyler was slowly returning on the arm of Miss Bowers.

A little farther away Mrs. Allerton was standing laughing at the little Nubian row of heads. Mrs. Otterbourne was with her.

The others were nowhere in sight.

Poirot shook his head as he followed Simon slowly on to the boat.

Chapter Eleven

'Will you explain to me, Madame, the meaning of the word "fey"?'

Mrs. Allerton looked slightly surprised. She and Poirot were toiling slowly up to the rock overlooking the Second Cataract. Most of the others had gone up on camels, but Poirot had felt that the motion of the camel was slightly reminiscent of that of a ship. Mrs. Allerton had put it on the grounds of personal dignity.

They had arrived at Wâdi Halfa the night before. This morning two launches had conveyed all the party to the Second Cataract, with the exception of Signor Richetti, who had insisted on making an excursion of his own to a remote spot called Semna, which, he explained, was of paramount interest as being the gateway of Nubia in the time of Amenemhet III, and where there was a stele recording the fact that on entering Egypt Negroes must pay customs duties. Everything had been done to discourage this example of individuality, but with no avail. Signor Richetti was determined and had waved aside each objection: (1) that the expedition was not worth making, (2) that the expedition could not be made, owing to the impossibility of getting a car there, (3) that no car could be obtained to do the trip, (4) that a car would be a prohibitive price. Having scoffed at (1), expressed incredulity at (2), offered to find a car himself to (3), and bargained fluently in Arabic for (4), Signor Richetti had at last departed—his departure being arranged in a secret and furtive manner, in case some of the other tourists should take it into their heads to stray from the appointed paths of sight-seeing.

'Fey?' Mrs. Allerton put her head on one side as she considered her reply. 'Well, it's a Scotch word, really. It means the kind of exalted happiness that comes before disaster. You know—it's too good to be true.'

She enlarged on the theme. Poirot listened attentively.

'I thank you, Madame. I understand now. It is odd that you should have said that yesterday—when Madame Doyle was to escape death so shortly afterwards.'

Mrs. Allerton gave a little shiver.

'It must have been a very near escape. Do you think some of these little black wretches rolled it over for fun? It's the sort of thing boys might do all over the world—not perhaps really meaning any harm.'

Poirot shrugged his shoulders.

'It may be, Madame.'

He changed the subject, talking of Majorca and asking various practical questions from the point of view of a possible visit.

Mrs. Allerton had grown to like the little man very much —partly perhaps out of a contradictory spirit. Tim, she felt, was always trying to make her less friendly to Hercule Poirot, whom he summarised firmly as 'the worst kind of bounder.' But she herself did not call him a bounder; she supposed it was his somewhat foreign exotic clothing which roused her son's prejudices. She herself found him an intelligent and stimulating companion. He was also extremely sympathetic. She found herself suddenly confiding in him her dislike of Joanna Southwood. It eased her to talk of the matter. And after all, why not? He did not know Joanna— would probably never meet her. Why should she not ease herself of that constantly borne burden of jealous thought?

At that same moment Tim and Rosalie Otterbourne were talking of her. Tim had just been half jestingly abusing his luck. His rotten health, never bad enough to be really interesting, yet not good enough for him to have led the life he would have chosen. Very little money, no congenial occupation.

'A thoroughly lukewarm, tame existence,' he finished discontentedly.

Rosalie said abruptly, 'You've got something heaps of people would envy you.'

'What's that?'

'Your mother.'

Tim was surprised and pleased.

'Mother? Yes, of course she is quite unique. It's nice of you to see it.'

'I think she's marvellous. She looks so lovely—so composed and calm—as though nothing could ever touch her, and yet—and yet somehow she's always ready to be funny about things too. . . .'

Rosalie was stammering slightly in her earnestness.

Tim felt a rising warmth towards the girl. He wished he could return the compliment, but, lamentably, Mrs. Otterbourne was his idea of the world's greatest menace. The inability to respond in kind made him embarrassed.

Miss Van Schuyler had stayed in the launch. She could not risk the ascent either on a camel or on her legs. She had said snappily:

'I'm sorry to have to ask you to stay with me, Miss Bowers. I intended you to go and Cornelia to stay, but girls are so selfish. She rushed off without a word to me. And I actually saw her talking to that very unpleasant and ill-bred young man, Ferguson. Cornelia has disappointed me sadly. She has absolutely no social sense.'

Miss Bowers replied in her usual matter-of-fact fashion:

'That's quite all right, Miss Van Schuyler. It would have been a hot walk up there, and I don't fancy the look of those saddles on the camels. Fleas, as likely as not.'

She adjusted her glasses, screwed up her eyes to look at the party descending the hill and remarked: 'Miss Robson isn't with that young man any more. She's with Dr. Bessner.'

Miss Van Schuyler grunted.

Since she had discovered that Dr. Bessner had a large clinic in Czechoslovakia and a European reputation as a fashionable physician, she was disposed to be gracious to him. Besides, she might need his professional services before the journey was over.

When the party returned to the *Karnak* Linnet gave a cry of surprise.

'A telegram for me.'

She snatched it off the board and tore it open.

'Why—I don't understand—potatoes, beetroots—what does it mean, Simon?'

Simon was just coming to look over her shoulder when a furious voice said: 'Excuse me, that telegram is for me,' and Signor Richetti snatched it rudely from her hand, fixing her with a furious glare as he did so.

Linnet stared in surprise for a moment, then turned over the envelope.

'Oh, Simon, what a fool I am! It's Richetti—not Ridgeway —and anyway of course my name isn't Ridgeway now. I must apologise.'

She followed the little archæologist up to the stern of the boat.

'I am so sorry, Signor Richetti. You see my name was Ridgeway before I married, and I haven't been married very long, and so——'

She paused, her face dimpled with smiles, inviting him to smile upon a young bride's *faux pas*.

But Richetti was obviously 'not amused.' Queen Victoria at her most disapproving could not have looked more grim. 'Names should be read carefully. It is inexcusable to be careless in these matters.'

Linnet bit her lip and her colour rose. She was not accustomed to have her apologies received in this fashion. She turned away and, rejoining Simon, said angrily, 'These Italians are really insupportable.'

'Never mind, darling; let's go and look at that big ivory crocodile you liked.'

They went ashore together.

Poirot, watching them walk up the landing-stage, heard a sharp indrawn breath. He turned to see Jacqueline de Bellefort at his side. Her hands were clenched on the rail. The expression on her face, as she turned it towards him, quite startled him. It was no longer gay or malicious. She looked devoured by some inner consuming fire.

'They don't care any more.' The words came low and fast. 'They've got beyond me. I can't reach them. . . . They don't mind if I'm here or not . . . I can't—I can't hurt them any more. . . .'

Her hands on the rail trembled.

'Mademoiselle——'

She broke in: 'Oh, it's too late now—too late for warning. . . . You were right. I ought not to have come. Not on this journey. What did you call it? A journey of the soul? I can't go back; I've got to go on. And I'm going on. They shan't be happy together; they shan't. I'd kill him sooner. . . .'

She turned abruptly away. Poirot, staring after her, felt a hand on his shoulder.

'Your girl friend seems a trifle upset, Monsieur Poirot.'

Poirot turned. He stared in surprise, seeing an old acquaintance.

'Colonel Race.'

The tall bronzed man smiled.

'Bit of a surprise, eh?'

Hercule Poirot had come across Colonel Race a year previously in London. They had been fellow guests at a very strange dinner party—a dinner party that had ended in death for that strange man, their host.

Poirot knew that Race was a man of unadvertised goings and comings. He was usually to be found in one of the outposts of Empire where trouble was brewing.

'So you are here at Wâdi Halfa,' he remarked thoughtfully.

'I am here on this boat.'

'You mean?'

'That I am making the return journey with you to Shellâl.'

Hercule Poirot's eyebrows rose.

'That is very interesting. Shall we, perhaps, have a little drink?'

They went into the observation saloon, now quite empty. Poirot ordered a whisky for the Colonel and a double orangeade full of sugar for himself.

'So you make the return journey with us,' said Poirot as he sipped. 'You would go faster, would you not, on the Government steamer, which travels by night as well as day?'

Colonel Race's face creased appreciatively.

'You're right on the spot as usual, Monsieur Poirot,' he said pleasantly.

'It is, then, the passengers?'

'One of the passengers.'

'Now which one, I wonder?' Hercule Poirot asked of the ornate ceiling.

'Unfortunately I don't know myself,' said Race ruefully.

Poirot looked interested.

Race said: 'There's no need to be mysterious to you. We've had a good deal of trouble out here—one way and another.

It isn't the people who ostensibly lead the rioters that we're after. It's the men who very cleverly put the match to the gunpowder. There were three of them. One's dead. One's in prison. I want the third man—a man with five or six cold-blooded murders to his credit. He's one of the cleverest paid agitators that ever existed. . . . He's on this boat. I know that from a passage in a letter that passed through our hands. Decoded it said: "X will be on the *Karnak* trip seventh to thirteenth." It didn't say under what name X would be passing.'

'Have you any description of him?'

'No. American, Irish, and French descent. Bit of a mongrel. That doesn't help us much. Have you got any ideas?'

'An idea—it is all very well,' said Poirot meditatively.

Such was the understanding between them that Race pressed him no further. He knew that Hercule Poirot did not ever speak unless he was sure.

Poirot rubbed his nose and said unhappily: 'There passes itself something on this boat that causes me much inquietude.'

Race looked at him inquiringly.

'Figure to yourself,' said Poirot, 'a person A who has grievously wronged a person B. The person B desires the revenge. The person B makes the threats.'

'A and B being both on this boat?'

Poirot nodded. 'Precisely.'

'And B, I gather, being a woman?'

'Exactly.'

Race lit a cigarette.

'I shouldn't worry. People who go about talking of what they are going to do don't usually do it.'

'And particularly is that the case with *les femmes,* you would say! Yes, that is true.'

But he still did not look happy.

'Anything else?' asked Race.

'Yes, there is something. Yesterday the person A had a very near escape from death, the kind of death that might very conveniently be called an accident.'

'Engineered by B?'

'No, that is just the point. B could have had nothing to do with it.'

'Then it *was* an accident.'

'I suppose so—but I do not like such accidents.'

'You're quite sure B could have had no hand in it?'

'Absolutely.'

'Oh, well, coincidences do happen. Who is A, by the way? A particularly disagreeable person?'

'On the contrary. A is a charming, rich, and beautiful young lady.'

Race grinned.

'Sounds quite like a novelette.'

'*Peut-être*. But I tell you, I am not happy, my friend. If I am right, and after all I am constantly in the habit of being right'—Race smiled into his moustache at this typical utterance —'then there is matter for grave inquiétude. And now, *you* come to add yet another complication. You tell me that there is a man on the *Karnak* who kills.'

'He doesn't usually kill charming young ladies.'

Poirot shook his head in a dissatisfied manner.

'I am afraid, my friend,' he said. 'I am afraid. . . . To-day, I advised this lady, Madame Doyle, to go with her husband to Khartoum, not to return on this boat. But they would not agree. I pray to Heaven that we may arrive at Shellâl without catastrophe.'

'Aren't you taking rather a gloomy view?'

Poirot shook his head.

'I am afraid,' he said simply. 'Yes, I, Hercule Poirot, I'm afraid. . . .'

Chapter Twelve

Cornelia Robson stood inside the temple of Abu Simbel. It was the evening of the following day—a hot still evening. The *Karnak* was anchored once more at Abu Simbel to permit a second visit to be made to the temple, this time by artificial light. The difference this made was considerable, and Cornelia commented wonderingly on the fact to Mr. Ferguson, who was standing by her side.

'Why, you see it ever so much better now!' she exclaimed. 'All those enemies having their heads cut off by the King —they just stand right out. That's a cute kind of castle there that I never noticed before. I wish Dr. Bessner was here, he'd tell me what it was.'

'How you can stand that old fool beats me,' said Ferguson gloomily.

'Why, he's just one of the kindest men I've ever met.'

'Pompous old bore.'

'I don't think you ought to speak that way.'

The young man gripped her suddenly by the arm. They were just emerging from the temple into the moonlight.

'Why do you stick being bored by fat old men—and bullied and snubbed by a vicious old harridan?'

'Why, Mr. Ferguson!'

'Haven't you got any spirit? Don't you know you're just as good as she is?'

'But I'm not!' Cornelia spoke with honest conviction.

'You're not as rich; that's all you mean.'

'No, it isn't. Cousin Marie's very cultured, and——'

'Cultured!' The young man let go of her arm as suddenly as he had taken it. 'That word makes me sick.'

Cornelia looked at him in alarm.

'She doesn't like you talking to me, does she?' asked the young man.

Cornelia blushed and looked embarrassed.

'Why? Because she thinks I'm not her social equal! Pah! Doesn't that make you see red?'

Cornelia faltered out: 'I wish you wouldn't get so mad about things.'

'Don't you realise—and you an American—that everyone is born free and equal?'

'They're not,' said Cornelia with calm certainty.

'My good girl, it's part of your constitution!'

'Cousin Marie says politicians aren't gentlemen,' said Cornelia. 'And of course people aren't equal. It doesn't make sense. I know I'm kind of homely-looking, and I used to feel mortified about it sometimes, but I've got over that. I'd like to have been born elegant and beautiful like Mrs. Doyle, but I wasn't, so I guess it's no use worrying.'

'Mrs. Doyle!' exclaimed Ferguson with deep contempt. 'She's the sort of woman who ought to be shot as an example.'

Cornelia looked at him anxiously.

'I believe it's your digestion,' she said kindly. 'I've got a special kind of pepsin that Cousin Marie tried once. Would you like to try it?'

Mr. Ferguson said: 'You're impossible!'

He turned and strode away. Cornelia went on towards the boat. Just as she was crossing on to the gangway he caught her up once more.

'You're the nicest person on the boat,' he said. 'And mind you remember it.'

Blushing with pleasure Cornelia repaired to the observation

saloon. Miss Van Schuyler was conversing with Dr. Bessner —an agreeable conversation dealing with certain royal patients of his.

Cornelia said guiltily: 'I do hope I haven't been a long time, Cousin Marie.'

Glancing at her watch, the old lady snapped: 'You haven't exactly hurried, my dear. And what have you done with my velvet stole?'

Cornelia looked round.

'Shall I see if it's in the cabin, Cousin Marie?'

'Of course it isn't! I had it just after dinner in here, and I haven't moved out of the place. It was on that chair.'

Cornelia made a desultory search.

'I can't see it anywhere, Cousin Marie.'

'Nonsense!' said Miss Van Schuyler. 'Look about.' It was an order such as one might give to a dog, and in her doglike fashion Cornelia obeyed. The quiet Mr. Fanthorp, who was sitting at a table near by, rose and assisted her. But the stole could not be found.

The day had been such an unusually hot and sultry one that most people had retired early after going ashore to view the temple. The Doyles were playing bridge with Pennington and Race at a table in a corner. The only other occupant of the saloon was Hercule Poirot, who was yawning his head off at a small table near the door.

Miss Van Schuyler, making a Royal Progress bedward, with Cornelia and Miss Bowers in attendance, paused by his chair. He sprang politely to his feet, stifling a yawn of gargantuan dimensions.

Miss Van Schuyler said: 'I have only just realised who you are, Monsieur Poirot. I may tell you that I have heard of you from my old friend Rufus Van Aldin. You must tell me about your cases sometime.'

Poirot, his eyes twinkling a little through their sleepiness, bowed in an exaggerated manner. With a kindly but condescending nod, Miss Van Schuyler passed on.

Poirot yawned once more. He felt heavy and stupid with sleep and could hardly keep his eyes open. He glanced over at the bridge players, absorbed in their game, then at young Fanthorp, who was deep in a book. Apart from them the saloon was empty.

He passed through the swinging door out on to the deck. Jacqueline de Bellefort, coming precipitately along the deck, almost collided with him.

'Pardon, Mademoiselle.'

She said: 'You look sleepy, Monsieur Poirot.'

He admitted it frankly:

'*Mais oui*—I am consumed with sleep. I can hardly keep my eyes open. It has been a day very close and oppressive.'

'Yes.' She seemed to brood over it. 'It's been the sort of day when things—snap! Break! When one can't go on. . . .'

Her voice was low and charged with passion. She looked not at him, but towards the sandy shore. Her hands were clenched, rigid. . . .

Suddenly the tension relaxed. She said: 'Good-night, Monsieur Poirot.'

'Good-night, Mademoiselle.'

Her eyes met his, just for a swift moment. Thinking it over the next day, he came to the conclusion that there had been appeal in that glance. He was to remember it afterwards.

Then he passed on to his cabin and she went towards the saloon.

Cornelia, having dealt with Miss Van Schuyler's many needs and fantasies, took some needlework with her back to the saloon. She herself did not feel in the least sleepy. On the contrary she felt wide awake and slightly excited.

The bridge four were still at it. In another chair the quiet Fanthorp read a book. Cornelia sat down to her needlework.

Suddenly the door opened and Jacqueline de Bellefort came in. She stood in the doorway, her head thrown back. Then she pressed a bell and sauntered across to Cornelia and sat down.

'Been ashore?' she asked.

'Yes. I thought it was just fascinating in the moonlight.' Jacqueline nodded.

'Yes, lovely night. . . . A real honeymoon night.'

Her eyes went to the bridge table—rested a moment on Linnet Doyle.

The boy came in answer to the bell. Jacqueline ordered a double gin. As she gave the order Simon Doyle shot a quick glance at her. A faint line of anxiety showed between his eyebrows.

His wife said: 'Simon, we're waiting for you to call.'

Jacqueline hummed a little tune to herself. When the drink came, she picked it up, said: 'Well, here's to crime,' drank it off and ordered another.

Again Simon looked across from the bridge table. His

calls became slightly absent-minded. His partner, Pennington, took him to task.

Jacqueline began to hum again, at first under her breath, then louder:

'*He was her man and he did her wrong. . . .*'

'Sorry,' said Simon to Pennington. 'Stupid of me not to return your lead. That gives 'em rubber.'

Linnet rose to her feet.

'I'm sleepy. I think I'll go to bed.'

'About time to turn in,' said Colonel Race.

'I'm with you,' agreed Pennington.

'Coming, Simon?'

Doyle said slowly: 'Not just yet. I think I'll have a drink first.'

Linnet nodded and went out. Race followed her. Pennington finished his drink and then followed suit.

Cornelia began to gather up her embroidery.

'Don't go to bed, Miss Robson,' said Jacqueline. 'Please don't. I feel like making a night of it. Don't desert me.'

Cornelia sat down again.

'We girls must stick together,' said Jacqueline.

She threw back her head and laughed—a shrill laugh without merriment.

The second drink came.

'Have something,' said Jacqueline.

'No, thank you very much,' replied Cornelia.

Jacqueline tilted back her chair. She hummed now loudly: '*He was her man and he did her wrong . . .*'

Mr. Fanthorp turned a page of *Europe from Within*.

Simon Doyle picked up a magazine.

'Really, I think I'll go to bed,' said Cornelia. 'It's getting very late.'

'You can't go to bed yet,' Jacqueline declared. 'I forbid you to. Tell me all about yourself.'

'Well—I don't know. There isn't much to tell,' Cornelia faltered. 'I've just lived at home, and I haven't been around much. This is my first trip to Europe. I'm just loving every minute of it.'

Jacqueline laughed.

'You're a happy sort of person, aren't you? God, I'd like to be you.'

'Oh, would you? But I mean—I'm sure——'

Cornelia felt flustered. Undoubtedly Miss de Bellefort was drinking too much. That wasn't exactly a novelty to Cornelia.

She had seen plenty of drunkenness during Prohibition years. But there was something else. . . . Jacqueline de Bellefort was talking to her—was looking at her—and yet, Cornelia felt, it was as though, somehow, she was talking to someone else. . . .

But there were only two other people in the room, Mr. Fanthorp and Mr. Doyle. Mr. Fanthorp seemed quite absorbed in his book. Mr. Doyle was looking rather odd—a queer sort of watchful look on his face. . . .

Jacqueline said again: 'Tell me all about yourself.'

Always obedient, Cornelia tried to comply. She talked, rather heavily, going into unnecessary small details about her daily life. She was so unused to being the talker. Her rôle was so constantly that of listener. And yet Miss de Bellefort seemed to want to know. When Cornelia faltered to a standstill, the other girl was quick to prompt her.

'Go on—tell me more.'

And so Cornelia went on ('Of course, Mother's very delicate —some days she touches nothing but cereals——') unhappily conscious that all she said was supremely uninteresting, yet flattered by the other girl's seeming interest. But was she interested? Wasn't she, somehow, listening to something else—or, perhaps, *for* something else? She was looking at Cornelia, yes, but wasn't there *someone else,* sitting in the room?

'And of course we get very good art classes, and last winter I had a course of——'

(How late was it? Surely very late. She had been talking and talking. If only something definite would happen——)

And immediately, as though in answer to the wish, something did happen. Only, at that moment, it seemed very natural.

Jacqueline turned her head and spoke to Simon Doyle.

'Ring the bell, Simon. I want another drink.'

Simon Doyle looked up from his magazine and said quietly: 'The stewards have gone to bed. It's after midnight.'

'I tell you I want another drink.'

Simon said: 'You've had quite enough drink, Jackie.'

She swung round at him.

'What damned business is it of yours?'

He shrugged his shoulders. 'None.'

She watched him for a minute or two. Then she said: 'What's the matter, Simon? Are you afraid?'

Simon did not answer. Rather elaborately he picked up his magazine again.

Cornelia murmured: 'Oh, dear—as late as that—I—must ——'

She began to fumble, dropped a thimble. . . .

Jacqueline said: 'Don't go to bed. I'd like another woman here—to support me.' She began to laugh again. 'Do you know what Simon over there is afraid of? He's afraid *I'm* going to tell you the story of *my* life.'

'Oh, really?'

Cornelia was the prey of conflicting emotions. She was deeply embarrassed but at the same time pleasurably thrilled. How—how *black* Simon Doyle was looking.

'Yes, it's a very sad story,' said Jacqueline; her soft voice was low and mocking. 'He treated me rather badly, didn't you, Simon?'

Simon Doyle said brutally: 'Go to bed, Jackie. You're drunk.'

'If you're embarrassed, Simon dear, you'd better leave the room.'

Simon Doyle looked at her. The hand that held the magazine shook a little, but he spoke bluntly.

'I'm staying,' he said.

Cornelia murmured for the third time, 'I really must—it's so late——'.

'You're not to go,' said Jacqueline. Her hand shot out and held the other girl in her chair. 'You're to stay and hear what I've got to say.'

'Jackie,' said Simon sharply, 'you're making a fool of yourself! For God's sake, go to bed.'

Jacqueline sat up suddenly in her chair. Words poured from her rapidly in a soft hissing stream.

'You're afraid of a scene, aren't you? That's because you're so English—so reticent! You want me to behave "decently," don't you? But I don't care whether I behave decently or not! You'd better get out of here quickly—because I'm going to talk—a lot.'

Jim Fanthorp carefully shut his book, yawned, glanced at his watch, got up and strolled out. It was a very British and utterly unconvincing performance.

Jacqueline swung round in her chair and glared at Simon.

'You damned fool,' she said thickly, 'do you think you can treat me as you have done and get away with it?'

Simon Doyle opened his lips, then shut them again. He sat quite still as though he were hoping that her outburst would exhaust itself if he said nothing to provoke her further.

Jacqueline's voice came thick and blurred. It fascinated Cornelia, totally unused to naked emotions of any kind.

'I told you,' said Jacqueline, 'that I'd kill you sooner than see you go to another woman. . . . You don't think I meant that? *You're wrong.* I've only been—waiting! You're my man! Do you hear? You belong to me. . . .'

Still Simon did not speak. Jacqueline's hand fumbled a moment or two on her lap. She leant forward.

'I told you I'd kill you and I meant it. . . .' Her hand came up suddenly with something in it that flashed and gleamed. 'I'll shoot you like a dog—like the dirty dog you are. . . .'

Now at last Simon acted. He sprang to his feet, but at the same moment she pulled the trigger. . . .

Simon half twisted—fell across a chair. . . . Cornelia screamed and rushed to the door. Jim Fanthorp was on the deck leaning over the rail. She called to him.

'Mr. Fanthorp . . . Mr. Fanthorp . . .'

He ran to her; she clutched at him incoherently. . . .

'She's shot him—Oh! she's shot him. . . .'

Simon Doyle still lay as he had fallen half into and across a chair. . . . Jacqueline stood as though paralysed. She was trembling violently, and her eyes, dilated and frightened, were staring at the crimson stain slowly soaking through Simon's trouser leg just below the knee where he held a handkerchief close against the wound. . . .

She stammered out:

'I didn't mean . . . Oh, my God, I didn't really mean . . .'

The pistol dropped from her nervous fingers with a clatter on the floor. She kicked it away with her foot. It slid under one of the settees.

Simon, his voice faint, murmured: 'Fanthorp, for heaven's sake—there's someone coming . . . Say it's all right—an accident —something. There mustn't be a scandal over this.'

Fanthorp nodded in quick comprehension. He wheeled round to the door where a startled Nubian face showed. He said: 'All right—all right! Just fun!'

The black face looked doubtful, puzzled, then reassured. The teeth showed in a wide grin. The boy nodded and went off.

Fanthorp turned back.

'That's all right. Don't think anybody else heard. Only sounded like a cork, you know. Now the next thing——'

He was startled. Jacqueline suddenly began to weep hysterically.

'Oh, God, I wish I were dead. . . . I'll kill myself. I'll be better dead. . . . Oh, what have I done—what have I done?'

Cornelia hurried to her.

'Hush, dear, hush.'

Simon, his brow wet, his face twisted with pain, said urgently:

'Get her away. For God's sake, get her out of here! Get her to her cabin, Fanthorp. Look here, Miss Robson, get that hospital nurse of yours.' He looked appealingly from one to the other of them. 'Don't leave her. Make quite sure she's safe with the nurse looking after her. Then get hold of old Bessner and bring him here. For God's sake, don't let any news of this get to my wife.'

Jim Fanthorp nodded comprehendingly. The quiet young man was cool and competent in an emergency.

Between them he and Cornelia got the weeping, struggling girl out of the saloon and along the deck to her cabin. There they had more trouble with her. She fought to free herself; her sobs redoubled.

'I'll drown myself . . . I'll drown myself. . . . I'm not fit to live. . . . Oh, Simon—Simon!'

Fanthorp said to Cornelia: 'Better get hold of Miss Bowers. I'll stay while you get her.'

Cornelia nodded and hurried out.

As soon as she left, Jacqueline clutched Fanthorp.

'His leg—it's bleeding—broken. . . . He may bleed to death. I must go to him. . . . Oh, Simon—Simon—how could I?'

Her voice rose. Fanthorp said urgently: 'Quietly—quietly. . . . He'll be all right.'

She began to struggle again.

'Let me go! Let me throw myself overboard. . . . Let me kill myself!'

Fanthorp, holding her by the shoulders, forced her back on to the bed.

'You must stay here. Don't make a fuss. Pull yourself together. It's all right, I tell you.'

To his relief, the distraught girl did manage to control herself a little, but he was thankful when the curtains were pushed aside and the efficient Miss Bowers, neatly dressed in a hideous kimono, entered, accompanied by Cornelia.

'Now then,' said Miss Bowers briskly, 'what's all this?'

She took charge without any sign of surprise and alarm.

Fanthorp thankfully left the overwrought girl in her capable hands and hurried along to the cabin occupied by Dr. Bessner. He knocked and entered on top of the knock.

'Dr. Bessner?'

A terrific snore resolved itself, and a startled voice asked: 'So? What is it?'

By this time Fanthorp had switched the light on. The doctor blinked up at him, looking rather like a large owl.

'It's Doyle. He's been shot. Miss de Bellefort shot him. He's in the saloon. Can you come?'

The stout doctor reacted promptly. He asked a few curt questions, pulled on his bedroom slippers and a dressing-gown, picked up a little case of necessaries and accompanied Fanthorp to the lounge.

Simon had managed to get the window beside him open. He was leaning his head against it, inhaling the air. His face was a ghastly colour.

Dr. Bessner came over to him.

'Ha? So? What have we here?'

A handkerchief sodden with blood lay on the carpet, and on the carpet itself was a dark stain.

The doctor's examination was punctuated with Teutonic grunts and exclamations.

'Yes, it is bad this. . . . The bone is fractured. And a big loss of blood. Herr Fanthorp, you and I must get him to my cabin. So—like this. He cannot walk. We must carry him, thus.'

As they lifted him Cornelia appeared in the doorway. Catching sight of her, the doctor uttered a grunt of satisfaction.

'Ach, it is you? Goot. Come with us. I have need of assistance. You will be better than my friend here. He looks a little pale already.'

Fanthorp emitted a rather sickly smile.

'Shall I get Miss Bowers?' he asked.

Dr. Bessner threw a considering glance over Cornelia.

'You will do very well, young lady,' he announced. 'You will not faint or be foolish, hein?'

'I can do what you tell me,' said Cornelia eagerly.

Bessner nodded in a satisfied fashion.

The procession passed along the deck.

The next ten minutes were purely surgical and Mr. Jim Fanthorp did not enjoy it at all. He felt secretly ashamed of the superior fortitude exhibited by Cornelia.

'So, that is the best I can do,' announced Dr. Bessner at last. 'You have been a hero, my friend.' He patted Simon approvingly on the shoulder. Then he rolled up his sleeve and produced a hypodermic needle.

'And now I will give you something to make you sleep. Your wife, what about her?'

Simon said weakly: 'She needn't know till the morning. . . .' He went on: 'I—you mustn't blame Jackie. . . . It's been all my fault. I treated her disgracefully . . . poor kid— she didn't know what she was doing. . . .'

Dr. Bessner nodded comprehendingly.

'Yes, yes—I understand. . . .'

'My fault——' Simon urged. His eyes went to Cornelia. 'Someone—ought to stay with her. She might—hurt herself ——'

Dr. Bessner injected the needle. Cornelia said, with quiet competence: 'It's all right, Mr. Doyle. Miss Bowers is going to stay with her all night. . . .'

A grateful look flashed over Simon's face. His body relaxed. His eyes closed. Suddenly he jerked them open. 'Fanthorp?'

'Yes, Doyle.'

'The pistol . . . ought not to leave it . . . lying about. The boys will find it in the morning. . . .'

Fanthorp nodded. 'Quite right. I'll go and get hold of it now.'

He went out of the cabin and along the deck. Miss Bowers appeared at the door of Jacqueline's cabin.

'She'll be all right now,' she announced. 'I've given her a morphine injection.'

'But you'll stay with her?'

'Oh, yes. Morphia excites some people. I shall stay all night.'

Fanthorp went on to the lounge.

Some three minutes later there was a tap on Bessner's cabin door.

'Dr. Bessner?'

'Yes?' The stout man appeared.

Fanthorp beckoned him out on the deck.

'Look here—I can't find that pistol. . . .'

'What is that?'

'The pistol. It dropped out of the girl's hand. She kicked it away and it went under a settee. It isn't under that settee now.'

They stared at each other.

'But who can have taken it?'

Fanthorp shrugged his shoulders.

Bessner said: 'It is curious, that. But I do not see what we can do about it.'

Puzzled and vaguely alarmed, the two men separated.

Chapter Thirteen

Hercule Poirot was just wiping the lather from his freshly shaved face when there was a quick tap on the door, and hard on top of it Colonel Race entered unceremoniously. He closed the door behind him.

He said: 'Your instinct was quite correct. It's happened.'

Poirot straightened up and asked sharply: 'What has happened?'

'Linnet Doyle's dead—shot through the head last night.'

Poirot was silent for a minute, two memories vividly before him—a girl in a garden at Assuan saying in a hard breathless voice: 'I'd like to put my dear little pistol against her head and just press the trigger,' and another more recent memory, the same voice saying: 'One feels one can't go on—the kind of day when something breaks'—and that strange momentary flash of appeal in her eyes. What had been the matter with him not to respond to that appeal? He had been blind, deaf, stupid with his need for sleep. . . .

Race went on: 'I've got some slight official standing; they sent for me, put it in my hands. The boat's due to start in half an hour, but it will be delayed till I give the word. There's a possibility, of course, that the murderer came from the shore.'

Poirot shook his head.

Race acquiesced in the gesture.

'I agree. One can pretty well rule that out. Well, man, it's up to you. This is your show.'

Poirot had been attiring himself with a neat-fingered celerity. He said now: 'I am at your disposal.'

The two men stepped out on the deck.

Race said: 'Bessner should be there by now. I sent the steward for him.'

There were four cabins de luxe, with bathrooms, on the boat. Of the two on the port side one was occupied by Dr.

Bessner, the other by Andrew Pennington. On the starboard side the first was occupied by Miss Van Schuyler, and the one next to it by Linnet Doyle. Her husband's dressing cabin was next door.

A white-faced steward was standing outside the door of Linnet Doyle's cabin. He opened the door for them and they passed inside. Dr. Bessner was bending over the bed. He looked up and grunted as the other two entered.

'What can you tell us, Doctor, about this business?' asked Race.

Bessner rubbed his unshaven jaw meditatively.

'Ach! She was shot—shot at close quarters. See—here, just above the ear—that is where the bullet entered. A very little bullet—I should say a twenty-two. The pistol, it was held close against her head, see, there is blackening here, the skin is scorched.'

Again in a sick wave of memory Poirot thought of those words uttered at Assuan.

Bessner went on: 'She was asleep; there was no struggle; the murderer crept up in the dark and shot her as she lay there.'

'Ah! *non*!' Poirot cried out. His sense of psychology was outraged. Jacqueline de Bellefort creeping into a darkened cabin, pistol in hand—no, it did not 'fit,' that picture.

Bessner stared at him through his thick lenses.

'But that is what happened, I tell you.'

'Yes, yes. I did not mean what you thought. I was not contradicting you.'

Bessner gave a satisfied grunt.

Poirot came up and stood beside him. Linnet Doyle was lying on her side. Her attitude was natural and peaceful. But above the ear was a tiny hole with an incrustation of dried blood round it.

Poirot shook his head sadly.

Then his gaze fell on the white painted wall just in front of him and he drew in his breath sharply. Its white neatness was marred by a big wavering letter J scrawled in some brownish-red medium.

Poirot stared at it, then he leaned over the dead girl and very gently picked up her right hand. One finger of it was stained a brownish-red.

'*Nom d'un nom d'un nom!*' ejaculated Hercule Poirot.

'Eh? What is that?'

Dr. Bessner looked up.

'Ach! *That.*'

Race said: 'Well, I'm damned. What do you make of that, Poirot?'

Poirot swayed a little on his toes.

'You ask me what I make of it. *Eh bien,* it is very simple, is it not? Madame Doyle is dying; she wishes to indicate her murderer, and so she writes with her finger, dipped in her own blood, the initial letter of her murderer's name. Oh, yes, it is astonishingly simple.'

'Ach, but——'

Dr. Bessner was about to break out, but a peremptory gesture from Race silenced him.

'So it strikes you like that?' he asked slowly.

Poirot turned round on him nodding his head.

'Yes, yes. It is, as I say, of an astonishing simplicity! It is so familiar, is it not? It has been done so often, in the pages of the romance of crime! It is now, indeed, a little *vieux jeu!* It leads one to suspect that our murderer is—old-fashioned!'

Race drew a long breath.

'I see,' he said. 'I thought at first——' He stopped.

Poirot said with a very faint smile: 'That I believed in all the old clichés of melodrama? But pardon, Dr. Bessner, you were about to say——?'

Bessner broke out gutturally: 'What do I say? Pah! I say it is absurd; it is the nonsense! The poor lady she died instantaneously. To dip her finger in the blood (and as you see, there is hardly any blood) and write the letter J upon the wall—Bah—it is the nonsense—the melodramatic nonsense!'

'*C'est de l'enfantillage,*' agreed Poirot.

'But it was done with a purpose,' suggested Race.

'That—naturally,' agreed Poirot, and his face was grave.

'What does J stand for?' asked Race.

Poirot replied promptly: 'J stands for Jacqueline de Bellefort, a young lady who declared to me less than a week ago that she would like nothing better than to——' he paused and then deliberately quoted, ' "to put my dear little pistol close against her head and then just press with my finger——" '

'*Gott im Himmel!*' exclaimed Dr. Bessner.

There was a momentary silence. Then Race drew a deep breath and said: 'Which is just what was done here?'

Bessner nodded.

'That is so, yes. It was a pistol of very small calibre—as

I say, probably a twenty-two. The bullet has got to be extracted, of course, before we can say definitely.'

Race nodded in swift comprehension. Then he asked: 'What about time of death?'

Bessner stroked his jaw again. His fingers made a rasping sound.

'I would not care to be too precise. It is now eight o'clock. I will say, with due regard to the temperature last night, that she has been dead certainly six hours and probably not longer than eight.'

'That puts it between midnight and two a.m.'

'That is so.'

There was a pause. Race looked round.

'What about her husband? I suppose he sleeps in the cabin next door.'

'At the moment,' said Dr. Bessner, 'he is asleep in my cabin.' Both men looked very surprised.

Bessner nodded his head several times.

'Ach, so. I see you have not been told about that. Mr. Doyle was shot last night in the saloon.'

'Shot? By whom?'

'By the young lady, Jacqueline de Bellefort.'

Race asked sharply, 'Is he badly hurt?'

'Yes, the bone was splintered. I have done all that is possible at the moment, but it is necessary, you understand, that the fracture should be X-rayed as soon as possible and proper treatment given such as is impossible on this boat.'

Poirot murmured: 'Jacqueline de Bellefort.'

His eyes went again to the J on the wall.

Race said abruptly: 'If there is nothing more we can do here for the moment, let's go below. The management has put the smoking-room at our disposal. We must get the details of what happened last night.'

They left the cabin. Race locked the door and took the key with him.

'We can come back later,' he said. 'The first thing to do is to get all the facts clear.'

They went down to the deck below, where they found the manager of the *Karnak* waiting uneasily in the doorway of the smoking-room. The poor man was terribly upset and worried over the whole business, and was eager to leave everything in Colonel Race's hands.

'I feel I can't do better than leave it to you, sir, seeing

your official position. I'd had orders to put myself at your disposal in the—er—other matter. If you will take charge, I'll see that everything is done as you wish.'

'Good man! To begin with I'd like this room kept clear for me and for Monsieur Poirot during the inquiry.'

'Certainly, sir.'

'That's all at present. Go on with your own work. I know where to find you.'

Looking slightly relieved, the manager left the room.

Race said, 'Sit down, Bessner, and let's have the whole story of what happened last night.'

They listened in silence to the doctor's rumbling voice.

'Clear enough,' said Race, when he had finished. 'The girl worked herself up, helped by a drink or two, and finally took a pot shot at the man with a twenty-two pistol. Then she went along to Linnet Doyle's cabin and shot her as well.'

But Dr. Bessner was shaking his head.

'No, no, I do not think so. I do not think that was *possible*. For one thing she would not write her own initial on the wall; it would be ridiculous, *nicht wahr*?'

'She might,' Race declared, 'if she were as blindly mad and jealous as she sounds; she might want to—well—sign her name to the crime, so to speak.'

Poirot shook his head. 'No, no, I do not think she would be as—as *crude* as that.'

'Then there's only one reason for that J. It was put there by someone else deliberately to throw suspicion on her.'

Bessner nodded. 'Yes, and the criminal was unlucky, because, you see, it is not only *unlikely* that the young Fräulein did the murder; it is also I think *impossible*.'

'How's that?'

Bessner explained Jacqueline's hysterics and the circumstances which had led Miss Bowers to take charge of her.

'And I think—I am sure—that Miss Bowers stayed with her all night.'

Race said: 'If that's so, it's going to simplify matters very much.'

'Who discovered the crime?' Poirot asked.

'Mrs. Doyle's maid, Louise Bourget. She went to call her mistress as usual, found her dead, and came out and flopped into the steward's arms in a dead faint. He went to the manager, who came to me. I got hold of Bessner and then came for you.'

Poirot nodded.

Race said: 'Doyle's got to know. You say he's asleep still?'

Bessner nodded. 'Yes, he's still asleep in my cabin. I gave him a strong opiate last night.'

Race turned to Poirot.

'Well,' he said, 'I don't think we need detain the doctor any longer, eh? Thank you, Doctor.'

Bessner rose. 'I will have my breakfast, yes. And then I will go back to my cabin and see if Mr. Doyle is ready to wake.'

'Thanks.'

Bessner went out. The two men looked at each other.

'Well, what about it, Poirot?' Race asked. 'You're the man in charge. I'll take my orders from you. You say what's to be done.'

Poirot bowed.

'*Eh bien!*' he said, 'we must hold the court of inquiry. First of all, I think we must verify the story of the affair last night. That is to say, we must question Fanthorp and Miss Robson, who were the actual witnesses of what occurred. The disappearance of the pistol is very significant.'

Race rang a bell and sent a message by the steward.

Poirot sighed and shook his head. 'It is bad, this,' he murmured. 'It is bad.'

'Have you any ideas?' asked Race curiously.

'My ideas conflict. They are not well arranged; they are not orderly. There is, you see, the big fact that this girl hated Linnet Doyle and wanted to kill her.'

'You think she's capable of it?'

'I think so—yes.' Poirot sounded doubtful.

'But not in this way? That's what's worrying you, isn't it? Not to creep into her cabin in the dark and shoot her while she was sleeping. It's the cold-bloodedness that strikes you as not ringing true?'

'In a sense, yes.'

'You think that this girl, Jacqueline de Bellefort, is incapable of a premeditated cold-blooded murder?'

Poirot said slowly: 'I am not sure, you see. She would have the brains—yes. But I doubt if, physically, she could bring herself to do the *act. . . .*'

Race nodded. 'Yes, I see. . . . Well, according to Bessner's story, it would also have been physically impossible.'

'If that is true it clears the ground considerably. Let us

hope it is true.' Poirot paused and then added simply: 'I shall be glad if it is so, for I have for that little one much sympathy.'

The door opened and Fanthorp and Cornelia came in. Bessner followed them.

Cornelia gasped out: 'Isn't this just awful? Poor, poor Mrs. Doyle! And she was so lovely too. It must have been a real *fiend* who could hurt her! And poor Mr. Doyle; he'll just go half crazy when he knows! Why, even last night he was so frightfully worried lest she should hear about his accident.'

'That is just what we want you to tell us about, Miss Robson,' said Race. 'We want to know exactly what happened last night.'

Cornelia began a little confusedly, but a question or two from Poirot helped matters.

'Ah, yes, I understand. After the bridge, Madame Doyle went to her cabin. Did she really go to her cabin, I wonder?'

'She did,' said Race. 'I actually saw her. I said good-night to her at the door.'

'And the time?'

'Mercy, I couldn't say,' replied Cornelia.

'It was twenty past eleven,' said Race.

'*Bien.* Then at twenty past eleven, Madame Doyle was alive and well. At that moment there was, in the saloon, who?'

Fanthorp answered: 'Doyle was there. And Miss de Bellefort. Myself and Miss Robson.'

'That's so,' agreed Cornelia. 'Mr. Pennington had a drink and then went off to bed.'

'That was how much later?'

'Oh, about three or four minutes.'

'Before half-past eleven, then?'

'Oh, yes.'

'So that there were left in the saloon you, Mademoiselle Robson, Mademoiselle de Bellefort, Monsieur Doyle and Monsieur Fanthorp. What were you all doing?'

'Mr. Fanthorp was reading a book. I'd got some embroidery. Miss de Bellefort was—she was——'

Fanthorp came to the rescue. 'She was drinking pretty heavily.'

'Yes,' agreed Cornelia. 'She was talking to me mostly and asking me about things at home. And she kept saying things—to me mostly, but I think they were kind of meant for Mr. Doyle. He was getting kind of mad at her, but he didn't say anything. I think he thought if he kept quiet she might simmer down.'

'But she didn't?'

Cornelia shook her head.

'I tried to go once or twice, but she made me stay, and I was getting very, very uncomfortable. And then Mr. Fanthorp got up and went out——'

'It was a little embarrassing,' said Fanthorp. 'I thought I'd make an unobtrusive exit. Miss de Bellefort was clearly working up for a scene.'

'And then she pulled out the pistol,' went on Cornelia, 'and Mr. Doyle jumped up to try and get it away from her, and it went off and shot him through the leg; and then she began to sob and cry—and I was scared to death and ran out after Mr. Fanthorp, and he came back with me, and Mr. Doyle said not to make a fuss, and one of the Nubian boys heard the noise of the shot and came along, but Mr. Fanthorp told him it was all right; and then we got Jacqueline away to her cabin, and Mr. Fanthorp stayed with her while I got Miss Bowers.' Cornelia paused breathless.

'What time was this?' asked Race.

Cornelia said again, 'Mercy, I don't know,' but Fanthorp answered promptly:

'It must have been about twenty minutes past twelve. I know that it was actually half-past twelve when I finally got to my cabin.'

'Now let me be quite sure on one or two points,' said Poirot. 'After Madame Doyle left the saloon, did any of you four leave it?'

'No.'

'You are quite certain Mademoiselle de Bellefort did not leave the saloon at all?'

Fanthorp answered promptly: 'Positive. Neither Doyle, Miss de Bellefort, Miss Robson, nor myself left the saloon.'

'Good. That establishes the fact that Mademoiselle de Bellefort could not possibly have shot Madame Doyle before—let us say—twenty past twelve. Now, Mademoiselle Robson, you went to fetch Mademoiselle Bowers. Was Mademoiselle de Bellefort alone in her cabin during that period?'

'No. Mr. Fanthorp stayed with her.'

'Good! So far, Mademoiselle de Bellefort has a perfect alibi. Mademoiselle Bowers is the next person to interview, but, before I send for her, I should like to have your opinion on one or two points. Monsieur Doyle, you say, was very anxious that Mademoiselle de Bellefort should not be left alone. Was he afraid, do you think, that she was contemplating some further rash act?'

'That is my opinion,' said Fanthorp.

'He was definitely afraid she might attack Madame Doyle?'

'No.' Fanthorp shook his head. 'I don't think that was his idea at all. I think he was afraid she might—er—do something rash to herself.'

'Suicide?'

'Yes.. You see, she seemed completely sobered and heart-broken at what she had done. She was full of self-reproach. She kept saying she would be better dead.'

Cornelia said timidly: 'I think he was rather upset about her. He spoke—quite nicely. He said it was all his fault—that he'd treated her badly. He—he was really very nice.'

Hercule Poirot nodded thoughtfully. 'Now about the pistol,' he went on. 'What happened to that?'

'She dropped it,' said Cornelia.

'And afterwards?'

Fanthorp explained how he had gone back to search for it, but had not been able to find it.

'Aha!' said Poirot. 'Now we begin to arrive. Let us, I pray you, be very precise. Describe to me exactly what happened.'

'Miss de Bellefort let it fall. Then she kicked it away from her with her foot.'

'She sort of hated it,' explained Cornelia. 'I know just what she felt.'

'And it went under a settee, you say. Now be very careful. Mademoiselle de Bellefort did not recover that pistol before she left the saloon?'

Both Fanthorp and Cornelia were positive on that point.

'Précisément. I seek only to be very exact, you comprehend. Then we arrive at this point. When Mademoiselle de Bellefort leaves the saloon the pistol is under the settee, and, since Mademoiselle de Bellefort is not left alone—Monsieur Fanthorp, Mademoiselle Robson or Mademoiselle Bowers being with her—she has no opportunity to get back the pistol after she left the saloon. What time was it, Monsieur Fanthorp, when you went back to look for it?'

'It must have been just before half-past twelve.'

'And how long would have elapsed between the time you and Dr. Bessner carried Monsieur Doyle out of the saloon until you returned to look for the pistol?'

'Perhaps five minutes—perhaps a little more.'

'Then in that five minutes someone removes that pistol from where it lay out of sight under the settee. That someone was *not* Mademoiselle de Bellefort. Who was it? It seems highly probable that the person who removed it was the murderer of Madame Doyle. We may assume, too, that that person had overheard or seen something of the events immediately preceding.'

'I don't see how you make that out,' objected Fanthorp.

'Because,' said Hercule Poirot, 'you have just told us that the pistol was out of sight under the settee. Therefore it is hardly credible that it was discovered by *accident*. It was taken by someone who knew it was there. Therefore that someone must have assisted at the scene.'

Fanthorp shook his head. 'I saw no one when I went out on the deck just before the shot was fired.'

'Ah, but you went out by the door on the starboard side.'

'Yes. The same side as my cabin.'

'Then if there had been anybody at the port door looking through the glass you would not have seen him?'

'No,' admitted Fanthorp.

'Did anyone hear the shot except the Nubian boy?'

'Not as far as I know.'

Fanthorp went on: 'You see, the windows in here were all closed. Miss Van Schuyler felt a draught earlier in the evening. The swing doors were shut. I doubt if the shot would be at all clearly heard. It would only sound like the pop of a cork.'

Race said: 'As far as I know, no one seems to have heard the other shot—the shot that killed Mrs. Doyle.'

'That we will inquire into presently,' said Poirot. 'For the moment we still concern ourselves with Mademoiselle de Bellefort. We must speak to Mademoiselle Bowers. But first, before you go'—he arrested Fanthorp and Cornelia with a gesture—'you will give me a little information about yourselves. Then it will not be necessary to call you again later. You first, Monsieur—your full name.'

'James Lechdale Fanthorp.'

'Address?'

'Glasmore House, Market Donnington, Northamptonshire.'

'Your profession?'

'I am a lawyer.'

'And your reasons for visiting this country?'

There was a pause. For the first time the impassive Mr.

Fanthorp seemed taken aback. He said at last, almost mumbling the words, 'Er—pleasure.'

'Aha!' said Poirot. 'You take the holiday; that is it, yes?'

'Er—yes.'

'Very well, Monsieur Fanthorp. Will you give me a brief account of your own movements last night after the events we have just been narrating?'

'I went straight to bed.'

'That was at——?'

'Just after half-past twelve.'

'Your cabin is number twenty-two on the starboard side —the one nearest the saloon?'

'Yes.'

'I will ask you one more question. Did you hear anything —anything at all—after you went to your cabin?'

Fanthorp considered.

'I turned in very quickly. I *think* I heard a kind of splash just as I was dropping off to sleep. Nothing else.'

'You heard a kind of splash? Near at hand?'

Fanthorp shook his head.

'Really, I couldn't say. I was half asleep.'

'And what time would that be?'

'It might have been about one o'clock. I can't really say.'

'Thank you, Monsieur Fanthorp. That is all.'

Poirot turned his attention to Cornelia.

'And now, Mademoiselle Robson. Your full name?'

'Cornelia Ruth. And my address is The Red House, Bell-field, Connecticut.'

'What brought you to Egypt?'

'Cousin Marie, Miss Van Schuyler, brought me along on a trip.'

'Had you ever met Madame Doyle previous to this journey?'

'No, never.'

'And what did you do last night?'

'I went right to bed after helping Dr. Bessner with Mr. Doyle's leg.'

'Your cabin is——?'

'Forty-three on the port side—right next door to Miss de Bellefort.'

'And did you hear anything?'

Cornelia shook her head. 'I didn't hear a thing.'

'No splash?'

'No, but then I wouldn't, because the boat's against the bank on my side.'

Poirot nodded. 'Thank you, Mademoiselle Robson. Now perhaps you will be so kind as to ask Mademoiselle Bowers to come here.'

Fanthorp and Cornelia went out.

'That seems clear enough,' said Race. 'Unless three independent witnesses are lying, Jacqueline de Bellefort couldn't have got hold of the pistol. But somebody did. And somebody overheard the scene. And somebody was B.F. enough to write a big J on the wall.'

There was a tap on the door and Miss Bowers entered. The hospital nurse sat down in her usual composed efficient manner. In answer to Poirot she gave her name, address, and qualifications, adding: 'I've been looking after Miss Van Schuyler for over two years now.'

'Is Mademoiselle Van Schuyler's health very bad?'

'Why, no, I wouldn't say that,' replied Miss Bowers. 'She's not very young, and she's nervous about herself, and she likes to have a nurse around handy. There's nothing serious the matter with her. She just likes plenty of attention, and she's willing to pay for it.'

Poirot nodded comprehendingly. Then he said: 'I understand that Mademoiselle Robson fetched you last night?'

'Why, yes, that's so.'

'Will you tell me exactly what happened?'

'Well, Miss Robson just gave me a brief outline of what had occurred, and I came along with her. I found Miss de Bellefort in a very excited, hysterical condition.'

'Did she utter any threats against Madame Doyle?'

'No, nothing of that kind. She was in a condition of morbid self-reproach. She'd taken a good deal of alcohol, I should say, and she was suffering from reaction. I didn't think she ought to be left. I gave her a shot of morphia and sat up with her.'

'Now, Mademoiselle Bowers, I want you to answer this. Did Mademoiselle de Bellefort leave her cabin at all?'

'No, she did not.'

'And you yourself?'

'I stayed with her until early this morning.'

'You are quite sure of that?'

'Absolutely sure.'

'Thank you, Mademoiselle Bowers.'

The nurse went out. The two men looked at each other. Jacqueline de Bellefort was definitely cleared of the crime. Who then had shot Linnet Doyle?

Chapter Fourteen

Race said: 'Someone pinched the pistol. It wasn't Jacqueline de Bellefort. Someone knew enough to feel that his crime would be attributed to her. But that someone did not know that a hospital nurse was going to give her morphia and sit up with her all night. And one thing more. Someone had already attempted to kill Linnet Doyle by rolling a boulder over the cliff; that someone was *not* Jacqueline de Bellefort. Who was it?'

Poirot said: 'It will be simpler to say who it could not have been. Neither Monsieur Doyle, Madame Allerton, Monsieur Allerton, Mademoiselle Van Schuyler, nor Mademoiselle Bowers could have had anything to do with it. They were all within my sight.'

'H'm,' said Race; 'that leaves rather a large field. What about motive?'

'That is where I hope Monsieur Doyle may be able to help us. There have been several incidents——'

The door opened and Jacqueline de Bellefort entered. She was very pale and she stumbled a little as she walked.

'I didn't do it,' she said. Her voice was that of a frightened child. 'I didn't do it. Oh, please believe me. Everyone will think I did it—but I didn't—I didn't. It's—it's awful. I wish it hadn't happened. I might have killed Simon last night; I was mad, I think. But I didn't do the other. . . .'

She sat down and burst into tears.

Poirot patted her on the shoulder.

'There, there. We know that you did not kill Madame Doyle. It is proved—yes, proved, *mon enfant*. It was not you.'

Jackie sat up suddenly, her wet handkerchief clasped in her hand.

'But who did?'

'That,' said Poirot, 'is just the question we are asking ourselves. You cannot help us there, my child?'

Jacqueline shook her head.

'I don't know . . . I can't imagine. . . . No, I haven't the faintest idea.' She frowned deeply. 'No,' she said at last. 'I can't think of anyone who wanted her dead.' Her voice faltered a little. 'Except me.'

Race said: 'Excuse me a minute—just thought of something.' He hurried out of the room.

Jacqueline de Bellefort sat with her head downcast, nervously twisting her fingers. She broke out suddenly: 'Death's horrible —horrible! I—hate the thought of it.'

Poirot said: 'Yes. It is not pleasant to think, is it, that now, at this very moment, someone is rejoicing at the successful carrying out of his or her plan.'

'Don't—don't!' cried Jackie. 'It sounds horrible, the way you put it.'

Poirot shrugged his shoulders. 'It is true.'

Jackie said in a low voice: 'I—I wanted her dead—and she *is* dead. . . . And, what is worse . . . she died—just like I said.'

'Yes, Mademoiselle. She was shot through the head.'

She cried out: 'Then I was right, that night at the Cataract Hotel. There *was* someone listening!'

'Ah!' Poirot nodded his head. 'I wondered if you would remember that. Yes, it is altogether too much of a coincidence— that Madame Doyle should be killed in just the way you described.'

Jackie shuddered.

'That man that night—who can he have been?'

Poirot was silent for a minute or two, then he said in quite a different tone of voice: 'You are sure it was a man, Mademoiselle?'

Jackie looked at him in surprise.

'Yes, of course. At least——'

'Well, Mademoiselle?'

She frowned, half closing her eyes in an effort to remember. She said slowly: 'I *thought* it was a man. . . .'

'But now you are not so sure?'

Jackie said slowly: 'No, I can't be certain. I just assumed it was a man—but it was really just a—a figure—a shadow. . . .'

She paused and then, as Poirot did not speak, she added: 'You think it must have been a woman? But surely none of the women on this boat can have wanted to kill Linnet?'

Poirot merely moved his head from side to side.

The door opened and Bessner appeared.

'Will you come and speak with Mr. Doyle, please, Monsieur Poirot? He would like to see you.'

Jackie sprang up. She caught Bessner by the arm.

'How is he? Is he—all right?'

'Naturally he is not all right,' replied Dr. Bessner reproachfully. 'The bone is fractured, you understand.'

'But he's not going to die?' cried Jackie.

'Ach, who said anything about dying? We will get him to civilisation and there we will have an X-ray and proper treatment.'

'Oh!' The girl's hands came together in convulsive pressure. She sank down again on a chair.

Poirot stepped out on to the deck with the doctor and at that moment Race joined them. They went up to the promenade deck and along to Bessner's cabin.

Simon Doyle was lying propped with cushions and pillows, an improvised cage over his leg. His face was ghastly in colour, the ravages of pain with shock on top of it. But the predominant expression on his face was bewilderment—the sick bewilderment of a child.

He muttered: 'Please come in. The doctor's told me—told me—about Linnet. . . . I can't believe it. I simply can't believe it's true.'

'I know. It's a bad knock,' said Race.

Simon stammered: 'You know—Jackie didn't do it. I'm certain Jackie didn't do it! It looks black against her, I dare say, but she *didn't* do it. She—she was a bit tight last night, and all worked up, and that's why she went for me. But she wouldn't—she wouldn't do *murder* . . . not cold-blooded murder. . . .'

Poirot said gently: 'Do not distress yourself, Monsieur Doyle. Whoever shot your wife, it was not Mademoiselle de Bellefort.'

Simon looked at him doubtfully.

'Is that on the square?'

'But since it was not Mademoiselle de Bellefort,' continued Poirot, 'can you give us any idea of who it might have been?'

Simon shook his head. The look of bewilderment increased.

'It's crazy—impossible. Apart from Jackie nobody could have wanted to do her in.'

'Reflect, Monsieur Doyle. Had she no enemies? Is there no one who had a grudge against her?'

Again Simon shook his head with the same hopeless gesture.

'It sounds absolutely fantastic. There's Windlesham, of course. She more or less chucked him to marry me—but I can't see a polite stick like Windlesham committing murder, and anyway he's miles away. Same thing with old Sir George Wode. He'd got a down on Linnet over the house—disliked the way she was pulling it about; but he's miles away in London, and anyway to think of murder in such a connection would be fantastic.'

'Listen, Monsieur Doyle.' Poirot spoke very earnestly. 'On the first day we came on board the *Karnak* I was impressed by a little conversation which I had with Madame your wife. She was very upset—very distraught. She said—mark this well—that *everybody* hated her. She said she felt afraid—unsafe—as though *everyone* round her were an enemy.'

'She was pretty upset at finding Jackie aboard. So was I,' said Simon.

'That is true, but it does not quite explain those words. When she said she was surrounded by enemies, she was almost certainly exaggerating, but all the same she did mean more than one person.'

'You may be right there,' admitted Simon. 'I think I can explain that. It was a name in the passenger list that upset her.'

'A name in the passenger list? What name?'

'Well, you see, she didn't actually tell me. As a matter of fact I wasn't even listening very carefully. I was going over the Jacqueline business in my mind. As far as I remember, Linnet said something about doing people down in business, and that it made her uncomfortable to meet anyone who had a grudge against her family. You see, although I don't really know the family history very well, I gather that Linnet's mother was a millionaire's daughter. Her father was only just ordinary plain wealthy, but after his marriage he naturally began playing the markets or whatever you call it. And as a result of that, of course, several people got it in the neck. You know, affluence one day, the gutter the next. Well, I gather there was someone on board whose father had got up against Linnet's father and taken a pretty hard knock. I remember Linnet saying: "It's pretty awful when people hate you without even knowing you." '

'Yes,' said Poirot thoughtfully. 'That would explain what she said to me. For the first time she was feeling the burden of her inheritance and not its advantages. You are quite sure, Monsieur Doyle, that she did not mention this man's name?'

Simon shook his head ruefully.

'I didn't really pay much attention. Just said: "Oh, nobody

minds what happened to their fathers nowadays. Life goes too fast for that." Something of that kind.'

Bessner said dryly: 'Ach, but I can have a guess. There is certainly a young man with a grievance on board.'

'You mean Ferguson?' asked Poirot.

'Yes. He spoke against Mrs. Doyle once or twice. I myself have heard him.'

'What can we do to find out?' asked Simon.

Poirot replied: 'Colonel Race and I must interview all the passengers. Until we have got their stories it would be unwise to form theories. Then there is the maid. We ought to interview her first of all. It would, perhaps, be as well if we did that here. Monsieur Doyle's presence might be helpful.'

'Yes, that's a good idea,' said Simon.

'Had she been with Mrs. Doyle long?'

'Just a couple of months, that's all.'

'Only a couple of months!' exclaimed Poirot.

'Why, you don't think——'

'Had Madame any valuable jewellery?'

'There were her pearls,' said Simon. 'She once told me they were worth forty or fifty thousand.' He shivered. 'My God, do you think those damned pearls——?'

'Robbery is a possible motive,' said Poirot. 'All the same it seems hardly credible. . . . Well, we shall see. Let us have the maid here.'

Louise Bourget was that same vivacious Latin brunette whom Poirot had seen one day and noticed.

She was anything but vivacious now. She had been crying and looked frightened. Yet there was a kind of sharp cunning apparent in her face which did not prepossess the two men favourably towards her.

'You are Louise Bourget?'

'Yes, Monsieur.'

'When did you last see Madame Doyle alive?'

'Last night, Monsieur. I was in her cabin to undress her.'

'What time was that?'

'It was some time after eleven, Monsieur. I cannot say exactly when. I undress Madame and put her to bed, and then I leave.'

'How long did all that take?'

'Ten minutes, Monsieur. Madame was tired. She told me to put the lights out when I went.'

'And when you had left her, what did you do?'

'I went to my own cabin, Monsieur, on the deck below.'

'And you heard or saw nothing more that can help us?'

'How could I, Monsieur?'

'That, Mademoiselle, is for you to say, not for us,' Hercule Poirot retorted.

She stole a sideways glance at him.

'But, Monsieur, I was nowhere near. . . . What could I have seen or heard? I was on the deck below. My cabin, it was on the other side of the boat, even. It is impossible that I should have heard anything. Naturally if I had been unable to sleep, if I had mounted the stairs, *then* perhaps I might have seen this assassin, this monster, enter or leave Madame's cabin, but as it is——'

She threw out her hands appealingly to Simon.

'Monsieur, I implore you—you see how it is? What can I say?'

'My good girl,' said Simon harshly, 'don't be a fool. Nobody thinks you saw or heard anything. You'll be quite all right. I'll look after you. Nobody's accusing you of anything.'

Louise murmured, 'Monsieur is very good,' and dropped her eyelids modestly.

'We take it, then, that you saw and heard nothing?' asked Race impatiently.

'That is what I said, Monsieur.'

'And you know of no one who had a grudge against your mistress?'

To the surprise of her listeners Louise nodded her head vigorously.

'Oh, yes. That I do know. To that question I can answer Yes most emphatically.'

Poirot said, 'You mean Mademoiselle de Bellefort?'

'She, certainly. But it is not of her I speak. There was someone else on this boat who disliked Madame, who was very angry because of the way Madame had injured him.'

'Good lord!' Simon exclaimed. 'What's all this?'

Louise went on, still emphatically nodding her head with the utmost vigour.

'Yes, yes, yes, it is as I say! It concerns the former maid of Madame—my predecessor. There was a man, one of the engineers on this boat, who wanted her to marry him. And my predecessor, Marie her name was, she would have done so. But Madame Doyle, she made inquiries and she discovered that this Fleetwood already had a wife—a wife of colour you understand, a wife of this country. She had gone back to her own people, but he was still married to her, you understand. And so Madame she told all this to Marie, and Marie she was very unhappy and she would not see Fleetwood any more. And this Fleetwood, he was infuriated, and when he found out that this Madame Doyle had formerly been Mademoiselle Linnet Ridgeway he tells me that he would like to kill her! Her interference ruined his life, he said.'

Louise paused triumphantly.

'This is interesting,' said Race.

Poirot turned to Simon.

'Had you any idea of this?'

'None whatever,' Simon replied with patent sincerity. 'I doubt if Linnet even knew the man was on the boat. She had probably forgotten all about the incident.'

He turned sharply to the maid.

'Did you say anything to Mrs. Doyle about this?'

'No, Monsieur, of course not.'

Poirot asked: 'Do you know anything about your mistress's pearls?'

'Her pearls?' Louise's eyes opened very wide. 'She was wearing them last night.'

'You saw them when she came to bed?'

'Yes, Monsieur.'

'Where did she put them?'

'On the table by the side as always.'

'That is where you last saw them?'

'Yes, Monsieur.'

'Did you see them there this morning?'

A startled look came into the girl's face.

'*Mon Dieu!* I did not even look. I come up to the bed, I see—I see Madame; and then I cry out and rush out of the door, and I faint.'

Hercule Poirot nodded his head.

'You did not look. But I, I have the eyes which notice, and there were no pearls on the table beside the bed this morning.'

Chapter Fifteen

Hercule Poirot's observation had not been at fault. There were no pearls on the table by Linnet Doyle's bed.

Louise Bourget was bidden to make a search among Linnet's belongings. According to her, all was in order. Only the pearls had disappeared.

As they emerged from the cabin a steward was waiting to tell them that breakfast had been served in the smoking-room. As they passed along the deck, Race paused to look over the rail.

'Aha! I see you have had an idea, my friend.'

'Yes. It suddenly came to me, when Fanthorp mentioned thinking he had heard a splash, that I too had been awakened some time last night by a splash. It's perfectly possible that, after the murder, the murderer threw the pistol overboard.'

Poirot said slowly: 'You really think that is possible, my friend?' Race shrugged his shoulders.

'It's a suggestion. After all, the pistol wasn't anywhere in the cabin. First thing I looked for.'

'All the same,' said Poirot, 'it is incredible that it should have been thrown overboard.'

Race asked: 'Where is it then?'

Poirot replied thoughtfully, 'If it is not in Madame Doyle's cabin, there is, logically, only one other place where it could be.'

'Where's that?'

'In Mademoiselle de Bellefort's cabin.'

Race said thoughtfully: 'Yes. I see——'

He stopped suddenly.

'She's out of her cabin. Shall we go and have a look now?'

Poirot shook his head. 'No, my friend, that would be precipitate. It may not yet have been put there.'

'What about an immediate search of the whole boat?'

'That way we should show our hand. We must work with great care. It is very delicate, our position, at the moment. Let us discuss the situation as we eat.'

Race agreed. They went into the smoking-room.

'Well,' said Race as he poured himself out a cup of coffee, 'we've got two definite leads. There's the disappearance of the pearls. And there's the man Fleetwood. As regards the pearls, robbery seems indicated, but—I don't know whether you'll agree with me——'

Poirot said quickly: 'But it was an odd moment to choose?'

'Exactly. To steal the pearls at such a moment invites a close search of everybody on board. How then could the thief hope to get away with his booty?'

'He might have gone ashore and dumped it.'

'The company always has a watchman on the bank.'

'Then that is not feasible. Was the murder committed to divert attention from the robbery? No, that does not make sense; it is profoundly unsatisfactory. But supposing that Madame Doyle woke up and caught the thief in the act?'

'And therefore the thief shot her? But she was shot whilst she slept.'

'So that too does not make sense. . . . You know, I have a little idea about those pearls—and yet—no—it is impossible. Because if my idea was right the pearls would not have disappeared. Tell me, what did you think of the maid?'

'I wondered,' said Race slowly, 'if she knew more than she said.'

'Ah, you too had that impression?'

'Definitely not a nice girl,' said Race.

Hercule Poirot nodded. 'Yes, I would not trust her.'

'You think she had something to do with the murder?'

'No. I would not say that.'

'With the theft of the pearls, then?'

'That is more probable. She had only been with Madame Doyle a very short time. She may be a member of a gang that specialises in jewel robberies. In such a case there is often a maid with excellent references. Unfortunately we are not in a position to seek information on these points. And yet that explanation does not quite satisfy me. . . . Those pearls— ah, *sacré*, my little idea *ought* to be right. And yet nobody would be so imbecile——' He broke off.

'What about the man Fleetwood?'

'We must question him. It may be that we have there the solution. If Louise Bourget's story is true, he had a definite motive for revenge. He could have overheard the scene between Jacqueline and Monsieur Doyle, and when they had left the saloon he could have darted in and secured the gun. Yes, it is all quite possible. And that letter J scrawled in blood. That, too, would accord with a simple, rather crude nature.'

'In fact, he's just the person we are looking for?'

'Yes—only——' Poirot rubbed his nose. He said with a slight

grimace: 'See you, I recognise my own weaknesses. It has been said of me that I like to make a case difficult. This solution that you put to me—it is too simple, too easy. I cannot feel that it really happened. And yet, that may be sheer prejudice on my part.'

'Well, we'd better have the fellow here.'

Race rang the bell and gave the order. Then he asked, 'Any other—possibilities?'

'Plenty, my friend. There is, for example, the American trustee.'

'Pennington?'

'Yes, Pennington. There was a curious little scene in here the other day.' He narrated the happenings to Race. 'You see —it is significant. Madame, she wanted to read all the papers before signing. So he makes the excuse of another day. And then, the husband, he makes a very significant remark.'

'What was that?'

'He says—"I never read anything. I sign where I am told to sign." You perceive the significance of that. Pennington did. I saw it in his eye. He looked at Doyle as though an entirely new idea had come into his head. Just imagine, my friend, that you have been left trustee to the daughter of an intensely wealthy man. You use, perhaps, that money to speculate with. I know it is so in all detective novels—but you read of it too in the newspapers. It happens, my friend, it *happens*.'

'I don't dispute it,' said Race.

'There is, perhaps, still time to make good by speculating wildly. Your ward is not yet of age. And then—she marries! The control passes from your hands into hers at a moment's notice! A disaster! But there is still a chance. She is on a honeymoon. She will perhaps be careless about business. A casual paper, slipped in among others, signed without reading. . . . But Linnet Doyle was not like that. Honeymoon or no honeymoon, she was a business woman. And then her husband makes a remark, and a new idea comes to that desperate man who is seeking a way out from ruin. If Linnet Doyle were to die, her fortune would pass to her husband—and he would be easy to deal with; he would be a child in the hands of an astute man like Andrew Pennington. *Mon cher Colonel,* I tell you I *saw* the thought pass through Andrew Pennington's head. "If only it were *Doyle* I had got to deal with . . ." That is what he was thinking.'

'Quite possible, I daresay,' said Race dryly, 'but you've no evidence.'

'Alas, no.'

'Then there's young Ferguson,' said Race. 'He talks bitterly enough. Not that I go by talk. Still, he *might* be the fellow whose father was ruined by old Ridgeway. It's a little far-fetched but it's *possible*. People do brood over bygone wrongs sometimes.' He paused a minute and then said: 'And there's my fellow.'

'Yes, there is "your fellow" as you call him.'

'He's a killer,' said Race. 'We know that. On the other hand, I can't see any way in which he could have come up against Linnet Doyle. Their orbits don't touch.'

Poirot said slowly: 'Unless, accidentally, she had become possessed of evidence showing his identity.'

'That's possible, but it seems highly unlikely.' There was a knock at the door. 'Ah, here's our would-be bigamist.'

Fleetwood was a big, truculent-looking man. He looked suspiciously from one to the other of them as he entered the room. Poirot recognised him as the man he had seen talking to Louise Bourget.

Fleetwood asked suspiciously: 'You wanted to see me?'

'We did,' said Race. 'You probably know that a murder was committed on this boat last night?'

Fleetwood nodded.

'And I believe it is true that you had reason to feel anger against the woman who was killed.'

A look of alarm sprang up in Fleetwood's eyes.

'Who told you that?'

'You considered that Mrs. Doyle had interfered between you and a young woman.'

'I know who told you that—that lying French hussy. She's a liar through and through, that girl.'

'But this particular story happens to be true.'

'It's a dirty lie!'

'You say that, although you don't know what it is yet.' The shot told. The man flushed and gulped.

'It is true, is it not, that you were going to marry the girl Marie, and that she broke it off when she discovered that you were a married man already?'

'What business was it of hers?'

'You mean, what business was it of Mrs. Doyle's? Well, you know, bigamy is bigamy.'

'It wasn't like that. I married one of the locals out here. It didn't answer. She went back to her people. I've not seen her for a half a dozen years.'

'Still you were married to her.'

The man was silent. Race went on: 'Mrs. Doyle, or Miss Ridgeway as she then was, found out all this?'

'Yes, she did, curse her! Nosing about where no one ever asked her to. I'd have treated Marie right. I'd have done anything for her. And she'd never have known about the other, if it hadn't been for that meddlesome young lady of hers. Yes, I'll say it, I *did* have a grudge against the lady, and I felt bitter about it when I saw her on this boat, all dressed up in pearls and diamonds and lording it all over the place, with never a thought that she'd broken up a man's life for him! I felt bitter all right, but if you think I'm a dirty murderer—if you think I went and shot her with a gun, well, that's a damned lie! I never touched her. And that's God's truth.'

He stopped. The sweat was rolling down his face.

'Where were you last night between the hours of twelve and two?'

'In my bunk asleep—and my mate will tell you so.'

'We shall see,' said Race. He dismissed him with a curt nod. 'That'll do.'

'*Eh bien?*' inquired Poirot as the door closed behind Fleetwood.

Race shrugged his shoulders. 'He tells quite a straight story. He's nervous, of course, but not unduly so. We'll have to investigate his alibi—though I don't suppose it will be decisive. His mate was probably asleep, and this fellow could have slipped in and out if he wanted to. It depends whether anyone else saw him.'

'Yes, one must inquire as to that.'

'The next thing, I think,' said Race, 'is whether anyone heard anything which might give a clue as to the time of the crime. Bessner places it as having occurred between twelve and two. It seems reasonable to hope that someone among the passengers may have heard the shot—even if they did not recognise it for what it was. I didn't hear anything of the kind myself. What about you?'

Poirot shook his head.

'Me, I slept absolutely like the log. I heard nothing—but nothing at all. I might have been drugged, I slept so soundly.'

'A pity,' said Race. 'Well, let's hope we have a bit of luck with the people who have cabins on the starboard side. Fanthorp we've done. The Allertons come next. I'll send the steward to fetch them.'

Mrs. Allerton came in briskly. She was wearing a soft grey striped silk dress. Her face looked distressed.

'It's too horrible,' she said as she accepted the chair that Poirot placed for her. 'I can hardly believe it. That lovely creature, with everything to live for—dead. I almost feel I can't believe it.'

'I know how you feel, Madame,' said Poirot sympathetically.

'I'm glad *you* are on board,' said Mrs. Allerton simply. 'You'll be able to find out who did it. I'm so glad it isn't that poor tragic girl.'

'You mean Mademoiselle de Bellefort. Who told you she did not do it?'

'Cornelia Robson,' replied Mrs. Allerton, with a faint smile. 'You know, she's simply thrilled by it all. It's probably the only exciting thing that has ever happened to her, and probably the only exciting thing that ever will happen to her. But she's so nice that she's terribly ashamed of enjoying it. She thinks it's awful of her.'

Mrs. Allerton gave a look at Poirot and then added: 'But I mustn't chatter. You want to ask me questions.'

'If you please. You went to bed at what time, Madame?'

'Just after half-past ten.'

'And you went to sleep at once?'

'Yes. I was sleepy.'

'And did you hear anything—anything at all—during the night?'

Mrs. Allerton wrinkled her brows.

'Yes, I think I heard a splash and someone running—or was it the other way about? I'm rather hazy. I just had a vague idea that someone had fallen overboard at sea—a dream, you know—and then I woke up and listened, but it was all quite quiet.'

'Do you know what time that was?'

'No, I'm afraid I don't. But I don't think it was very long after I went to sleep. I mean it was within the first hour or so.'

'Alas, Madame, that is not very definite.'

'No, I know it isn't. But it's no good my trying to guess, is it, when I haven't really the vaguest idea?'

'And that is all you can tell us, Madame?'

'I'm afraid so.'

'Had you ever actually met Madame Doyle before?'

'No, Tim had met her. And I'd heard a good deal about

her—through a cousin of ours, Joanna Southwood, but I'd never spoken to her till we met at Assuan.'

'I have one other question, Madame, if you will pardon me for asking.'

Mrs. Allerton murmured with a faint smile, 'I should love to be asked an indiscreet question.'

'It is this. Did you, or your family, ever suffer any financial loss through the operations of Madame Doyle's father, Melhuish Ridgeway?'

Mrs. Allerton looked thoroughly astonished.

'Oh, no! The family finances have never suffered except by dwindling . . . you know, everything paying less interest than it used to. There's never been anything melodramatic about our poverty. My husband left very little money, but what he left I still have, though it doesn't yield as much as it used to yield.'

'I thank you, Madame. Perhaps you will ask your son to come to us.'

Tim said lightly, when his mother came: 'Ordeal over? My turn now! What sort of things did they ask you?'

'Only whether I heard anything last night,' said Mrs. Allerton. 'And unluckily I didn't hear anything at all. I can't think why not. After all, Linnet's cabin is only one away from mine. I should think I'd have been bound to hear the shot. Go along, Tim; they're waiting for you.'

To Tim Allerton Poirot repeated his previous questions.

Tim answered: 'I went to bed early, half-past ten or so. I read for a bit. Put out my light just after eleven.'

'Did you hear anything after that?'

'Heard a man's voice saying good-night, I think, not far away.'

'That was me saying good-night to Mrs. Doyle,' said Race.

'Yes. After that I went to sleep. Then, later, I heard a kind of hullabaloo going on, somebody calling Fanthorp, I remember.'

'Mademoiselle Robson when she ran out from the observation saloon.'

'Yes, I suppose that was it. And then a lot of different voices. And then somebody running along the deck. And then a splash. And then I heard old Bessner booming out something about "Careful now" and "Not too quick."'

'You heard a splash?'

'Well, something of that kind.'

'You are sure it was not a *shot* you heard?'

'Yes, I suppose it might have been . . . I did hear a cork

pop. Perhaps that was the shot. I may have imagined the splash from connecting the idea of the cork with liquid pouring into a glass. . . . I know my foggy idea was that there was some kind of party on, and I wished they'd all go to bed and shut up.'

'Anything more after that?'

Tim thought. 'Only Fanthorp barging round in his cabin next door. I thought he'd never get to bed.'

'And after that?'

Tim shrugged his shoulders. 'After that—oblivion.'

'You heard nothing more?'

'Nothing whatever.'

'Thank you, Monsieur Allerton.'

Tim got up and left the cabin.

Chapter Sixteen

Race pored thoughtfully over a plan of the promenade deck of the *Karnak*.

'Fanthorp, young Allerton, Mrs. Allerton. Then an empty cabin—Simon Doyle's. Now who's on the other side of Mrs. Doyle's? The old American dame. If anyone heard anything she would have done. If she's up we'd better have her along.'

Miss Van Schuyler entered the room. She looked even older and yellower than usual this morning. Her small dark eyes had an air of venomous displeasure in them.

Race rose and bowed.

'We're very sorry to trouble you, Miss Van Schuyler. It's very good of you. Please sit down.'

Miss Van Schuyler said sharply: 'I dislike being mixed up in this. I resent it very much. I do not wish to be associated in any way with this—er—very unpleasant affair.'

'Quite—quite. I was just saying to Monsieur Poirot that the sooner we took your statement the better, as then you need have no further trouble.'

Miss Van Schuyler looked at Poirot with something approaching favour.

'I'm glad you both realise my feelings. I am not accustomed to anything of this kind.'

Poirot said soothingly: 'Precisely, Mademoiselle. That is why we wish to free you from unpleasantness as quickly as possible. Now you went to bed last night—at what time?'

'Ten o'clock is my usual time. Last night I was rather later, as Cornelia Robson, very inconsiderately, kept me waiting.'

'*Très bien*, Mademoiselle. Now what did you hear after you had retired?'

Miss Van Schuyler said: 'I sleep very lightly.'

'*A merveille!* That is very fortunate for us.'

'I was awakened by that rather flashy young woman, Mrs. Doyle's maid, who said, "*Bonne nuit, Madame*" in what I cannot but think an unnecessarily loud voice.'

'And after that?'

'I went to sleep again. I woke up thinking someone was in my cabin, but I realised that it was someone in the cabin next door.'

'In Madame Doyle's cabin?'

'Yes. Then I heard someone outside on the deck and then a splash.'

'You have no idea what time this was?'

'I can tell you the time exactly. It was ten minutes past one.'

'You are sure of that?'

'Yes. I looked at my little clock that stands by my bed.'

'You did not hear a shot?'

'No, nothing of the kind.'

'But it might possibly have been a shot that awakened you?'

Miss Van Schuyler considered the question, her toadlike head on one side.

'It might,' she admitted rather grudgingly.

'And you have no idea what caused the splash you heard?'

'Not at all—I know perfectly.'

Colonel Race sat up alertly. 'You know?'

'Certainly. I did not like this sound of prowling around. I got up and went to the door of my cabin. Miss Otterbourne was leaning over the side. She had just dropped something into the water.'

'Miss Otterbourne?' Race sounded really surprised.

'Yes.'

'You are quite sure it was Miss Otterbourne?'

'I saw her face distinctly.'

'She did not see you?'

'I do not think so.'

Poirot leant forward.

'And what did her face look like, Mademoiselle?'

'She was in a condition of considerable emotion.'

Race and Poirot exchanged a quick glance.

'And then?' Race prompted.

'Miss Otterbourne went away round the stern of the boat and I returned to bed.'

There was a knock at the door and the manager entered. He carried in his hand a dripping bundle.

'We've got it, Colonel.'

Race took the package. He unwrapped fold after fold of sodden velvet. Out of it fell a coarse handkerchief, faintly stained with pink, wrapped round a small pearl-handled pistol.

Race gave Poirot a glance of slightly malicious triumph.

'You see,' he said, 'my idea was right. It *was* thrown overboard.'

He held the pistol out on the palm of his hand.

'What do you say, Monsieur Poirot? Is this the pistol you saw at the Cataract Hotel that night?'

Poirot examined it carefully; then he said quietly: 'Yes—that is it. There is the ornamental work on it—and the initials J.B. It is an *article de luxe,* a very feminine production, but it is none the less a lethal weapon.'

'Twenty-two,' murmured Race. He took out the clip. 'Two bullets fired. Yes, there doesn't seem much doubt about it.'

Miss Van Schuyler coughed significantly.

'And what about my stole?' she demanded.

'Your stole, Mademoiselle?'

'Yes, that is my velvet stole you have here.'

Race picked up the dripping folds of material.

'This is yours, Miss Van Schuyler?'

'Certainly it's mine!' the old lady snapped. 'I missed it last night. I was asking everyone if they'd seen it.'

Poirot questioned Race with a glance, and the latter gave a slight nod of assent.

'Where did you see it last, Miss Van Schuyler?'

'I had it in the saloon yesterday evening. When I came to go to bed I could not find it anywhere.'

Race said quietly: 'You realise what it's been used for?' He spread it out, indicating with a finger the scorching and several small holes. 'The murderer wrapped it round the pistol to deaden the noise of the shot.'

'Impertinence!' snapped Miss Van Schuyler. The colour rose in her wizened cheeks.

Race said: 'I shall be glad, Miss Van Schuyler, if you will tell me the extent of your previous acquaintance with Mrs. Doyle.'

'There was no previous acquaintance.'

'But you knew of her?'

'I knew who she was, of course.'

'But your families were not acquainted?'

'As a family we have always prided ourselves on being exclusive, Colonel Race. My dear mother would never have dreamed of calling upon any of the Hartz family, who, outside their wealth, were nobodies.'

'That is all you have to say, Miss Van Schuyler?'

'I have nothing to add to what I have told you. Linnet Ridgeway was brought up in England and I never saw her till I came aboard this boat.'

She rose. Poirot opened the door and she marched out.

The eyes of the two men met.

'That's her story,' said Race, 'and she's going to stick to it! It may be true. I don't know. But—Rosalie Otterbourne? I hadn't expected that.'

Poirot shook his head in a perplexed manner. Then he brought down his hand on the table with a sudden bang.

'But it does not make sense,' he cried. '*Nom d'un nom d'un nom!* It does not make sense.'

Race looked at him.

'What do you mean exactly?'

'I mean that up to a point it is all the clear sailing. Someone wished to kill Linnet Doyle. Someone overheard the scene in the saloon last night. Someone sneaked in there and retrieved the pistol—Jacqueline de Bellefort's pistol, remember. Somebody shot Linnet Doyle with that pistol and wrote the letter J on the wall. . . . All so clear, is it not? All pointing to Jacqueline de Bellefort as the murderess. And then what does the murderer do? Leave the pistol—the damning pistol—Jacqueline de Bellefort's pistol, for everyone to find? No, he—or she—throws the pistol, that particularly damning bit of evidence, overboard. Why, my friend, why?'

Race shook his head. 'It's odd.'

'It is more than odd—it is *impossible*!'

'Not impossible, since it happened!'

'I do not mean that. I mean that the sequence of events is impossible. Something is wrong.'

Chapter Seventeen

Colonel Race glanced curiously at his colleague. He respected —he had reason to respect—the brain of Hercule Poirot. Yet for the moment he did not follow the other's process of thought. He asked no question, however. He seldom did ask questions. He proceeded straightforwardly with the matter in hand.

'What's the next thing to be done? Question the Otterbourne girl?'

'Yes, that may advance us a little.'

Rosalie Otterbourne entered ungraciously. She did not look nervous or frightened in any way—merely unwilling and sulky.

'Well,' she asked, 'what is it?'

Race was the spokesman.

'We're investigating Mrs. Doyle's death,' he explained.

Rosalie nodded.

'Will you tell me what you did last night?'

Rosalie reflected a minute.

'Mother and I went to bed early—before eleven. We didn't hear anything in particular, except a bit of fuss outside Dr. Bessner's cabin. I heard the old man's German voice booming away. Of course I didn't know what it was all about till this morning.'

'You didn't hear a shot?'

'No.'

'Did you leave your cabin at all last night?'

'No.'

'You are quite sure of that?'

Rosalie stared at him.

'What do you mean? Of course I'm sure of it.'

'You did not, for instance, go round to the starboard side of the boat and throw something overboard?'

The colour rose in her face.

'Is there any rule against throwing things overboard?'

'No, of course not. Then you did?'

'No, I didn't. I never left my cabin, I tell you.'

'Then if anyone says that they saw you——?'

She interrupted him. 'Who says they saw me?'

'Miss Van Schuyler.'

'Miss Van Schuyler?' She sounded genuinely astonished.

'Yes. Miss Van Schuyler says she looked out of her cabin and saw you throw something over the side.'

Rosalie said clearly, 'That's a damned lie.' Then, as though struck by a sudden thought, she asked: 'What time was this?'

It was Poirot who answered.

'It was ten minutes past one, Mademoiselle.'

She nodded her head thoughtfully. 'Did she see anything else?'

Poirot looked at her curiously. He stroked his chin.

'See—no,' he replied, 'but she heard something.'

'What did she hear?'

'Someone moving about in Madame Doyle's cabin.'

'I see,' muttered Rosalie.

She was pale now—deadly pale.

'And you persist in saying that you threw nothing overboard, Mademoiselle?'

'What on earth should I run about throwing things overboard for in the middle of the night?'

'There might be a reason—an innocent reason.'

'Innocent?' repeated the girl sharply.

'That's what I said. You see, Mademoiselle, something *was* thrown overboard last night—something that was not innocent.'

Race silently held out the bundle of stained velvet, opening it to display its contents.

Rosalie Otterbourne shrank back. 'Was that—what—she was killed with?'

'Yes, Mademoiselle.'

'And you think that I—I did it? What utter nonsense! Why on earth should I want to kill Linnet Doyle? I don't even know her!'

She laughed and stood up scornfully. 'The whole thing is too ridiculous.'

'Remember, Miss Otterbourne,' said Race, 'that Miss Van Schuyler is prepared to swear she saw your face quite clearly in the moonlight.'

Rosalie laughed again. 'That old cat? She's probably half blind anyway. It wasn't me she saw.' She paused. 'Can I go now?'

Race nodded and Rosalie Otterbourne left the room.

The eyes of the two men met. Race lighted a cigarette.

'Well, that's that. Flat contradiction. Which of 'em do we believe?'

Poirot shook his head. 'I have a little idea that neither of them was being quite frank.'

'That's the worst of our job,' said Race despondently. 'So many people keep back the truth for positively futile reasons. What's our next move? Get on with the questioning of the passengers?'

'I think so. It is always well to proceed with order and method.'

Race nodded.

Mrs. Otterbourne, dressed in floating batik material, succeeded her daughter. She corroborated Rosalie's statement that they had both gone to bed before eleven o'clock. She herself had heard nothing of interest during the night. She could not say whether Rosalie had left their cabin or not. On the subject of the crime she was inclined to hold forth.

'The *crime passionel*!' she exclaimed. 'The primitive instinct —to kill! So closely allied to the sex instinct. That girl, Jacqueline, half Latin, hot-blooded, obeying the deepest instincts of her being, stealing forth, revolver in hand——'

'But Jacqueline de Bellefort did not shoot Madame Doyle. That we know for certain. It is proved,' explained Poirot.

'Her husband, then,' said Mrs. Otterbourne, rallying from the blow. 'The blood lust and the sex instinct—a sexual crime. There are many well-known instances.'

'Mr. Doyle was shot through the leg and he was quite unable to move—the bone was fractured,' explained Colonel Race. 'He spent the night with Dr. Bessner.'

Mrs. Otterbourne was even more disappointed. She searched her mind hopefully.

'Of course!' she said. 'How foolish of me! Miss Bowers!'

'Miss Bowers?'

'Yes. Naturally. It's so *clear* psychologically. Repression! The repressed virgin! Maddened by the sight of these two— a young husband and wife passionately in love with each other. Of course it was her! She's just the type—sexually unattractive, innately respectable. In my book, *The Barren Vine* ——'

Colonel Race interposed tactfully: 'Your suggestions have been most helpful, Mrs. Otterbourne. We must get on with our job now. Thank you so much.'

He escorted her gallantly to the door and came back wiping his brow.

'What a poisonous woman! Whew! Why didn't somebody murder *her*!'

'It may yet happen,' Poirot consoled him.

'There might be some sense in that. Whom have we got left? Pennington—we'll keep him for the end, I think. Richetti—Ferguson.'

Signor Richetti was very voluble, very agitated.

'But what a horror, what an infamy—a woman so young and so beautiful—indeed an inhuman crime!'

Signor Richetti's hands flew expressively up in the air.

His answers were prompt. He had gone to bed early—very early. In fact immediately after dinner. He had read for a while —a very interesting pamphlet lately published—*Prähistorische Forschung in Kleinasien*—throwing an entirely new light on the painted pottery of the Anatolian foothills.

He had put out his light some time before eleven. No, he had not heard any shot. Not any sound like the pop of a cork. The only thing he had heard—but that was later, in the middle of the night—was a splash, a big splash, just near his porthole.

'Your cabin is on the lower deck, on the starboard side, is it not?'

'Yes, yes, that is so. And I heard the big splash.' His arms flew up once more to describe the bigness of the splash.

'Can you tell me at all what time that was?'

Signor Richetti reflected.

'It was one, two, three hours after I go to sleep. Perhaps two hours.'

'About ten minutes past one, for instance?'

'It might very well be, yes. Ah! But what a terrible crime —how inhuman . . . So charming a woman . . .'

Exit Signor Richetti, still gesticulating freely.

Race looked at Poirot. Poirot raised his eyebrows expressively, then shrugged his shoulders. They passed on to Mr. Ferguson.

Ferguson was difficult. He sprawled insolently in a chair. 'Grand to-do about this business!' he sneered. 'What's it really matter? Lots of superfluous women in the world!'

Race said coldly: 'Can we have an account of your movements last night, Mr. Ferguson?'

'Don't see why you should, but I don't mind. I mooched around a good bit. Went ashore with Miss Robson. When she went back to the boat I mooched around by myself for a while. Came back and turned in round about midnight.'

'Your cabin is on the lower deck, starboard side?'

'Yes. I'm not up among the nobs.'

'Did you hear a shot? It might only have sounded like the popping of a cork.'

Ferguson considered. 'Yes, I think I did hear something like a cork. . . . Can't remember when—before I went to sleep. But there was still a lot of people about then—commotion, running about on the deck above.'

'That was probably the shot fired by Miss de Bellefort. You didn't hear another?'

Ferguson shook his head.

'Nor a splash?'

'A splash? Yes, I believe I did hear a splash. But there was so much row going on I can't be sure about it.'

'Did you leave your cabin during the night?'

Ferguson grinned. 'No, I didn't. And I didn't participate in the good work, worse luck.'

'Come, come, Mr. Ferguson, don't behave childishly.'

The young man reacted angrily.

'Why shouldn't I say what I think? I believe in violence.'

'But you don't practise what you preach?' murmured Poirot. 'I wonder.'

He leaned forward.

'It was the man, Fleetwood, was it not, who told you that Linnet Doyle was one of the richest women in England?'

'What's Fleetwood got to do with this?'

'Fleetwood, my friend, had an excellent motive for killing Linnet Doyle. He had a special grudge against her.'

Mr. Ferguson came up out of his seat like a jack-in-the-box.

'So that's your dirty game, is it?' he demanded wrathfully. 'Put it on to a poor devil like Fleetwood, who can't defend himself, who's got no money to hire lawyers. But I tell you this—if you try and saddle Fleetwood with this business you'll have me to deal with.'

'And who exactly are you?' asked Poirot sweetly.

Mr. Ferguson got rather red.

'I can stick by my friends anyway,' he said gruffly.

'Well, Mr. Ferguson, I think that's all we need for the present,' said Race.

As the door closed behind Ferguson he remarked unexpectedly: 'Rather a likeable young cub, really.'

'You don't think he is the man *you* are after?' asked Poirot.

'I hardly think so. I suppose he *is* on board. The information was very precise. Oh, well, one job at a time. Let's have a go at Pennington.'

Chapter Eighteen

Andrew Pennington displayed all the conventional reactions of grief and shock. He was, as usual, carefully dressed. He had changed into a black tie. His long clean-shaven face bore a bewildered expression.

'Gentlemen,' he said sadly, 'this business has got me right down! Little Linnet—why, I remember her as the cutest little thing you can imagine. How proud of her Melhuish Ridgeway used to be, too! Well, there's no point in going into that. Just tell me what I can do; that's all I ask.'

Race said: 'To begin wih, Mr. Pennington, did you hear anything last night?'

'No, sir, I can't say I did. I have the cabin right next to Dr. Bessner's number forty—forty-one, and I heard a certain commotion going on in there round about midnight or so. Of course I didn't know what it was at the time.'

'You heard nothing else? No shots?'

Andrew Pennington shook his head.

'Nothing whatever of that kind.'

'And you went to bed at what time?'

'Must have been some time after eleven.'

He leant forward.

'I don't suppose it's news to you to know that there's plenty of rumours going about the boat. That half-French girl—Jacqueline de Bellefort—there was something fishy there, you know. Linnet didn't tell me anything, but naturally I wasn't born blind and deaf. There'd been some affair between her and Simon, some time, hadn't there—*Cherchez la femme*—that's a pretty good sound rule, and I should say you wouldn't have to *cherchez* far.'

'You mean that in your belief Jacqueline de Bellefort shot Madame Doyle?' Poirot asked.

'That's what it looks like to me. Of course I don't *know* anything. . . .'

'Unfortunately we *do* know something!'

'Eh?' Mr. Pennington looked startled.

'We know that it is quite impossible for Mademoiselle de Bellefort to have shot Madame Doyle.'

He explained carefully the circumstances. Pennington seemed reluctant to accept them.

'I agree it looks all right on the face of it—but this hospital nurse woman, I'll bet she didn't stay awake all night. She dozed off and the girl slipped out and in again.'

'Hardly likely, Monsieur Pennington. She had administered a strong opiate, remember. And anyway a nurse is in the habit of sleeping lightly and waking when her patient wakes.'

'It all sounds rather fishy to me,' declared Pennington.

Race said, in a gently authoritative manner: 'I think you must take it from me, Mr. Pennington, that we have examined all the possibilities very carefully. The result is quite definite —Jacqueline de Bellefort did not shoot Mrs. Doyle. So we are forced to look elsewhere. That is where we hope you may be able to help us.'

'I?' Pennington gave a nervous start.

'Yes. You were an intimate friend of the dead woman. You know the circumstances of her life, in all probability, much better than her husband does, since he only made her acquaintance a few months ago. You would know, for instance, of anyone who had a grudge against her. You would know, perhaps, whether there was anyone who had a motive for desiring her death.'

Andrew Pennington passed his tongue over rather dry-looking lips.

'I assure you, I have no idea. . . . You see Linnet was brought up in England. I know very little of her surroundings and associations.'

'And yet,' mused Poirot, 'there was someone on board who was interested in Madame Doyle's removal. She had a near escape before, you remember, at this very place, when that boulder crashed down—ah! but you were not there, perhaps?'

'No. I was inside the temple at the time. I heard about it afterwards, of course. A very near escape. But possibly an accident, don't you think?'

Poirot shrugged his shoulders.

'One thought so at the time. Now—one wonders.'

'Yes—yes, of course.' Pennington wiped his face with a fine silk handkerchief.

Colonel Race went on: 'Mr. Doyle happened to mention someone being on board who bore a grudge—not against her personally, but against her family. Do you know who that could be?'

Pennington looked genuinely astonished.

'No, I've no idea.'

'She didn't mention the matter to you?'

'No.'

'You were an intimate friend of her father's—you cannot remember any business operations of his that might have resulted in ruin for some business opponent?'

Pennington shook his head helplessly. 'No outstanding case. Such operations were frequent, of course, but I can't recall anyone who uttered threats—nothing of that kind.'

'In short, Mr. Pennington, you cannot help us?'

'It seems so. I deplore my inadequacy, gentlemen.'

Race interchanged a glance with Poirot, then he said: 'I'm sorry too. We'd had hopes.'

He got up as a sign the interview was at an end.

Andrew Pennington said: 'As Doyle's laid up, I expect he'd like me to see to things. Pardon me, Colonel, but what exactly are the arrangements?'

'When we leave here we shall make a non-stop run to Shellâl, arriving there to-morrow morning.'

'And the body?'

'Will be removed to one of the cold storage chambers.'

Andrew Pennington bowed his head. Then he left the room.

Poirot and Race again interchanged a glance.

'Mr. Pennington,' said Race, lighting a cigarette, 'was not at all comfortable.'

Poirot nodded. 'And,' he said, 'Mr. Pennington was sufficiently perturbed to tell a rather stupid lie. He was *not* in the temple of Abu Simbel when that boulder fell. I—*moi qui vous parle*—can swear to that. I had just come from there.'

'A very stupid lie,' said Race, 'and a very revealing one.'

Again Poirot nodded.

'But for the moment,' he said, and smiled, 'we handle him with the gloves of kid, is it not so?'

'That was the idea,' agreed Race.

'My friend, you and I understand each other to a marvel.'

There was a faint grinding noise, a stir beneath their feet. The *Karnak* had started on her homeward journey to Shellâl.

'The pearls,' said Race. 'That is the next thing to be cleared up.'

'You have a plan?'

'Yes.' He glanced at his watch. 'It will be lunch time in half an hour. At the end of the meal I propose to make an announcement—just state the fact that the pearls have been stolen, and that I must request everyone to stay in the dining-saloon while a search is conducted.'

Poirot nodded approvingly.

'It is well imagined. Whoever took the pearls still has them. By giving no warning beforehand, there will be no chance of their being thrown overboard in a panic.'

Race drew some sheets of paper towards him. He murmured apologetically: 'I'd like to make a brief précis of the facts as I go along. It keeps one's mind free of confusion.'

'You do well. Method and order, they are everything,' replied Poirot.

Race wrote for some minutes in his small neat script. Finally he pushed the result of his labours towards Poirot.

'Anything you don't agree with there?'

Poirot took up the sheets. They were headed:

MURDER OF MRS. LINNET DOYLE

Mrs. Doyle was last seen alive by her maid, Louise Bourget. Time: 11.30 (approx.).

From 11.30-12.20 following have alibis: Cornelia Robson, James Fanthorp, Simon Doyle, Jacqueline de Bellefort—*nobody else*—but crime almost certainly committed *after* that time, since it is practically certain that pistol used was Jacqueline de Bellefort's, which was then in her handbag. That her pistol was used is not *absolutely* certain until after post mortem and expert evidence re bullet—but it may be taken as overwhelmingly probable.

Probable course of events: X (murderer) was witness of scene between Jacqueline and Simon Doyle in observation saloon and noted where pistol went under settee. After the saloon was vacant, X procured pistol—his or her idea being that Jacqueline de Bellefort would be thought guilty of crime. On this theory certain people are automatically cleared of suspicion:

Cornelia Robson, since she had no opportunity to take pistol before James Fanthorp returned to search for it.

Miss Bowers—same.

Dr. Bessner—same.

N.B.—Fanthorp is not definitely excluded from suspicion, since he could actually have pocketed pistol while declaring himself unable to find it.

Any other person could have taken the pistol during that ten minutes' interval.

Possible motives for the murder:

Andrew Pennington. This is on the assumption that he has been guilty of fraudulent practices. There is a certain amount of evidence in favour of that assumption, but not enough to justify making out a case against him. If it was he who rolled down the boulder, he is a man who can seize a chance when it presents itself. The crime, clearly, was not premeditated except in a *general* way. Last night's shooting scene was an ideal opportunity.

Objections to the theory of Pennington's guilt: *Why did he throw the pistol overboard, since it constituted a valuable clue against J.B.?*

Fleetwood. Motive, revenge. Fleetwood considered himself injured by Linnet Doyle. Might have overheard scene and noted position of pistol. He may have taken pistol because it was a handy weapon, rather than with the idea of throwing guilt on Jacqueline. This would fit in with throwing it overboard. *But if that were the case, why did he write J in blood on the wall?*

N.B.—Cheap handkerchief found with pistol more likely to have belonged to a man like Fleetwood than to one of the well-to-do passengers.

Rosalie Otterbourne. Are we to accept Miss Van Schuyler's evidence or Rosalie's denial? Something *was* thrown overboard at that time and that something was presumably the pistol wrapped up in the velvet stole.

Points to be noted. Had Rosalie any motive? She may have disliked Linnet Doyle and even been envious of her—but as a motive for murder that seems grossly inadequate. The evidence against her can be convincing only if we discover an adequate motive. As far as we know, there is no previous knowledge or link between Rosalie Otterbourne and Linnet Doyle.

Miss Van Schuyler. The velvet stole in which pistol was wrapped belongs to Miss Van Schuyler. According to her own statement she last saw it in the observation saloon. She drew attention to its loss during the evening, and a search was made for it without success.

How did the stole come into the possession of X? Did X purloin it some time early in the evening? But if so, why? Nobody could tell, in advance, that there was going to be a scene between Jacqueline and Simon. Did X find the stole in the saloon when he went to get the pistol from under the settee? But if so, why was it not found when the search for it was made? Did it never leave Miss Van Schuyler's possession? That is to say: Did Miss Van Schuyler murder Linnet Doyle? Is her accusation of Rosalie Otterbourne a deliberate lie? If she did murder her, what was her motive?

Other possibilities:

Robbery as a motive. Possible, since the pearls have disappeared, and Linnet Doyle was certainly wearing them last night.

Someone with a grudge against the Ridgeway family. Possible —again no evidence.

We know that there is a dangerous man on board—a killer Here we have a killer and a death. May not the two be connected? But we should have to show that Linnet Doyle possessed dangerous knowledge concerning this man.

Conclusions: We can group the persons on board into two classes—those who had a possible motive or against whom there is definite evidence, and those who, as far as we know, are free of suspicion.

Group I	Group II
Andrew Pennington	Mrs. Allerton
Fleetwood	Tim Allerton
Rosalie Otterbourne	Cornelia Robson
Miss Van Schuyler	Miss Bowers
Louise Bourget (Robbery?)	Dr. Bessner
Ferguson (Political?)	Signor Richetti
	Mrs. Otterbourne
	James Fanthorp

Poirot pushed the paper back.

'It is very just, very exact, what you have written there.'

'You agree with it?'

'Yes.'

'And now what is your contribution?'

Poirot drew himself up in an important manner.

'Me, I pose to myself one question: "*Why* was the pistol thrown overboard?" '

'That's all?'

'At the moment, yes. Until I can arrive at a satisfactory answer to that question, there is no sense anywhere. That is —that *must* be the starting point. You will notice, my friend, that, in your summary of where we stand, you have not attempted to answer that point.'

Race shrugged his shoulders.

'Panic.'

Poirot shook his head perplexedly. He picked up the sodden velvet wrap and smoothed it out, wet and limp, on the table. His fingers traced the scorched marks and the burnt holes.

'Tell me, my friend,' he said suddenly. 'You are more conversant with firearms than I am. Would such a thing as this, wrapped round a pistol, make much difference in muffling the sound?'

'No, it wouldn't. Not like a silencer, for instance.'

Poirot nodded. He went on: 'A man—certainly a man who had had much handling of firearms—would know that. But a woman—a woman would *not* know.'

Race looked at him curiously. 'Probably not.'

'No. She would have read the detective stories where they are not always very exact as to details.'

Race flicked the little pearl-handled pistol with his finger. 'This little fellow wouldn't make much noise anyway,' he said. 'Just a pop, that's all. With any other noise around, ten to one you wouldn't notice it.'

'Yes, I have reflected as to that.'

Poirot picked up the handkerchief and examined it.

'A man's handkerchief—but not a gentleman's handkerchief. *Ce cher* Woolworth, I imagine. Threepence at most.'

'The sort of handkerchief a man like Fleetwood would own.'

'Yes. Andrew Pennington, I notice, carries a very fine silk handkerchief.'

'Ferguson?' suggested Race.

'Possibly. As a gesture. But then it ought to be a bandana.'

'Used it instead of a glove, I suppose, to hold the pistol and obviate fingerprints.' Race added, with slight facetiousness, ' "The Clue of the Blushing Handkerchief." '

'Ah, yes. Quite a *jeune fille* colour, is it not?' He laid it down and returned to the stole, once more examining the powder marks.

'All the same,' he murmured, 'it is odd . . .'

'What's that?'

Poirot said gently: '*Cette pauvre* Madame Doyle. Lying there so peacefully . . . with the little hole in her head. You remember how she looked?'

Race looked at him curiously. 'You know,' he said, 'I've got an idea you're trying to tell me something—but I haven't the faintest idea what it is.'

Chapter Nineteen

There was a tap on the door.

'Come in,' Race called.

A steward entered.

'Excuse me, sir,' he said to Poirot, 'but Mr. Doyle is asking for you.'

'I will come.'

Poirot rose. He went out of the room and up the companionway to the promenade deck and along it to Dr. Bessner's cabin.

Simon, his face flushed and feverish, was propped up with pillows. He looked embarrassed.

'Awfully good of you to come along, Monsieur Poirot. Look here, there's something I want to ask you.'

'Yes?'

Simon got still redder in the face.

'It's—it's about Jackie. I want to see her. Do you think—would you mind—would she mind, d'you think, if you asked her to come along here? You know I've been lying here thinking. . . . That wretched kid—she is only a kid after all —and I treated her damn' badly—and——' He stammered to silence.

Poirot looked at him with interest.

'You desire to see Mademoiselle Jacqueline? I will fetch her.'

'Thanks. Awfully good of you.'

Poirot went on his quest. He found Jacqueline de Bellefort sitting huddled up in a corner of the observation saloon. There was an open book on her lap but she was not reading.

Poirot said gently: 'Will you come with me, Mademoiselle? Monsieur Doyle wants to see you.'

She started up. Her face flushed—then paled. She looked bewildered.

'Simon? He wants to see me—to see *me*?'

He found her incredulity moving.

'Will you come, Mademoiselle?'

She went with him in a docile fashion, like a child, but like a puzzled child.

'I—yes, of course I will.'

Poirot passed into the cabin.

'Here is Mademoiselle.'

She stepped in after him, wavered, stood still . . . standing there mute and dumb, her eyes fixed on Simon's face.

'Hullo, Jackie.' He, too, was embarrassed. He went on: 'Awfully good of you to come. I wanted to say—I mean—what I mean is——'

She interrupted him then. Her words came out in a rush—breathless, desperate.

'Simon—I didn't kill Linnet. You know I didn't do that . . . I—I—was mad last night. Oh, can you ever forgive me?' Words came more easily to him now.

'Of course. That's all right! Absolutely all right! That's what I wanted to say. Thought you might be worrying a bit, you know. . . .'

'*Worrying? A bit?* Oh! Simon!'

'That's what I wanted to see you about. It's quite all right, see, old girl? You just got a bit rattled last night—a shade tight. All perfectly natural.'

'Oh, Simon! I might have killed you!'

'Not you. Not with a rotten little peashooter like that. . . .'

'And your leg! Perhaps you'll never walk again. . . .'

'Now, look here, Jackie, don't be maudlin. As soon as we get to Assuan they're going to put the X-ray to work, and dig out that tin-pot bullet, and everything will be as right as rain.'

Jacqueline gulped twice, then she rushed forward and knelt down by Simon's bed, burying her face and sobbing. Simon patted her awkwardly on the head. His eyes met Poirot's and, with a reluctant sigh, the latter left the cabin.

He heard broken murmurs as he went:

'How could I be such a devil? Oh, Simon! . . . I'm so dreadfully sorry.'

Outside Cornelia Robson was leaning over the rail. She turned her head.

'Oh, it's you, Monsieur Poirot. It seems so awful somehow that it should be such a lovely day.'

Poirot looked up at the sky.

'When the sun shines you cannot see the moon,' he said. 'But when the sun is gone—ah, when the sun is gone.'

Cornelia's mouth fell open.

'I beg your pardon?'

'I was saying, Mademoiselle, that when the sun has gone down, we shall see the moon. That is so, is it not?'

'Why—why, yes—certainly.'

She looked at him doubtfully.

Poirot laughed gently.

'I utter the imbecilities,' he said. 'Take no notice.'

He strolled gently towards the stern of the boat. As he passed the next cabin he paused for a minute. He caught fragments of speech from within:

'Utterly ungrateful—after all I've done for you—no consideration for your wretched mother—no idea of what I suffer. . . .'

Poirot's lips stiffened as he pressed them together. He raised a hand and knocked.

There was a startled silence and Mrs. Otterbourne's voice called out: 'Who's that?'

'Is Mademoiselle Rosalie there?'

Rosalie appeared in the doorway. Poirot was shocked at her appearance. There were dark circles under her eyes and drawn lines round her mouth.

'What's the matter?' she said ungraciously. 'What do you want?'

'The pleasure of a few minutes' conversation with you, Mademoiselle. Will you come?'

Her mouth went sulky at once. She shot him a suspicious look.

'Why should I?'

'I entreat you, Mademoiselle.'

'Oh, I suppose——'

She stepped out on the deck, closing the door behind her. 'Well?'

Poirot took her gently by the arm and drew her along the deck, still in the direction of the stern. They passed the bathrooms and round the corner. They had the stern part of the deck to themselves. The Nile flowed away behind them.

Poirot rested his elbows on the rail. Rosalie stood up straight and stiff.

'Well?' she asked again, and her voice held the same ungracious tone.

Poirot spoke slowly, choosing his words. 'I could ask you certain questions, Mademoiselle, but I do not think for one moment that you would consent to answer them.'

'Seems rather a waste to bring me along here then.'

Poirot drew a finger slowly along the wooden rail.

'You are accustomed, Mademoiselle, to carrying your own burdens. . . . But you can do that too long. The strain becomes too great. For you, Mademoiselle, the strain is becoming too great.'

'I don't know what you are talking about,' said Rosalie.

'I am talking about facts, Mademoiselle—plain ugly facts. Let us call the spade the spade and say it in one little short sentence. Your mother drinks, Mademoiselle.'

Rosalie did not answer. Her mouth opened; then she closed it again. For once she seemed at a loss.

'There is no need for you to talk, Mademoiselle. I will do all the talking. I was interested at Assuan in the relations existing between you. I saw at once that, in spite of your carefully studied unfilial remarks, you were in reality passionately protecting her from something. I very soon knew what that something was. I knew it long before I encountered your mother one morning in an unmistakable state of intoxication. Moreover, her case, I could see, was one of secret bouts of drinking—by far the most difficult kind of case with which to deal. You were coping with it manfully. Nevertheless, she had all the secret drunkard's cunning. She managed to get hold of a secret supply of spirits and to keep it successfully hidden from you. I should not be surprised if you discovered its hiding place only yesterday. Accordingly, last night, as soon as your mother was really soundly asleep, you stole out with the contents of the *cache,* went round to the other side of the boat (since your own side was up against the bank) and cast it overboard into the Nile.'

He paused.

'I am right, am I not?'

'Yes—you're quite right.' Rosalie spoke with sudden passion. 'I was a fool not to say so, I suppose! But I didn't want everyone to know. It would go all over the boat. And it seemed so—so silly—I mean—that I——'

Poirot finished the sentence for her.

'So silly that you should be suspected of committing a murder?'

Rosalie nodded.

Then she burst out again: 'I've tried so hard to—keep everyone from knowing. . . . It isn't really her fault. She got discouraged. Her books didn't sell any more. People are tired of all that cheap sex stuff. . . . It hurt her—it hurt her dreadfully. And so she began to—to drink. For a long time I didn't know why she was so queer. Then, when I found out, I tried to—to stop it. She'd be all right for a bit, and then, suddenly, she'd start, and there would be dreadful quarrels and rows with people. It was awful.' She shuddered. 'I had always to be on the watch—to get her away. . . .

147

'And then—she began to dislike me for it. She—she's turned right against me. I think she almost hates me sometimes.'

'*Pauvre petite*,' said Poirot.

She turned on him vehemently.

'Don't be sorry for me. Don't be kind. It's easier if you're not.' She sighed—a long heartrending sigh. 'I'm so tired . . . I'm so deadly, deadly tired.'

'I know,' said Poirot.

'People think I'm awful. Stuck-up and cross and bad-tempered. I can't help it. I've forgotten how to be—to be nice.'

'That is what I said to you; you have carried your burden by yourself too long.'

Rosalie said slowly: 'It's a relief—to talk about it. You—you've always been kind to me, Monsieur Poirot. I'm afraid I've been rude to you often.'

'*La politesse*, it is not necessary between friends.'

The suspicion came back to her face suddenly.

'Are you—are you going to tell everyone? I suppose you must, because of those damned bottles I threw overboard.'

'No, no, it is not necessary. Just tell me what I want to know. At what time was this? Ten minutes past one?'

'About that, I should think. I don't remember exactly.'

'Now tell me, Mademoiselle. Mademoiselle Van Schuyler saw *you*, did you see *her*?'

Rosalie shook her head.

'No, I didn't.'

'She says that she looked out of the door of her cabin.'

'I don't think I should have seen her. I just looked along the deck and then out to the river.'

Poirot nodded.

'And did you see anyone—anyone at all, when you looked down the deck?'

There was a pause—quite a long pause. Rosalie was frowning. She seemed to be thinking earnestly.

At last she shook her head quite decisively.

'No,' she said. 'I saw nobody.'

Hercule Poirot slowly nodded his head. But his eyes were grave.

Chapter Twenty

People crept into the dining-saloon by ones and twos in a very subdued manner. There seemed a general feeling that to sit down eagerly to food displayed an unfortunate heartlessness. It was with an almost apologetic air that one passenger after another came and sat down at their tables.

Tim Allerton arrived some few minutes after his mother had taken her seat. He was looking in a thoroughly bad temper.

'I wish we'd never come on this blasted trip,' he growled.

Mrs. Allerton shook her head sadly.

'Oh, my dear, so do I. That beautiful girl! It all seems such a *waste*. To think that anyone could shoot her in cold blood. It seems awful to me that anyone could do such a thing. And that other poor child.'

'Jacqueline?'

'Yes; my heart aches for her. She looks so dreadfully unhappy.'

'Teach her not to go round loosing off toy firearms,' said Tim unfeelingly as he helped himself to butter.

'I expect she was badly brought up.'

'Oh, for God's sake, Mother, don't go all maternal about it.'

'You're in a shocking bad temper, Tim.'

'Yes, I am. Who wouldn't be?'

'I don't see what there is to be cross about. It's just frightfully sad.'

Tim said crossly: 'You're taking the romantic point of view! What you don't seem to realise is that it's no joke being mixed up in a murder case.'

Mrs. Allerton looked a little startled.

'But surely——'

'That's just it. There's no "But surely" about it. Everyone on this damned boat is under suspicion—you and I as well as the rest of them.'

Mrs. Allerton demurred. 'Technically we are, I suppose—but actually it's ridiculous!'

'There's nothing ridiculous where murder's concerned! You may sit there, darling, just exuding virtue and conscious rectitude, but a lot of unpleasant policemen at Shellâl or Assuan won't take you at your face value.'

'Perhaps the truth will be known before then.'

'Why should it be?'

'Monsieur Poirot may find out.'

'That old mountebank? He won't find out anything. He's all talk and moustaches.'

'Well, Tim,' said Mrs. Allerton, 'I daresay everything you say is true, but, even if it is, we've got to go through with it, so we might as well make up our minds to it and go through with it as cheerfully as we can.'

But her son showed no abatement of gloom.

'There's this blasted business of the pearls being missing, too.'

'Linnet's pearls?'

'Yes. It seems somebody must have pinched 'em.'

'I suppose that was the motive for the crime,' said Mrs. Allerton.

'Why should it be? You're mixing up two perfectly different things.'

'Who told you that they were missing?'

'Ferguson. He got it from his tough friend in the engine room, who got it from the maid.'

'They were lovely pearls,' declared Mrs. Allerton.

Poirot sat down at the table, bowing to Mrs. Allerton.

'I am a little late,' he said.

'I expect you have been busy,' Mrs. Allerton replied.

'Yes, I have been much occupied.'

He ordered a fresh bottle of wine from the waiter.

'We're very catholic in our tastes,' said Mrs. Allerton. 'You drink wine always; Tim drinks whisky and soda, and I try all the different brands of mineral water in turn.'

'*Tiens!*' said Poirot. He stared at her for a moment. He murmured to himself: 'It is an idea, that . . .'

Then, with an impatient shrug of his shoulders, he dismissed the sudden preoccupation that had distracted him and began to chat lightly of other matters.

'Is Mr. Doyle badly hurt?' asked Mrs. Allerton.

'Yes, it is a fairly serious injury. Dr. Bessner is anxious to reach Assuan so that his leg can be X-rayed and the bullet removed. But he hopes there will be no permanent lameness.'

'Poor Simon,' said Mrs. Allerton. 'Once yesterday he looked such a happy boy, with everything in the world he wanted. And now his beautiful wife killed and he himself laid up and helpless. I do hope, though——'

'What do you hope, Madame?' asked Poirot as Mrs. Allerton paused.

'I hope he's not too angry with that poor child.'

'With Mademoiselle Jacqueline? Quite the contrary. He was full of anxiety on her behalf.'

He turned to Tim.

'You know, it is a pretty little problem of psychology, that. All the time that Mademoiselle Jacqueline was following them from place to place, he was absolutely furious; but now, when she has actually shot him, and wounded him dangerously—perhaps made him lame for life—all his anger seems to have evaporated. Can you understand that?'

'Yes,' said Tim thoughtfully, 'I think I can. The first thing made him feel a fool——'

Poirot nodded. 'You are right. It offended his male dignity.'

'But now—if you look at it a certain way, it's *she* who's made a fool of herself. Everyone's down on her, and so——'

'He can be generously forgiving,' finished Mrs. Allerton. 'What children men are!'

'A profoundly untrue statement that women always make,' murmured Tim.

Poirot smiled. Then he said to Tim: 'Tell me, Madame Doyle's cousin, Miss Joanna Southwood, did she resemble Madame Doyle?'

'You've got it a little wrong, Monsieur Poirot. She was our cousin and Linnet's friend.'

'Ah, pardon—I was confused. She is a young lady much in the news, that. I have been interested in her for some time.'

'Why?' asked Tim sharply.

Poirot half rose to bow to Jacqueline de Bellefort, who had just come in and passed their table on the way to her own. Her cheeks were flushed and her eyes bright, and her breath came a little unevenly. As he resumed his seat Poirot seemed to have forgotten Tim's question. He murmured vaguely: 'I wonder if all young ladies with valuable jewels are as careless as Madame Doyle was?'

'It is true, then, that they were stolen?' asked Mrs. Allerton.

'Who told you so, Madame?'

'Ferguson said so,' Tim volunteered.

Poirot nodded gravely.

'It is quite true.'

'I suppose,' said Mrs. Allerton nervously, 'that this will mean a lot of unpleasantness for all of us. Tim says it will.'

Her son scowled, but Poirot had turned to him.

'Ah! you have had previous experience, perhaps? You have been in a house where there was a robbery?'

'Never,' said Tim.

'Oh, yes, darling, you were at the Portarlingtons' that time —when that awful woman's diamonds were stolen.'

'You always get things hopelessly wrong, Mother. I was there when it was discovered that the diamonds she was wearing round her fat neck were only paste! The actual substitution was probably done months earlier. As a matter of fact, a lot of people said she'd had it done herself!'

'Joanna said so, I expect.'

'Joanna wasn't there.'

'But she knew them quite well. And it's very like her to make that kind of suggestion.'

'You're always down on Joanna, Mother.'

Poirot hastily changed the subject. He had it in mind to make a really big purchase at one of the Assuan shops. Some very attractive purple and gold material at one of the Indian merchants. There would, of course, be the duty to pay, but——

'They tell me that they can—how do you say—expedite it for me. And that the charges will not be too high. How think you, will it arrive all right?'

Mrs. Allerton said that many people, so she had heard, had had things sent straight to England from the shops in question and that everything had arrived safely.

'Bien. Then I will do that. But the trouble one has, when one is abroad, if a parcel comes out from England! Have you had experience of that? Have you had any parcels arrive since you have been on your travels?'

'I don't think we have, have we, Tim? You get books sometimes, but of course there is never any trouble about them.'

'Ah, no, books are different.'

Dessert had been served. Now, without any previous warning, Colonel Race stood up and made his speech.

He touched on the circumstances of the crime and announced the theft of the pearls. A search of the boat was about to be instituted, and he would be obliged if all the passengers would remain in the saloon until this was completed. Then, after that, if the passengers agreed, as he was sure they would, they themselves would be kind enough to submit to a search.

Poirot slipped nimbly along to his side. There was a little buzz and hum all round them. Voices doubtful, indignant, excited. . . .

Poirot reached Race's side and murmured something in his ear just as the latter was about to leave the dining-saloon.

Race listened, nodded assent, and beckoned a steward. He said a few brief words to him; then, together with Poirot, he passed out on to the deck, closing the door behind him.

They stood for a minute or two by the rail. Race lit a cigarette. 'Not a bad idea of yours,' he said. 'We'll soon see if there's anything in it. I'll give 'em three minutes.'

The door of the dining-saloon opened and the same steward to whom they had spoken came out. He saluted Race and said: 'Quite right, sir. There's a lady who says it's urgent she should speak to you at once without delay.'

'Ah!' Race's face showed satisfaction. 'Who is it?'

'Miss Bowers, sir, the hospital nurse lady.'

A slight shade of surprise showed on Race's face. He said. 'Bring her to the smoking-room. Don't let anyone else leave.'

'No, sir—the other steward will attend to that.'

He went back into the dining-room. Poirot and Race went to the smoking-room.

'Bowers, eh?' muttered Race.

They had hardly got inside the smoking-room before the steward reappeared with Miss Bowers. He ushered her in and left, shutting the door behind him.

'Well, Miss Bowers?' Colonel Race looked at her inquiringly. 'What's all this?'

Miss Bowers looked her usual composed, unhurried self. She displayed no particular emotion.

'You'll excuse me, Colonel Race,' she said, 'but under the circumstances I thought the best thing to do would be to speak to you at once'—she opened her neat black handbag —'and to return you these.'

She took out a string of pearls and laid them on the table.

Chapter Twenty-one

If Miss Bowers had been the kind of woman who enjoyed creating a sensation, she would have been richly repaid by the result of her action.

A look of utter astonishment passed over Colonel Race's face as he picked up the pearls from the table.

'This is most extraordinary,' he said. 'Will you kindly explain, Miss Bowers?'

'Of course. That's what I've come to do.' Miss Bowers settled herself comfortably in a chair. 'Naturally it was a little difficult for me to decide what it was best for me to do. The family would naturally be averse to scandal of any kind, and they trusted my discretion, but the circumstances are so very unusual that it really leaves me no choice. Of course, when you didn't find anything in the cabins, your next move would be a search of the passengers, and, if the pearls were then found in my possession, it would be rather an awkward situation and the truth would come out just the same.'

'And just what is the truth? Did you take these pearls from Mrs. Doyle's cabin?'

'Oh, no, Colonel Race, of course not. Miss Van Schuyler did.'

'Miss Van Schuyler?'

'Yes. She can't help it, you know, but she does—er—take things. Especially jewellery. That's really why I'm always with her. It's not her health at all; it's this little idiosyncrasy. I keep on the alert, and fortunately there's never been any trouble since I've been with her. It just means being watchful, you know. And she always hides the things she takes in the same place—rolled up in a pair of stockings—so that it makes it very simple. I look each morning. Of course I'm a light sleeper, and I always sleep next door to her, and with the communicating door open if it's in a hotel, so that I usually hear. Then I go after her and persuade her to go back to bed. Of course it's been rather more difficult on a boat. But she doesn't usually do it at night. It's more just picking up things that she sees left about. Of course, pearls have a great attraction for her always.'

Miss Bowers ceased speaking.

Race asked: 'How did you discover they had been taken?'

'They were in her stockings this morning. I knew whose they were, of course. I've often noticed them. I went along to put them back, hoping that Mrs. Doyle wasn't up yet and hadn't discovered her loss. But there was a steward standing there, and he told me about the murder and that no one could go in. So then, you see, I was in a regular quandary. But I still hoped to slip them back in the cabin later, before their absence had been noticed. I can assure you I've passed a very unpleasant morning wondering what was the best thing to do. You see, the Van Schuyler family is so *very* particular and exclusive. It would never do if this got into the newspapers. But that won't be necessary, will it?'

Miss Bowers really looked worried.

'That depends on circumstances,' said Colonel Race cautiously.

'But we shall do our best for you, of course. What does Miss Van Schuyler say to this?'

'Oh, she'll deny it, of course. She always does. Says some wicked person has put it there. She never admits taking anything. That's why if you catch her in time she goes back to bed like a lamb. Says she just went out to look at the moon. Something like that.'

'Does Miss Robson know about this—er—failing?'

'No, she doesn't. Her mother knows, but she's a very simple kind of girl and her mother thought it best she should know nothing about it. I was quite equal to dealing with Miss Van Schuyler,' added the competent Miss Bowers.

'We have to thank you, Mademoiselle, for coming to us so promptly,' said Poirot.

Miss Bowers stood up.

'I'm sure I hope I acted for the best.'

'Be assured that you have.'

'You see, what with there being a murder as well——'

Colonel Race interrupted her. His voice was grave.

'Miss Bowers, I am going to ask you a question, and I want to impress upon you that it has got to be answered truthfully. Miss Van Schuyler is unhinged mentally to the extent of being a kleptomaniac. Has she also a tendency to homicidal mania?'

Miss Bowers' answer came immediately: 'Oh, dear me, no! Nothing of that kind. You can take my word for it absolutely. The old lady wouldn't hurt a fly.'

The reply came with such positive assurance that there seemed nothing more to be said. Nevertheless Poirot did interpolate one mild inquiry.

'Does Miss Van Schuyler suffer at all from deafness?'

'As a matter of fact she does, Monsieur Poirot. Not so that you'd notice in any way, not if you were speaking to her, I mean. But quite often she doesn't hear you when you come into a room. Things like that.'

'Do you think she would have heard anyone moving about in Mrs. Doyle's cabin, which is next door to her own?'

'Oh, I shouldn't think so—not for a minute. You see, the bunk is the other side of the cabin, not even against the partition wall. No, I don't think she would have heard anything.'

'Thank you, Miss Bowers.'

Race said: 'Perhaps you will now go back to the dining-saloon and wait with the others?'

He opened the door for her and watched her go down the

staircase and enter the saloon. Then he shut the door and came back to the table. Poirot had picked up the pearls.

'Well,' said Race grimly, 'that reaction came pretty quickly. That's a very cool-headed and astute young woman—perfectly capable of holding out on us and still further if she thinks it suits her book. What about Miss Marie Van Schuyler now? I don't think we can eliminate her from the possible suspects. You know, she *might* have committed murder to get hold of those jewels. We can't take the nurse's word for it. She's all out to do the best for the family.'

Poirot nodded in agreement. He was very busy with the pearls, running them through his fingers, holding them up to his eyes.

He said: 'We may take it, I think, that part of the old lady's story to us was true. She *did* look out of her cabin and she *did* see Rosalie Otterbourne. But I don't think she *heard* anything or anyone in Linnet Doyle's cabin. I think she was just peering out from *her* cabin preparatory to slipping along and purloining the pearls.'

'The Otterbourne girl was there, then?'

'Yes. Throwing her mother's secret *cache* of drink overboard.'

Colonel Race shook his head sympathetically.

'So that's it! Tough on a young 'un.'

'Yes, her life has not been very gay, *cette pauvre petite Rosalie.*'

'Well, I'm glad that's been cleared up. *She* didn't see or hear anything?'

'I asked her that. She responded—after a lapse of quite twenty seconds—that she saw nobody.'

'Oh?' Race looked alert.

'Yes, it is suggestive, that.'

Race said slowly: 'If Linnet Doyle was shot round about ten minutes past one, or indeed any time after the boat had quieted down, it has seemed amazing to me that no one heard the shot. I grant you that a little pistol like that wouldn't make much noise, but all the same the boat would be deadly quiet, and any noise, even a gentle pop, should have been heard. But I begin to understand better now. The cabin on the forward side of hers was unoccupied—since her husband was in Dr. Bessner's cabin. The one aft was occupied by the Van Schuyler woman, who was deaf. That leaves only——'

He paused and looked expectantly at Poirot, who nodded.

'The cabin next to her on the other side of the boat. In

other words—Pennington. We always seem to come back to Pennington.'

'We will come back to him presently with the kid gloves removed! Ah, yes, I am promising myself that pleasure.'

'In the meantime we'd better get on with our search of the boat. The pearls still make a convenient excuse, even though they have been returned—but Miss Bowers is not likely to advertise that fact.'

'Ah, these pearls!' Poirot held them up against the light once more. He stuck out his tongue and licked them; he even gingerly tried one of them between his teeth. Then, with a sigh, he threw them down on the table.

'Here are more complications, my friend,' he said. 'I am not an expert on precious stones, but I have had a good deal to do with them in my time and I am fairly certain of what I say. These pearls are only a clever imitation.'

Chapter Twenty-two

Colonel Race swore hastily.

'This damned case gets more and more involved.' He picked up the pearls. 'I suppose you've not made a mistake? They look all right to me.'

'They are a very good imitation—yes.'

'Now where does that lead us? I suppose Linnet Doyle didn't deliberately have an imitation made and bring it aboard with her for safety. Many women do.'

'I think, if that were so, her husband would know about it.'

'She may not have told him.'

Poirot shook his head in a dissatisfied manner.

'No, I do not think that is so. I was admiring Madame Doyle's pearls the first evening on the boat—their wonderful sheen and lustre. I am sure that she was wearing the genuine ones then.'

'That brings us up against two possibilities. First, that Miss Van Schuyler only stole the imitation string after the real ones had been stolen by someone else. Second, that the whole kleptomaniac story is a fabrication. Either Miss Bowers is a thief, and quickly invented the story and allayed suspicion by handing over the false pearls, or else that whole party is in it together. That is to say, they are a gang of clever jewel thieves masquerading as an exclusive American family.'

'Yes,' Poirot murmured. 'It is difficult to say. But I will point out to you one thing—to make a perfect and exact copy of the pearls, clasp and all, good enough to stand a chance of deceiving Madame Doyle, is a highly skilled technical performance. It could not be done in a hurry. Whoever copied those pearls must have had a good opportunity of studying the original.'

Race rose to his feet.

'Useless to speculate about it any further now. Let's get on with the job. We've got to find the real pearls. And at the same time we'll keep our eyes open.'

They disposed first of the cabins occupied on the lower deck. That of Signor Richetti contained various archæological works in different languages, a varied assortment of clothing, hair lotions of a highly scented kind and two personal letters—one from an archæological expedition in Syria, and one from, apparently, a sister in Rome. His handkerchiefs were all of coloured silk.

They passed on to Ferguson's cabin.

There was a sprinkling of communistic literature, a good many snapshots, Samuel Butler's *Erewhon* and a cheap edition of Pepys' *Diary*. His personal possessions were not many. Most of what outer clothing there was was torn and dirty; the underclothing, on the other hand, was of really good quality. The handkerchiefs were expensive linen ones.

'Some interesting discrepancies,' murmured Poirot.

Race nodded. 'Rather odd that there are absolutely no personal papers, letters, etc.'

'Yes; that gives one to think. An odd young man, Monsieur Ferguson.' He looked thoughtfully at a signet ring he held in his hand, before replacing it in the drawer where he had found it.

They went along to the cabin, occupied by Louis Bourget. The maid had her meals after the other passengers, but Race had sent word that she was to be taken to join the others. A cabin steward met them.

'I'm sorry, sir,' he apologised, 'but I've not been able to find the young woman anywhere. I can't think where she can have got to.'

Race glanced inside the cabin. It was empty.

They went up to the promenade deck and started on the starboard side. The first cabin was that occupied by James Fanthorp. Here all was in meticulous order. Mr. Fanthorp travelled light, but all that he had was of good quality.

'No letters,' said Poirot thoughtfully. 'He is careful, our Mr. Fanthorp, to destroy his correspondence.'

They passed on to Tim Allerton's cabin, next door.

There were evidences here of an Anglo-Catholic turn of mind—an exquisite little triptych, and a big rosary of intricately carved wood. Besides personal clothing, there was a half-completed manuscript, a good deal annotated and scribbled over, and a good collection of books, most of them recently published. There were also a quantity of letters thrown carelessly into a drawer. Poirot, never in the least scrupulous about reading other people's correspondence, glanced through them. He noted that amongst them there were no letters from Joanna Southwood. He picked up a tube of Seccotine, fingered it absently for a minute or two, then said: 'Let us pass on.'

'No Woolworth handkerchiefs,' reported Race, rapidly replacing the contents of a drawer.

Mrs. Allerton's cabin was the next. It was exquisitely neat, and a faint old-fashioned smell of lavender hung about it. The two men's search was soon over. Race remarked as they left it: 'Nice woman, that.'

The next cabin was that which had been used as a dressing-room by Simon Doyle. His immediate necessities—pyjamas, toilet things, etc.—had been moved to Bessner's cabin, but the remainder of his possessions were still there—two good-sized leather suitcases and a kitbag. There were also some clothes in the wardrobe.

'We will look carefully here, my friend,' said Poirot, 'for it is possible that the thief hid the pearls here.'

'You think it is likely?'

'But yes, indeed. Consider! The thief, whoever he or she may be, must know that sooner or later a search will be made, and therefore a hiding-place in his or her own cabin would be injudicious in the extreme. The public rooms present other difficulties. But here is a cabin belonging to a man who cannot possibly visit it himself so that, if the pearls are found here, it tells us nothing at all.' But the most meticulous search failed to reveal any trace of the missing necklace.

Poirot murmured 'Zut!' to himself and they emerged once more on the deck.

Linnet Doyle's cabin had been locked after the body was removed, but Race had the key with him. He unlocked the door and the two men stepped inside.

Except for the removal of the girl's body, the cabin was exactly as it had been that morning.

'Poirot,' said Race, 'if there's anything to be found here, for God's sake go ahead and find it. You can if anyone can—I know that.'

'This time you do not mean the pearls, *mon ami*?'

'No. The murder's the main thing. There may be something I overlooked this morning.'

Quietly, deftly, Poirot went about his search. He went down on his knees and scrutinised the floor inch by inch. He examined the bed. He went rapidly through the wardrobe and chest of drawers. He went through the wardrobe trunk and the two costly suitcases. He looked through the expensive gold-fitted dressing-case. Finally he turned his attention to the washstand. There were various creams, powders, face lotions. But the only thing that seemed to interest Poirot were two little bottles labelled Nailex. He picked them up at last and brought them to the dressing-table. One, which bore the inscription Nailex Rose, was empty but for a drop or two of dark red fluid at the bottom. The other, the same size, but labelled Nailex Cardinal, was nearly full. Poirot uncorked first the empty, then the full one, and sniffed them both delicately.

An odour of peardrops billowed into the room. With a slight grimace he recorked them.

'Get anything?' asked Race.

Poirot replied by a French proverb: '*On no prend pas les mouches avec le vinaigre.*' Then he said with a sigh: 'My friend, we have not been fortunate. The murderer has not been obliging. He has not dropped for us the cuff link, the cigarette end, the cigar ash—or, in the case of a woman, the handkerchief, the lipstick, or the hair slide.'

'Only the bottle of nail polish?'

Poirot shrugged his shoulders. 'I must ask the maid. There is something—yes—a little curious there.'

'I wonder where the devil the girl's got to?' said Race.

They left the cabin, locking the door behind them, and passed on to that of Miss Van Schuyler.

Here again were all the appurtenances of wealth, expensive toilet fittings, good luggage, a certain number of private letters and papers all perfectly in order.

The next cabin was the double one occupied by Poirot, and beyond it that of Race. 'Hardly like to hide 'em in either of these,' said the Colonel.

Poirot demurred. 'It might be. Once, on the Orient Express, I investigated a murder. There was a little matter of a scarlet kimono. It had disappeared, and yet it must be on the train. I found it—where do you think? In my own locked suitcase! Ah! it was an impertinence, that!'

'Well, let's see if anybody has been impertinent with you or me this time.'

But the thief of the pearls had not been impertinent with Hercule Poirot or with Colonel Race.

Rounding the stern they made a very careful search of Miss Bowers' cabin but could find nothing of a suspicious nature. Her handkerchiefs were of plain linen with an initial.

The Otterbournes' cabin came next. Here, again, Poirot made a very meticulous search, but with no result.

The next cabin was Bessner's. Simon Doyle lay with an untasted tray of food beside him.

'Off my feed,' he said apologetically.

He was looking feverish and very much worse than earlier in the day. Poirot appreciated Bessner's anxiety to get him as swiftly as possible to hospital and skilled appliances. The little Belgian explained what the two of them were doing, and Simon nodded approval. On learning that the pearls had been restored by Miss Bowers, but proved to be merely imitation, he expressed the most complete astonishment.

'You are quite sure, Monsieur Doyle, that your wife did not have an imitation string which she brought aboard with her instead of the real ones?'

Simon shook his head decisively.

'Oh, no. I'm quite sure of that. Linnet loved those pearls and she wore 'em everywhere. They were insured against every possible risk, so I think that made her a bit careless.'

'Then we must continue our search.'

He started opening drawers. Race attacked a suitcase.

Simon stared. 'Look here, you surely don't suspect old Bessner pinched them?'

Poirot shrugged his shoulders.

'It might be so. After all, what do we know of Dr. Bessner? Only what he himself gives out.'

'But he couldn't have hidden them in here without my seeing him.'

'He could not have hidden anything to-day without your having seen him. But we do not know when the substitution took place. He may have effected the exchange some days ago.'

'I never thought of that.'

But the search was unavailing.

The next cabin was Pennington's. The two men spent

some time in their search. In particular, Poirot and Race examined carefully a case full of legal and business documents, most of them requiring Linnet's signature.

Poirot shook his head gloomily. 'These seem all square and aboveboard. You agree?'

'Absolutely. Still, the man isn't a born fool. If there *had* been a compromising document there—a power of attorney or something of that kind—he'd be pretty sure to have destroyed it first thing.'

'That is so, yes.'

Poirot lifted a heavy Colt revolver out of the top drawer of the chest of drawers, looked at it and put it back.

'So it seems there are still some people who travel with revolvers,' he murmured.

'Yes, a little suggestive, perhaps. Still, Linnet Doyle wasn't shot with a thing that size.' Race paused and then said: 'You know, I've thought of a possible answer to your point about the pistol being thrown overboard. Supposing that the actual murderer did leave it in Linnet Doyle's cabin, and that someone else—some second person—took it away and threw it into the river?'

'Yes, that is possible. I have thought of it. But it opens up a whole string of questions. Who was that second person? What interest had they in endeavouring to shield Jacqueline de Bellefort by taking away the pistol? What was the second person doing there? The only other person we know of who went into the cabin was Mademoiselle Van Schuyler. Was it conceivably Mademoiselle Van Schuyler who removed it? Why should *she* wish to shield Jacqueline de Bellefort? And yet— what other reason can there be for the removal of the pistol?'

Race suggested, 'She may have recognised the stole as hers, got the wind up, and thrown the whole bag of tricks over on that account.'

'The stole, perhaps, but would she have got rid of the pistol, too? Still, I agree that it is a possible solution. But it is always—*bon Dieu*! it is clumsy. And you still have not appreciated one point about the stole——'

As they emerged from Pennington's cabin Poirot suggested that Race should search the remaining cabins, those occupied by Jacqueline, Cornelia and two empty ones at the end, while he himself had a few words with Simon Doyle. Accordingly he retraced his steps along the deck and re-entered Bessner's cabin.

Simon said: 'Look here, I've been thinking. I'm perfectly sure that those pearls were all right yesterday.'

'Why is that, Monsieur Doyle?'

'Because Linnet'—he winced as he uttered his wife's name—'was passing them through her hands just before dinner and talking about them. She knew something about pearls. I feel certain she'd have known if they were a fake.'

'They were a very good imitation, though. Tell me, was Madame Doyle in the habit of letting those pearls out of her hands? Did she ever lend them to a friend, for instance?'

Simon flushed with slight embarrassment.

'You see, Monsieur Poirot, it's difficult for me to say. . . . I—I—well, you see, I hadn't known Linnet very long.'

'Ah, no, it was a quick romance—yours.'

Simon went on. 'And so—really—I shouldn't know a thing like that. But Linnet was awfully generous with her things. I should think she might have done.'

'She never, for instance'—Poirot's voice was very smooth—'she never, for instance, lent them to Mademoiselle de Bellefort?'

'What d'you mean?' Simon flushed brick-red, tried to sit up and, wincing, fell back. 'What are you getting at? That Jackie stole the pearls? She didn't. I'll swear she didn't. Jackie's as straight as a die. The mere idea of her being a thief is ridiculous—absolutely ridiculous.'

Poirot looked at him with gently twinkling eyes. 'Oh, la! la! la!' he said unexpectedly. 'That suggestion of mine, it has indeed stirred up the nest of hornets.'

Simon repeated doggedly, unmoved by Poirot's lighter note, 'Jackie's straight!'

Poirot remembered a girl's voice by the Nile in Assuan saying, 'I love Simon—and he loves me. . . .'

He had wondered which of the three statements he had heard that night was the true one. It seemed to him that it had turned out to be Jacqueline who had come closest to the truth.

The door opened and Race came in.

'Nothing,' he said brusquely. 'Well, we didn't expect it. I see the stewards coming along with their report as to the searching of the passengers.'

A steward and stewardess appeared in the doorway. The former spoke first. 'Nothing, sir.'

'Any of the gentlemen make any fuss?'

'Only the Italian gentleman, sir. He carried on a good deal. Said it was a dishonour—something of that kind. He'd got a gun on him, too.'

'What kind of a gun?'

'Mauser automatic twenty-five, sir.'

'Italians are pretty hot-tempered,' said Simon. 'Richetti got in no end of a stew at Wâdi Halfa just because of a mistake over a telegram. He was darned rude to Linnet over it.'

Race turned to the stewardess. She was a big handsome-looking woman.

'Nothing on any of the ladies, sir. They made a good deal of fuss—except for Mrs. Allerton, who was as nice as nice could be. Not a sign of the pearls. By the way, the young lady, Miss Rosalie Otterbourne, had a little pistol in her handbag.'

'What kind?'

'It was a very small one, sir, with a pearl handle. A kind of toy.'

Race stared. 'Devil take this case,' he muttered. 'I thought we'd got *her* cleared of suspicion, and now—— Does every girl on this blinking boat carry around pearl-handed toy pistols?'

He shot a question at the stewardess. 'Did she show any feeling over your finding it?'

The woman shook her head. 'I don't think she noticed. I had my back turned whilst I was going through the handbag.'

'Still, she must have known you'd come across it. Oh, well, it beats me. What about the maid?'

'We've looked all over the boat, sir. We can't find her anywhere.'

'What's this?' asked Simon.

'Mrs. Doyle's maid—Louise Bourget. She's disappeared.'

'*Disappeared?*'

Race said thoughtfully: 'She might have stolen the pearls. She is the one person who had ample opportunity to get a replica made.'

'And then, when she found a search was being instituted, she threw herself overboard?' suggested Simon.

'Nonsense,' replied Race, irritably. 'A woman can't throw herself overboard in broad daylight, from a boat like this, without somebody realising the fact. She's bound to be somewhere on board.' He addressed the stewardess once more. 'When was she last seen?'

'About half an hour before the bell went for lunch, sir.'

'We'll have a look at her cabin anyway,' said Race. 'That may tell us something.'

He led the way to the deck below. Poirot followed him. They unlocked the door of the cabin and passed inside.

Louise Bourget, whose trade it was to keep other people's

belongings in order, had taken a holiday where her own were concerned. Odds and ends littered the top of the chest of drawers; a suitcase gaped open, with clothes hanging out of the side of it and preventing it shutting; underclothing hung limply over the sides of the chairs.

As Poirot, with swift neat fingers, opened the drawers of the dressing-chest, Race examined the suitcase.

Louise's shoes were lined along by the bed. One of them, a black patent leather, seemed to be resting at an extraordinary angle, almost unsupported. The appearance of it was so odd that it attracted Race's attention.

He closed the suitcase and bent over the line of shoes. Then he uttered a sharp exclamation.

Poirot whirled round.

'*Qu'est-ce qu'il y a?*'

Race said grimly: 'She hasn't disappeared. She's here—under the bed. . . .'

Chapter Twenty-three

The body of a dead woman, who in life had been Louise Bourget, lay on the floor of her cabin. The two men bent over it.

Race straightened himself first.

'Been dead close on an hour, I should say. We'll get Bessner on to it. Stabbed to the heart. Death pretty well instantaneous, I should imagine. She doesn't look pretty, does she?'

'No.'

Poirot shook his head with a slight shudder.

The dark feline face was convulsed, as though with surprise and fury, the lips drawn back from the teeth.

Poirot bent again gently and picked up the right hand. Something just showed within the fingers. He detached it and held it out to Race, a little sliver of flimsy paper coloured a pale mauvish pink.

'You see what it is?'

'Money,' said Race.

'The corner of a thousand-franc note, I fancy.'

'Well, it's clear what happened,' said Race. 'She knew something—and she was blackmailing the murderer with her knowledge. We thought she wasn't being quite straight this morning.'

Poirot cried out: 'We have been idiots—fools! We should have known—then. What did she say? "What could I have seen or heard? I was on the deck below. Naturally, if I had been unable to sleep, if I had mounted the stairs, *then* perhaps I might have seen this assassin, this monster, enter or leave Madame's cabin, but as it is——" Of course, that is what did happen! She did come up. She did see someone gliding into Linnet Doyle's cabin—or coming out of it. And, because of her greed, her insensate greed, she lies here——'

'And we are no nearer to knowing who killed her,' finished Race disgustedly.

Poirot shook his head. 'No, no. We know much more now. We know—we know almost everything. Only what we know seems incredible. . . . Yet it must be so. Only I do not see. Pah! what a fool I was this morning! We felt—both of us felt—that she was keeping something back, and yet we never realised that logical reason, blackmail.'

'She must have demanded hush money straight away,' said Race. 'Demanded it with threats. The murderer was forced to accede to that request and paid her in French notes. Anything there?'

Poirot shook his head thoughtfully. 'I hardly think so. Many people take a reserve of money with them when travelling —sometimes five-pound notes, sometimes dollars, but very often French notes as well. Possibly the murderer paid her all he had in a mixture of currencies. Let us continue our reconstruction.'

'The murderer comes to her cabin, gives her the money, and then——'

'And then,' said Poirot, 'she counts it. Oh, yes, I know that class. She would count the money, and while she counted it she was completely off her guard. The murderer struck. Having done so successfully, he gathered up the money and fled—not noticing that the corner of one of the notes was torn.'

'We may get him that way,' suggested Race doubtfully.

'I doubt it,' said Poirot. 'He will examine those notes, and will probably notice the tear. Of course if he were of a parsimonious disposition he would not be able to bring himself to destroy a *mille* note—but I very much fear that his temperament is just the opposite.'

'How do you make that out?'

'Both this crime and the murder of Madame Doyle demanded certain qualities—courage, audacity, bold execution, lightning

166

action; those qualities do not accord with a saving, prudent disposition.'

Race shook his head sadly. 'I'd better get Bessner down,' he said.

The stout doctor's examination did not take long. Accompanied by a good many *Ach's* and *So's*, he went to work.

'She has been dead not more than an hour,' he announced. 'Death it was very quick—at once.'

'And what weapon do you think was used?'

'Ach, it is interesting that. It was something very sharp, very thin, very delicate. I could show you the kind of thing.'

Back again in his cabin he opened a case and extracted a long, delicate, surgical knife.

'It was something like that, my friend; it was not a common table knife.'

'I suppose,' suggested Race smoothly, 'that none of your own knives are—er—missing, Doctor?'

Bessner stared at him; then his face grew red with indignation.

'What is that you say? Do you think I—I, Carl Bessner—who is so well-known all over Austria—I with my clinics, my highly born patients—I have killed a miserable little *femme de chambre*? Ah, but it is ridiculous—absurd, what you say! None of my knives are missing—not one, I tell you. They are all here, correct, in their places. You can see for yourself. And this insult to my profession I will not forget.'

Dr. Bessner closed his case with a snap, flung it down and stamped out on to the deck.

'Whew!' said Simon. 'You've put the old boy's back up.'

Poirot shrugged his shoulders. 'It is regrettable.'

'You're on the wrong tack. Old Bessner's one of the best, even though he is a kind of Boche.'

Dr. Bessner reappeared suddenly.

'Will you be so kind as to leave me now my cabin? I have to do the dressing of my patient's leg.'

Miss Bowers had entered with him and stood, brisk and professional, waiting for the others to go.

Race and Poirot crept out meekly. Race muttered something and went off. Poirot turned to his left. He heard scraps of girlish conversation, a little laugh. Jacqueline and Rosalie were together in the latter's cabin.

The door was open and the two girls were standing near it. As his shadow fell on them they looked up. He saw Rosalie Otterbourne smile at him for the first time—a shy welcoming smile—a little uncertain in its lines, as of one who does a new and unfamiliar thing.

'You talk the scandal, Mesdemoiselles?' he accused them.

'No, indeed,' said Rosalie. 'As a matter of fact we were just comparing lipsticks.'

Poirot smiled. '*Les chiffons d'aujourd'hui,*' he murmured.

But there was something a little mechanical about his smile, and Jacqueline de Bellefort, quicker and more observant than Rosalie, saw it. She dropped the lipstick she was holding and came out upon the deck.

'Has something—what has happened now?'

'It is as you guess, Mademoiselle; something has happened.'

'What?' Rosalie came out too.

'Another death,' said Poirot.

Rosalie caught her breath sharply. Poirot was watching her narrowly. He saw alarm and something more—consternation—show for a minute or two in her eyes.

'Madame Doyle's maid has been killed,' he told them bluntly.

'Killed?' cried Jacqueline. '*Killed,* do you say?'

'Yes, that is what I said.' Though his answer was nominally to her, it was Rosalie whom he watched. It was Rosalie to whom he spoke as he went on: 'You see, this maid she saw something she was not intended to see. And so—she was silenced, in case she should not hold her tongue.'

'What was it she saw?'

Again it was Jacqueline who asked, and again Poirot's answer was to Rosalie. It was an odd little three-cornered scene.

'There is, I think, very little doubt what it was she saw,' said Poirot. 'She saw someone enter and leave Linnet Doyle's cabin on that fatal night.'

His ears were quick. He heard the sharp intake of breath and saw the eyelids flicker. Rosalie Otterbourne had reacted just as he intended she should.

'Did she say who it was she saw?' Rosalie asked.

Gently—regretfully—Poirot shook his head.

Footsteps pattered up the deck. It was Cornelia Robson, her eyes wide and startled.

'Oh, Jacqueline,' she cried, 'something awful has happened! Another dreadful thing!'

Jacqueline turned to her. The two moved a few steps forward. Almost unconsciously Poirot and Rosalie Otterbourne moved in the other direction.

Rosalie said sharply: 'Why do you look at me? What have you got in your mind?'

'That is two questions you ask me. I will ask you only one in return. Why do you not tell me all the truth, Mademoiselle?'

'I don't know what you mean. I told you—everything—this morning.'

'No, there were things you did not tell me. You did not tell me that you carry about in your handbag a small-calibre pistol with a pearl handle. You did not tell me all that you saw last night.'

She flushed. Then she said sharply: 'It's quite untrue. I haven't got a revolver.'

'I did not say a revolver. I said a small pistol that you carry about in your handbag.'

She wheeled round, darted into her cabin and out again and thrust her grey leather handbag into his hands.

'You're talking nonsense. Look for yourself if you like.'

Poirot opened the bag. There was no pistol inside.

He handed the bag back to her, meeting her scornful triumphant glance.

'No,' he said pleasantly. 'It is not there.'

'You see. You're not always right, Monsieur Poirot. And you're wrong about that other ridiculous thing you said.'

'No, I do not think so.'

'You're infuriating!' She stamped an angry foot. 'You get an idea into your head, and you go on and on and on about it.'

'Because I want you to tell me the truth.'

'What is the truth? You seem to know it better than I do.'

Poirot said: 'You want me to tell what it was you saw? If I am right, will you admit that I am right? I will tell you my little idea. I think that when you came round the stern of the boat you stopped involuntarily because you saw a man come out of a cabin about half-way down the deck—Linnet Doyle's cabin, as you realised next day. You saw him come out, close the door behind him, and walk away from you down the deck and—perhaps—enter one of the two end cabins. Now, then, am I right, Mademoiselle?'

She did not answer.

Poirot said: 'Perhaps you think it wiser not to speak. Perhaps you are afraid that, if you do, you too will be killed.'

For a moment he thought she had risen to the easy bait, that the accusation against her courage would succeed where more subtle arguments would have failed.

Her lips opened—trembled—then, 'I saw no one,' said Rosalie Otterbourne.

Chapter Twenty-four

Miss Bowers came out of Dr. Bessner's cabin, smoothing her cuffs over her wrists.

Jacqueline left Cornelia abruptly and accosted the hospital nurse.

'How is he?' she demanded.

Poirot came up in time to hear the answer. Miss Bowers was looking rather worried.

'Things aren't going too badly,' she said.

Jacqueline cried: 'You mean, he's worse?'

'Well, I must say I shall be relieved when we get in and can get a proper X-ray done and the whole thing cleaned up under an anæsthetic. When do you think we shall get to Shellâl, Monsieur Poirot?'

'To-morrow morning.'

Miss Bowers pursed her lips and shook her head.

'It's very unfortunate. We are doing all we can, but there's always such a danger of septicæmia.'

Jacqueline caught Miss Bowers' arm and shook it.

'Is he going to die? Is he going to die?'

'Dear me, no, Miss de Bellefort. That is, I hope not, I'm sure. The wound in itself isn't dangerous, but there's no doubt it ought to be X-rayed as soon as possible. And then, of course poor Mr. Doyle ought to have been kept absolutely quiet to-day. He's had far too much worry and excitement. No wonder his temperature is rising. What with the shock of his wife's death, and one thing and another——'

Jacqueline relinquished her grasp of the nurse's arm and turned away. She stood leaning over the side, her back to the other two.

'What I say is, we've got to hope for the best always,' said Miss Bowers. 'Of course Mr. Doyle has a very strong constitution—one can see that—probably never had a day's illness in his life. So that's in his favour. But there's no denying that this rise in temperature is a nasty sign and——'

She shook her head, adjusted her cuffs once more, and moved briskly away.

Jacqueline turned and walked gropingly, blinded by tears, towards her cabin. A hand below her elbow steadied and guided her. She looked up through the tears to find Poirot by her side. She leaned on him a little and he guided her through the cabin door.

She sank down on the bed and the tears came more freely, punctuated by great shuddering sobs.

'He'll die! He'll die! I know he'll die . . . And I shall have killed him. Yes, I shall have killed him. . . .'

Poirot shrugged his shoulders. He shook his head a little, sadly. 'Mademoiselle, what is done is done. One cannot take back the accomplished action. It is too late to regret.'

She cried out more vehemently: 'I shall have killed him! And I love him so . . . I love him so.'

Poirot sighed. 'Too much. . . .'

It had been his thought long ago in the restaurant of M. Blondin. It was his thought again now.

He said, hesitating a little: 'Do not, at all events, go by what Miss Bowers says. Hospital nurses, me, I find them always gloomy! The night nurse, always, she is astonished to find her patient alive in the evening; the day nurse, always, she is surprised to find him alive in the morning! They know too much, you see, of the possibilities that may arise. When one is motoring one might easily say to oneself: "If a car came out from that cross-road—or if that lorry backed suddenly —or if the wheel came off the car that is approaching—or if a dog jumped off the hedge on to my driving arm—*eh bien*, I should probably be killed!" But one assumes, and usually rightly, that none of these things *will* happen, and that one will get to one's journey's end. But if, of course, one has been in an accident, or seen one or more accidents, then one is inclined to take the opposite point of view.'

Jacqueline asked, half smiling through her tears: 'Are you trying to console me, Monsieur Poirot?'

'The *bon Dieu* knows what I am trying to do! You should not have come on this journey.'

'No—I wish I hadn't. It's been—so awful. But—it will be soon over now.'

'*Mais oui—mais oui.*'

'And Simon will go to the hospital, and they'll give the proper treatment and everything will be all right.'

'You speak like the child! "And they lived happily ever afterward." That is it, is it not?'

She flushed suddenly scarlet.

'Monsieur Poirot, I never meant—never——'

'It is too soon to think of such a thing! That is the proper hypocritical thing to say, is it not? But you are partly a

Latin, Mademoiselle Jacqueline. You should be able to admit facts even if they do not sound very decorous. *Le roi est mort—vive le roi!* The sun has gone and the moon rises. That is so, is it not?'

'You don't understand. He's just sorry for me—awfully sorry for me, because he knows how terrible it is for me to know I've hurt him so badly.'

'Ah, well,' said Poirot. 'The pure pity, it is a very lofty sentiment.'

He looked at her half mockingly, half with some other emotion.

He murmured softly under his breath words in French:

> *'La vie est vaine.*
> *Un peu d'amour,*
> *Un peu de haine,*
> *Et puis bonjour.*
>
> *La vie est brève.*
> *Un peu d'espoir,*
> *Un peu de rêve,*
> *Et puis bonsoir.'*

He went out again on to the deck. Colonel Race was striding along the deck and hailed him at once.

'Poirot. Good man! I want you. I've got an idea.'

Thrusting his arm through Poirot's he walked him up the deck.

'Just a chance remark of Doyle's. I hardly noticed it at the time. Something about a telegram.'

'*Tiens—c'est vrai.*'

'Nothing in it, perhaps, but one can't leave any avenue unexplored. Damn it all, man, two murders, and we're still in the dark.'

Poirot shook his head. 'No, not in the dark. In the light.'

Race looked at him curiously. 'You have an idea?'

'It is more than an idea now. *I am sure.*'

'Since—when?'

'Since the death of the maid, Louise Bourget.'

'Damned if I see it!'

'My friend, it is so clear—so clear. Only there are difficulties —embarrassments—impediments! See you, around a person like Linnet Doyle there is so much—so many conflicting hates and jealousies and envies and meannesses. It is like a cloud of flies, buzzing, buzzing. . . .'

'But you think you know?' The other looked at him curiously. 'You wouldn't say so unless you were sure. Can't say I've any real light, myself. I've suspicions, of course. . . .'

Poirot stopped. He laid an impressive hand on Race's arm. 'You are a great man, *mon Colonel*. . . . You do not say: "Tell me. What is it that you think?" You know that if I could speak now I would. But there is much to be cleared away first. But think, think for a moment along the lines that I shall indicate. There are certain points. . . . There is the statement of Mademoiselle de Bellefort that someone overheard our conversation that night in the garden at Assuan. There is the statement of Monsieur Tim Allerton as to what he heard and did on the night of the crime. There are Louise Bourget's significant answers to our questions this morning. There is the fact that Madame Allerton drinks water, that her son drinks whisky and soda and that I drink wine. Add to that the fact of two bottles of nail polish and the proverb I quoted. And finally we come to the crux of the whole business, the fact that the pistol was wrapped up in a cheap handkerchief and a velvet stole and thrown overboard. . . .'

Race was silent a minute or two, then he shook his head.

'No,' he said. 'I don't see it. Mind, I've got a faint idea what you're driving at, but as far as I can see, it doesn't work.'

'But yes—but yes. You are seeing only half the truth. And remember this—we must start again from the beginning, since our first conception was entirely wrong.'

Race made a slight grimace.

'I'm used to that. It often seems to me that's all detective work is, wiping out your false starts and beginning again.'

'Yes, it is very true, that. And it is just what some people will not do. They conceive a certain theory, and everything has to fit into that theory. If one little fact will not fit it, they throw it aside. But it is always the facts that will not fit in that are significant. All along I have realised the significance of that pistol being removed from the scene of the crime. I knew that it meant something, but what that something was I only realised one little half hour ago.'

'And I still don't see it!'

'But you will! Only reflect along the lines I indicated. And now let us clear up this matter of a telegram. That is, if the Herr Doktor will admit us.'

Dr. Bessner was still in a very bad humour. In answer to their knock he disclosed a scowling face.

'What is it? Once more you wish to see my patient? But I tell you it is not wise. He has fever. He has had more than enough excitement to-day.'

'Just one question,' said Race. 'Nothing more, I assure you.'

With an unwilling grunt the doctor moved aside and the two men entered the cabin. Dr. Bessner, growling to himself, pushed past them.

'I return in three minutes,' he said. 'And then—positively —you go!'

They heard him stumping down the deck.

Simon Doyle looked from one to the other of them inquiringly.

'Yes,' he said, 'what is it?'

'A very little thing,' Race replied. 'Just now, when the stewards were reporting to me, they mentioned that Signor Richetti had been particularly troublesome. You said that that didn't surprise you, as you knew he had a bad temper, and that he had been rude to your wife over some matter of a telegram. Now can you tell me about that incident?'

'Easily. It was at Wâdi Halfa. We'd just come back from the Second Cataract. Linnet thought she saw a telegram for her sticking up on the board. She'd forgotten, you see, that she wasn't called Ridgeway any longer, and Richetti and Ridgeway do look rather alike when written in an atrocious handwriting. So she tore it open, couldn't make head or tail of it, and was puzzling over it when this fellow Richetti came along, fairly tore it out of her hand and gibbered with rage. She went after him to apologise and he was frightfully rude to her about it.'

Race drew a deep breath. 'And do you know at all, Mr. Doyle, what was in that telegram?'

'Yes. Linnet read part of it out aloud. It said——'

He paused. There was a commotion outside. A high-pitched voice was rapidly approaching.

'Where are Monsieur Poirot and Colonel Race? I must see them *immediately*! It is most important. I have vital information. I—— Are they with Mr. Doyle?'

Bessner had not closed the door. Only the curtain hung across the open doorway. Mrs. Otterbourne swept it to one side and entered like a tornado. Her face was suffused with colour, her gait slightly unsteady, her command of words not quite under her control.

'Mr. Doyle,' she said dramatically, 'I know who killed your wife!'

'What?'

Simon stared at her. So did the other two.

Mrs. Otterbourne swept all three of them with a triumphant glance. She was happy—superbly happy.

'Yes,' she said. 'My theories are completely vindicated. The deep, primeval, primordial urges—it may appear impossible—fantastic—but it is the truth!'

Race said sharply: 'Do I understand that you have evidence in your possession to show who killed Mrs. Doyle?'

Mrs. Otterbourne sat down in a chair and leaned forward, nodding her head vigorously.

'Certainly I have. You will agree, will you not, that whoever killed Louise Bourget also killed Linnet Doyle—that the two crimes were committed by one and the same hand?'

'Yes, yes,' said Simon impatiently. 'Of course. That stands to reason. Go on.'

'Then my assertion holds. I know who killed Louise Bourget; therefore I know who killed Linnet Doyle.'

'You mean, you have a theory as to who killed Louise Bourget,' suggested Race sceptically.

Mrs. Otterbourne turned on him like a tiger.

'No, I have exact knowledge. I *saw* the person with my own eyes.'

Simon, fevered, shouted out: 'For God's sake, start at the beginning. You know the person who killed Louise Bourget, you say.'

Mrs. Otterbourne nodded.

'I will tell you exactly what occurred.'

Yes, she was very happy—no doubt of it! This was her moment, her triumph! What of it if her books were failing to sell, if the stupid public that once had bought them and devoured them voraciously now turned to newer favourites? Salome Otterbourne would once again be notorious. Her name would be in all the papers. She would be principal witness for the prosecution at the trial.

She took a deep breath and opened her mouth.

'It was when I went down to lunch. I hardly felt like eating—all the horror of the recent tragedy—— Well, I needn't go into that. Half-way down I remembered that I had—er—left something in my cabin. I told Rosalie to go on without me. She did.'

Mrs. Otterbourne paused a minute.

The curtain across the door moved slightly as though lifted by the wind, but none of the three men noticed it.

'I—er——' Mrs. Otterbourne paused. Thin ice to skate over here, but it must be done somehow. 'I—er—had an arrangement with one of the—er—*personnel* of the ship. He was to—er—get me something I needed, but I did not wish my daughter to know of it. She is inclined to be tiresome in certain ways——'

Not too good, this, but she could think of something that sounded better before it came to telling the story in court.

Race's eyebrows lifted as his eyes asked a question of Poirot.

Poirot gave an infinitesimal nod. His lips formed the word: 'Drink.'

The curtain across the door moved again. Between it and the door itself something showed with a faint steel-blue gleam.

Mrs. Otterbourne continued: 'The arrangement was that I should go round to the stern on the deck below this, and there I should find the man waiting for me. As I went along the deck a cabin door opened and somebody looked out. It was this girl—Louise Bourget, or whatever her name is. She seemed to be expecting someone. When she saw it was me, she looked disappointed and went abruptly inside again. I didn't think anything of it, of course. I went along just as I had said I would and got the—the stuff from the man. I paid him and—er—just had a word with him. Then I started back. Just as I came around the corner I saw someone knock on the maid's door and go into the cabin.'

Race said, 'And that person was——?'

Bang!

The noise of the explosion filled the cabin. There was an acrid sour smell of smoke. Mrs. Otterbourne turned slowly sideways, as though in supreme inquiry, then her body slumped forward and she fell to the ground with a crash. From just behind her ear the blood flowed from a round neat hole.

There was a moment's stupefied silence. Then both the able-bodied men jumped to their feet. The woman's body hindered their movements a little. Race bent over her while Poirot made a catlike jump for the door and the deck.

The deck was empty. On the ground just in front of the sill lay a big Colt revolver.

Poirot glanced in both directions. The deck was empty. He then sprinted towards the stern. As he rounded the corner he ran into Tim Allerton, who was coming full tilt from the opposite direction.

'What the devil was that?' cried Tim breathlessly.

Poirot said sharply: 'Did you meet anyone on your way here?'

'Meet anyone? No.'

'Then come with me.' He took the young man by the arm and retraced his steps. A little crowd had assembled by now. Rosalie, Jacqueline, and Cornelia had rushed out of their cabins. More people were coming along the deck from the saloon—Ferguson, Jim Fanthorp, and Mrs. Allerton.

Race stood by the revolver. Poirot turned his head and said sharply to Tim Allerton: 'Got any gloves in your pocket?'

Tim fumbled.

'Yes, I have.'

Poirot seized them from him, put them on, and bent to examine the revolver. Race did the same. The others watched breathlessly.

Race said: 'He didn't go the other way. Fanthorp and Ferguson were sitting on this deck lounge; they'd have seen him.'

Poirot responded, 'And Mr. Allerton would have met him if he'd gone aft.'

Race said, pointing to the revolver: 'Rather fancy we've seen this not so very long ago. Must make sure, though.'

He knocked on the door of Pennington's cabin. There was no answer. The cabin was empty. Race strode to the right-hand drawer of the chest and jerked it open. The revolver was gone.

'Settles that,' said Race. 'Now then, where's Pennington himself?'

They went out again on deck. Mrs. Allerton had joined the group. Poirot moved swiftly over to her.

'Madame, take Miss Otterbourne with you and look after her. Her mother has been'—he consulted Race with an eye and Race nodded—'killed.'

Dr. Bessner came bustling along.

'*Gott im Himmel!* What is there now?'

They made way for him. Race indicated the cabin. Bessner went inside.

'Find Pennington,' said Race. 'Any fingerprints on that revolver?'

'None,' said Poirot.

They found Pennington on the deck below. He was sitting in the little drawing-room writing letters. He lifted a handsome, clean-shaven face.

'Anything new?' he asked.

'Didn't you hear a shot?'

'Why—now you mention it—I believe I did hear a kind of a bang. But I never dreamed—— Who's been shot?'

'Mrs. Otterbourne.'

'Mrs. Otterbourne?' Pennington sounded quite astounded. 'Well, you do surprise me. Mrs. Otterbourne.' He shook his head. 'I can't see that at all.' He lowered his voice. 'Strikes me, gentlemen, we've got a homicidal maniac aboard. We ought to organise a defence system.'

'Mr. Pennington,' said Race, 'how long have you been in this room?'

'Why, let me see.' Mr. Pennington gently rubbed his chin. 'I should say a matter of twenty minutes or so.'

'And you haven't left it?'

'Why no—certainly not.'

He looked inquiringly at the two men.

'You see, Mr. Pennington,' said Race, 'Mrs. Otterbourne was shot with your revolver.'

Chapter Twenty-five

Mr. Pennington was shocked. Mr. Pennington could hardly believe it.

'Why, gentlemen,' he said, 'this is a very serious matter. Very serious indeed.'

'Extremely serious for you, Mr. Pennington.'

'For me?' Pennington's eyebrows rose in startled surprise. 'But, my dear sir, I was sitting quietly writing in here when that shot was fired.'

'You have, perhaps, a witness to prove that?'

Pennington shook his head.

'Why, no—I wouldn't say that. But it's clearly impossible that I should have gone to the deck above, shot this poor woman (and why should I shoot her anyway?) and come down again with no one seeing me. There are always plenty of people on the deck lounge this time of day.'

'How do you account for your pistol being used?'

'Well—I'm afraid I may be to blame there. Quite soon after getting aboard there was a conversation in the saloon one evening, I remember, about firearms, and I mentioned then that I always carried a revolver with me when I travel.'

'Who was there?'

'Well, I can't remember exactly. Most people, I think. Quite a crowd, anyway.'

He shook his head gently.

'Why, yes,' he said. 'I am certainly to blame there.'

He went on: 'First Linnet, then Linnet's maid, and now Mrs. Otterbourne. There seems no reason in it all!'

'There *was* reason,' said Race.

'There was?'

'Yes. Mrs. Otterbourne was on the point of telling us that she had seen a certain person go into Louise's cabin. Before she could name that person she was shot dead.'

Andrew Pennington passed a fine silk handkerchief over his brow.

'All this is terrible,' he murmured.

Poirot said: 'Monsieur Pennington, I would like to discuss certain aspects of the case with you. Will you come to my cabin in half an hour's time?'

'I should be delighted.'

Pennington did not sound delighted. He did not look delighted either. Race and Poirot exchanged glances and then abruptly left the room.

'Cunning old devil,' said Race, 'but he's afraid. Eh?'

Poirot nodded. 'Yes, he is not happy, our Monsieur Pennington.'

As they reached the promenade deck again, Mrs. Allerton came out of her cabin and, seeing Poirot, beckoned him imperiously.

'Madame?'

'That poor child! Tell me, Monsieur Poirot, is there a double cabin somewhere that I could share with her? She oughtn't to go back to the one she shared with her mother, and mine is only a single one.'

'That can be arranged, Madame. It is very good of you.'

'It's mere decency. Besides, I'm very fond of the girl. I've always liked her.'

'Is she very upset?'

'Terribly. She seems to have been absolutely devoted to that odious woman. That is what is so pathetic about it all. Tim says he believes she drank. Is that true?'

Poirot nodded.

'Oh, well, poor woman, one must not judge her, I suppose; but that girl must have had a terrible life.'

'She did, Madame. She is very proud and she was very loyal.'

'Yes, I like that—loyalty, I mean. It's out of fashion nowadays. She's an odd character, that girl—proud, reserved, stubborn, and terribly warm-hearted underneath, I fancy.'

'I see that I have given her into good hands, Madame.'

'Yes, don't worry. I'll look after her. She's inclined to cling to me in the most pathetic fashion.'

Mrs. Allerton went back into the cabin. Poirot returned to the scene of the tragedy.

Cornelia was still standing on the deck, her eyes wide. She said: 'I don't understand, Monsieur Poirot. How did the person who shot her get away without our seeing him?'

'Yes, how?' echoed Jacqueline.

'Ah,' said Poirot, 'it was not quite such a disappearing trick as you think, Mademoiselle. There were three distinct ways the murderer might have gone.'

Jacqueline looked puzzled. She said, 'Three?'

'He might have gone to the right, or he might have gone to the left, but I don't see any other way,' puzzled Cornelia.

Jacqueline too frowned. Then her brow cleared.

She said: 'Of course. He could move in two directions on one plane, but he could go at right angles to that plane too. That is, he couldn't go *up* very well, but he could go *down*.'

Poirot smiled. 'You have brains, Mademoiselle.'

Cornelia said: 'I know I'm just a plain mutt, but I still don't see.'

Jacqueline said: 'Monsieur Poirot means, darling, that he could swing himself over the rail and down on to the deck below.'

'My!' gasped Cornelia. 'I never thought of that. He'd have to be mighty quick about it, though. I suppose he could just do it?'

'He could do it easily enough,' said Tim Allerton. 'Remember, there's always a minute of shock after a thing like this. One hears a shot and one's too paralysed to move for a second or two.'

'That was your experience, Monsieur Allerton?'

'Yes, it was. I just stood like a dummy for quite five seconds. Then I fairly sprinted round the deck.'

Race came out of Bessner's cabin and said authoritatively: 'Would you mind all clearing off? We want to bring out the body.'

Everyone moved away obediently. Poirot went with them. Cornelia said to him with sad earnestness: 'I'll never forget this trip as long as I live. Three deaths. . . . It's just like living in a nightmare.'

Ferguson overheard her. He said aggressively: 'That's because you're over-civilised. You should look on death as the Oriental does. It's a mere incident—hardly noticeable.'

'That's all very well,' Cornelia said. 'They're not educated, poor creatures.'

'No, and a good thing too. Education has devitalised the white races. Look at America—goes in for an orgy of culture. Simply disgusting.'

'I think you're talking nonsense,' said Cornelia, flushing. 'I attend lectures every winter on Greek Art and the Renaissance, and I went to some on Famous Women of History.'

Mr. Ferguson groaned in agony: 'Greek Art; Renaissance! Famous Women of History! It makes me quite sick to hear you. It's the *future* that matters, woman, not the past. Three women are dead on this boat. Well, what of it? They're no loss! Linnet Doyle and her money! The French maid—a domestic parasite. Mrs. Otterbourne—a useless fool of a woman. Do you think anyone really cares whether they're dead or not? *I* don't. I think it's a damned good thing!'

'Then you're wrong!' Cornelia blazed out at him. 'And it makes me sick to hear you talk and talk, as though nobody mattered but *you*. I didn't like Mrs. Otterbourne much, but her daughter was ever so fond of her, and she's all broken up over her mother's death. I don't know much about the French maid, but I expect somebody was fond of her somewhere; and as for Linnet Doyle—well, apart from everything else, she was just lovely! She was so beautiful when she came into a room that it made a lump come in your throat. I'm homely myself, and that makes me appreciate beauty a lot more. She was as beautiful—just as a woman—as anything in Greek Art. And when anything beautiful's dead, it's a loss to the world. So there!'

Mr. Ferguson stepped back a space. He caught hold of his hair with both hands and tugged at it vehemently.

'I give it up,' he said. 'You're unbelievable. Just haven't got a bit of natural female spite in you anywhere.' He turned to Poirot. 'Do you know, sir, that Cornelia's father was practically ruined by Linnet Ridgeway's old man? But does the girl gnash her teeth when she sees the heiress sailing about in pearls and Paris models? No, she just bleats out:

"Isn't she beautiful?" like a blessed Baa Lamb. I don't believe she even felt sore at her.'

Cornelia flushed. 'I did—just for a minute. Poppa kind of died of discouragement, you know, because he hadn't made good.'

'Felt sore for a minute! I ask you.'

Cornelia flashed round on him.

'Well, didn't you say just now it was the future that mattered, not the past? All that was in the past, wasn't it? It's over.'

'Got me there,' said Ferguson. 'Cornelia Robson, you're the only nice woman I've ever come across. Will you marry me?'

'Don't be absurd.'

'It's a genuine proposal—even if it is made in the presence of Old Man Sleuth. Anyway, you're a witness, Monsieur Poirot. I've deliberately offered marriage to this female—against all my principles, because I don't believe in legal contracts between the sexes; but I don't think she'd stand for anything else, so marriage it shall be. Come on, Cornelia, say yes.'

'I think you're utterly ridiculous,' said Cornelia, flushing.

'Why won't you marry me?'

'You're not serious,' said Cornelia.

'Do you mean not serious in proposing or do you mean not serious in character?'

'Both, but I really meant character. You laugh at all sorts of serious things. Education and Culture—and—and Death. You wouldn't be *reliable*.'

She broke off, flushed again, and hurried along into her cabin.

Ferguson stared after her. 'Damn the girl! I believe she really means it. She wants a man to be reliable. *Reliable*—ye gods!' He paused and then said curiously: 'What's the matter with you, Monsieur Poirot? You seem very deep in thought.'

Poirot roused himself with a start.

'I reflect, that is all. I reflect.'

'Meditation on Death. Death, the Recurring Decimal, by Hercule Poirot. One of his well-known monographs.'

'Monsieur Ferguson,' said Poirot, 'you are a very impertinent young man.'

'You must excuse me. I like attacking established institutions.'

'And I am an established institution?'

'Precisely. What do you think of that girl?'

'Of Miss Robson?'

'Yes.'

'I think that she has a great deal of character.'

'You're right. She's got spirit. She looks meek, but she isn't. She's got guts. She's—oh, damn it, I want that girl. It mightn't be a bad move if I tackled the old lady. If I could once get her thoroughly against me, it might cut some ice with Cornelia.'

He wheeled and went into the observation saloon. Miss Van Schuyler was seated in her usual corner. She looked even more arrogant than usual. She was knitting. Ferguson strode up to her. Hercule Poirot, entering unobtrusively, took a seat a discreet distance away and appeared to be absorbed in a magazine.

'Good-afternoon, Miss Van Schuyler.'

Miss Van Schuyler raised her eyes for a bare second, dropped them again and murmured frigidly, 'Er—good-afternoon.'

'Look here, Miss Van Schuyler, I want to talk to you about something pretty important. It's just this. I want to marry your cousin.'

Miss Van Schuyler's ball of wool dropped on to the ground and ran wildly across the saloon.

She said in a venomous tone: 'You must be out of your senses, young man.'

'Not at all. I'm determined to marry her. I've asked her to marry me!'

Miss Van Schuyler surveyed him coldly, with the kind of speculative interest she might have accorded to an odd sort of beetle.

'Indeed? And I presume she sent you about your business.'

'She refused me.'

'Naturally.'

'Not "naturally" at all. I'm going to go on asking her till she agrees.'

'I can assure you, sir, that I shall take steps to see that my young cousin is not subjected to any such persecution,' said Miss Van Schuyler in a biting tone.

'What have you got against me?'

Miss Van Schuyler merely raised her eyebrows and gave a vehement tug to her wool, preparatory to regaining it and closing the interview.

'Come now,' persisted Mr. Ferguson, 'what have you got against me?'

'I should think that was quite obvious, Mr.—er—I don't know your name.'

'Ferguson.'

'Mr. Ferguson.' Miss Van Schuyler uttered the name with definite distaste. 'Any such idea is quite out of the question.'

'You mean,' said Ferguson, 'that I'm not good enough for her?'

'I should think that would have been obvious to you.'

'In what way am I not good enough?'

Miss Van Schuyler again did not answer.

'I've got two legs, two arms, good health, and quite reasonable brains. What's wrong with that?'

'There is such a thing as social position, Mr. Ferguson.'

'Social position is bunk!'

The door swung open and Cornelia came in. She stopped dead on seeing her redoubtable Cousin Marie in conversation with her would-be suitor.

The outrageous Mr. Ferguson turned his head, grinned broadly and called out: 'Come along, Cornelia. I'm asking for your hand in marriage in the best conventional manner.'

'Cornelia,' said Miss Van Schuyler, and her voice was truly awful in quality, *'have you encouraged this young man?'*

'I—no, of course not—at least—not exactly—I mean——'

'What do you mean?'

'She hasn't encouraged me,' said Mr. Ferguson helpfully. 'I've done it all. She hasn't actually pushed me in the face, because she's got too kind a heart. Cornelia, your cousin says I'm not good enough for you. That, of course, is true, but not in the way she means it. My moral nature certainly doesn't equal yours, but her point is that I'm hopelessly below you socially.'

'That, I think, is equally obvious to Cornelia,' said Miss Van Schuyler.

'Is it?' Mr. Ferguson looked at her searchingly. 'Is that why you won't marry me?'

'No, it isn't.' Cornelia flushed. 'If—if I liked you, I'd marry you no matter who you were.'

'But you don't like me?'

'I—I think you're just outrageous. The way you say things. . . . The *things* you say . . . I—I've never met anyone the least like you. I——'

Tears threatened to overcome her. She rushed from the room.

'On the whole,' said Mr. Ferguson, 'that's not too bad

for a start.' He leaned back in his chair, gazed at the ceiling, whistled, crossed his disreputable knees and remarked: 'I'll be calling you Cousin yet.'

Miss Van Schuyler trembled with rage. 'Leave this room at once, sir, or I'll ring for the steward.'

'I've paid for my ticket,' said Mr. Ferguson. 'They can't possibly turn me out of the public lounge. But I'll humour you.' He sang softly, 'Yo ho ho, and a bottle of rum.' Rising, he sauntered nonchalantly to the door and passed out.

Choking with anger Miss Van Schuyler struggled to her feet. Poirot, discreetly emerging from retirement behind his magazine, sprang up and retrieved the ball of wool.

'Thank you, Monsieur Poirot. If you would send Miss Bowers to me—I feel quite upset—that insolent young man.'

'Rather eccentric, I'm afraid,' said Poirot. 'Most of that family are. Spoilt, of course. Always inclined to tilt at windmills.' He added carelessly, 'You recognised him, I suppose?'

'Recognised him?'

'Calls himself Ferguson and won't use his title because of his advanced ideas.'

'His *title*?' Miss Van Schuyler's tone was sharp.

'Yes, that's young Lord Dawlish. Rolling in money, of course, but he became a communist when he was at Oxford.'

Miss Van Schuyler, her face a battleground of contradictory emotions, said: 'How long have you known this, Monsieur Poirot?'

Poirot shrugged his shoulders.

'There was a picture in one of these papers—I noticed the resemblance. Then I found a signet ring with a coat of arms on it. Oh, there's no doubt about it, I assure you.'

He quite enjoyed reading the conflicting expressions that succeeded each other on Miss Van Schuyler's face. Finally, with a gracious inclination of the head, she said, 'I am very much obliged to you, Monsieur Poirot.'

Poirot looked after her and smiled as she went out of the saloon. Then he sat down and his face grew grave once more. He was following out a train of thought in his mind. From time to time he nodded his head.

'*Mais oui*,' he said at last. 'It all fits in.'

Chapter Twenty-six

Race found him still sitting there.

'Well, Poirot, what about it? Pennington's due in ten minutes. I'm leaving this in your hands.'

Poirot rose quickly to his feet. 'First, get hold of young Fanthorp.'

'Fanthorp?' Race looked surprised.

'Yes. Bring him to my cabin.'

Race nodded and went off. Poirot went along to his cabin. Race arrived with young Fanthorp a minute or two afterward.

Poirot indicated chairs and offered cigarettes.

'Now, Monsieur Fanthorp,' he said, 'to our business! I perceive that you wear the same tie that my friend Hastings wears.'

Jim Fanthorp looked down at his neckwear with some bewilderment.

'It's an O.E. tie,' he said.

'Exactly. You must understand that, though I am a foreigner, I know something of the English point of view. I know, for instance, that there are "things which are done" and "things which are not done." '

Jim Fanthorp grinned.

'We don't say that sort of thing much nowadays, sir.'

'Perhaps not, but the custom, it still remains. The Old School Tie is the Old School Tie, and there are certain things (I know this from experience) that the Old School Tie does not do! One of those things, Monsieur Fanthorp, is to butt into a private conversation unasked when one does not know the people who are conducting it.'

Fanthorp stared.

Poirot went on: 'But the other day, Monsieur Fanthorp, that is exactly what you did do. Certain persons were quietly transacting some private business in the observation saloon. You strolled near them, obviously in order to overhear what it was that was in progress, and presently you actually turned round and congratulated a lady—Madame Simon Doyle—on the soundness of her business methods.'

Jim Fanthorp's face got very red. Poirot swept on, not waiting for a comment.

'Now that, Monsieur Fanthorp, was not at all the behaviour of one who wears a tie similar to that worn by my friend Hastings! Hastings is all delicacy, would die of shame before he did such a thing! Therefore, taking that action of yours in conjunction with the fact that you are a very young man to be able to afford an expensive holiday, that you are a member of a country solicitor's firm, and therefore probably not extravagantly well off, and that you show no signs of recent illness such as might necessitate a prolonged visit abroad, I ask myself—and am now asking you—what is the reason for your presence on this boat?'

Jim Fanthorp jerked his head back.

'I decline to give you any information whatever, Monsieur Poirot. I really think you must be mad.'

'I am not mad. I am very, very sane. Where is your firm? In Northampton; that is not very far from Wode Hall. What conversation did you try to overhear? One concerning legal documents. What was the object of your remark—a remark which you uttered with obvious embarrassment and *malaise*? Your object was to prevent Madame Doyle from signing any document unread.'

He paused.

'On this boat we have had a murder, and following that murder two other murders in rapid succession. If I further give you the information that the weapon which killed Madame Otterbourne was a revolver owned by Monsieur Andrew Pennington, then perhaps you will realise that it is actually your duty to tell us all you can.'

Jim Fanthorp was silent for some minutes. At last he said: 'You have rather an odd way of going about things, Monsieur Poirot, but I appreciate the points you have made. The trouble is that I have no exact information to lay before you.'

'You mean that it is a case, merely, of suspicion.'

'Yes.'

'And therefore you think it injudicious to speak? That may be true, legally speaking. But this is not a court of law. Colonel Race and myself are endeavouring to track down a murderer. Anything that can help us to do so may be valuable.'

Again Jim Fanthorp reflected. Then he said: 'Very well. What is it you want to know?'

'Why did you come on this trip?'

'My uncle, Mr. Carmichael, Mrs. Doyle's English solicitor, sent me. He handled a good many of her affairs. In this way, he was often in correspondence with Mr. Andrew Pennington, who was Mrs. Doyle's American trustee. Several small incidents (I cannot enumerate them all) made my uncle suspicious that all was not quite as it should be.'

'In plain language,' said Race, 'your uncle suspected that Pennington was a crook?'

Jim Fanthorp nodded, a faint smile on his face.

'You put it rather more bluntly than I should, but the main idea is correct. Various excuses made by Pennington, certain plausible explanations of the disposal of funds, aroused my uncle's distrust.

'While these suspicions of his were still nebulous, Miss Ridgeway married unexpectedly and went off on her honeymoon to Egypt. Her marriage relieved my uncle's mind, as he knew that on her return to England the estate would have to be formally settled and handed over.

'However, in a letter she wrote him from Cairo, she mentioned casually that she had unexpectedly run across Andrew Pennington. My uncle's suspicions became acute. He felt sure that Pennington, perhaps by now in a desperate position, was going to try and obtain signatures from her which would cover his own defalcations. Since my uncle had no definite evidence to lay before her, he was in a most difficult position. The only thing he could think of was to send me out here, travelling by air, with instruction to discover what was in the wind. I was to keep my eyes open and act summarily if necessary—a most unpleasant mission, I can assure you. As a matter of fact, on the occasion you mention I had to behave more or less as a cad! It was awkward, but on the whole I was satisfied with the result.'

'You mean you put Madame Doyle on her guard?' asked Race.

'Not so much that, but I think I put the wind up Pennington. I felt convinced he wouldn't try any more funny business for some time, and by then I hoped to have got intimate enough with Mr. and Mrs. Doyle to convey some kind of a warning. As a matter of fact I hoped to do so through Doyle. Mrs. Doyle was so attached to Mr. Pennington that it would have been a bit awkward to suggest things to her about him. It would have been easier for me to approach the husband.'

Race nodded.

Poirot asked: 'Will you give me a candid opinion on one point, Monsieur Fanthorp? If you were engaged in putting a swindle over, would you choose Madame Doyle or Monsieur Doyle as a victim?'

Fanthorp smiled faintly.

'Mr. Doyle, every time. Linnet Doyle was very shrewd in business matters. Her husband, I should fancy, is one of those trustful fellows who know nothing of business and are always ready to "sign on the dotted line" as he himself put it.'

'I agree,' said Poirot. He looked at Race. 'And there's your motive.'

Jim Fanthorp said: 'But this is all pure conjecture. It isn't *evidence*.'

Poirot replied, easily: '*Ah, bah!* we will get evidence!'

'How?'

'Possibly from Mr. Pennington himself.'

Fanthorp looked doubtful.

'I wonder. I very much wonder.'

Race glanced at his watch. 'He's about due now.'

Jim Fanthorp was quick to take the hint. He left them.

Two minutes later Andrew Pennington made his appearance. His manner was all smiling urbanity. Only the taut line of his jaw and the wariness of his eyes betrayed the fact that a thoroughly experienced fighter was on his guard.

'Well, gentlemen,' he said, 'here I am.'

He sat down and looked at them inquiringly.

'We asked you to come here, Monsieur Pennington,' began Poirot, 'because it is fairly obvious that you have a very special and immediate interest in the case.'

Pennington raised his eyebrows slightly.

'Is that so?'

Poirot said gently: 'Surely. You have known Linnet Ridgeway, I understand, since she was quite a child.'

'Oh! that——' His face altered, became less alert. 'I beg pardon, I didn't quite get you. Yes, as I told you this morning, I've known Linnet since she was a cute little thing in pinafores.'

'You were on terms of close intimacy with her father?'

'That's so. Melhuish Ridgeway and I were very close—very close.'

'You were so intimately associated that on his death he appointed you business guardian to his daughter and trustee to the vast fortune she inherited?'

'Why, roughly, that is so.' The wariness was back again. The note was more cautious. 'I was not the only trustee, naturally; others were associated with me.'

'Who have since died?'

'Two of them are dead. The other, Mr. Sterndale Rockford, is alive.'

'Your partner?'

'Yes.'

'Mademoiselle Ridgeway, I understand, was not yet of age when she married?'

'She would have been twenty-one next July.'

'And in the normal course of events she would have come into control of her fortune then?'

'Yes.'

'But her marriage precipitated matters?'

Pennington's jaw hardened. He shot out his chin at them aggressively.

'You'll pardon me, gentlemen, but what exact business is all this of yours?'

'If you dislike answering the question——'

'There's no dislike about it. I don't mind what you ask me. But I don't see the relevance of all this.'

'Oh, but surely, Monsieur Pennington'—Poirot leaned forward, his eyes green and catlike—'there is the question of motive. In considering that, financial considerations must always be taken into account.'

Pennington said sullenly: 'By Ridgeway's will, Linnet got control of her dough when she was twenty-one or when she married.'

'No conditions of any kind?'

'No conditions.'

'And it is a matter, I am credibly assured, of millions.'

'Millions it is.'

Poirot said softly: 'Your responsibility, Mr. Pennington, and that of your partner, has been a very grave one.'

Pennington replied curtly: 'We're used to responsibility. Doesn't worry us any.'

'I wonder.'

Something in his tone flicked the other man on the raw. He asked angrily: 'What the devil do you mean?'

Poirot replied with an air of engaging frankness: 'I was wondering, Mr. Pennington, whether Linnet Ridgeway's sudden marriage caused any—consternation, in your office?'

'Consternation?'

'That was the word I used.'

'What the hell are you driving at?'

'Something quite simple. Are Linnet Doyle's affairs in the perfect order they should be?'

Pennington rose to his feet.

'That's enough. I'm through.' He made for the door.

'But you will answer my question first?'

Pennington snapped: 'They're in perfect order.'

'You were not so alarmed when the news of Linnet Ridgeway's marriage reached you that you rushed over to Europe by the first boat and staged an apparently fortuitous meeting in Egypt?'

Pennington came back towards them. He had himself under control once more.

'What you are saying is absolute balderdash! I didn't even know that Linnet was married till I met her in Cairo. I was utterly astonished. Her letter must have missed me by a day in New York. It was forwarded and I got it about a week later.'

'You came over by the *Carmanic*, I think you said.'

'That's right.'

'And the letter reached New York after the *Carmanic* sailed?'

'How many times have I got to repeat it?'

'It is strange,' said Poirot.

'What's strange?'

'That on your luggage there are no labels of the *Carmanic*. The only recent labels of transatlantic sailing are the *Normandie*. The *Normandie*, I remember, sailed two days after the *Carmanic*.'

For a moment the other was at a loss. His eyes wavered. Colonel Race weighed in with telling effect.

'Come now, Mr. Pennington,' he said. 'We've several reasons for believing that you came over on the *Normandie* and not by the *Carmanic*, as you said. In that case, you received Mrs. Doyle's letter before you left New York. It's no good denying it, for it's the easiest thing in the world to check up the steamship companies.'

Andrew Pennington felt absent-mindedly for a chair and sat down. His face was impassive—a poker face. Behind that mask his agile brain looked ahead to the next move.

'I'll have to hand it to you, gentlemen. You've been too smart for me. But I had my reasons for acting as I did.'

'No doubt.' Race's tone was curt.

'If I give them to you, it must be understood I do so in confidence.'

'I think you can trust us to behave fittingly. Naturally I cannot give assurances blindly.'

'Well——' Pennington sighed. 'I'll come clean. There was some monkey business going on in England. It worried me. I couldn't do much about it by letter. The only thing was to come over and see for myself.'

'What do you mean by monkey business?'

'I'd good reason to believe that Linnet was being swindled.'

'By whom?'

'Her British lawyer. Now that's not the kind of accusation you can fling around anyhow. I made up my mind to come over right away and see into matters myself.'

'That does great credit to your vigilance, I am sure. But why the little deception about not having received the letter?'

'Well, I ask you——' Pennington spread out his hands. 'You can't butt in on a honeymoon couple without more or less coming down to brass tacks and giving your reasons. I thought it best to make the meeting accidental. Besides, I didn't know anything about the husband. He might have been mixed up in the racket for all I knew.'

'In fact all your actions were actuated by pure disinterestedness,' said Colonel Race dryly.

'You've said it, Colonel.'

There was a pause. Race glanced at Poirot. The little man leant forward.

'Monsieur Pennington, we do not believe a word of your story.'

'The hell you don't! And what the hell do you believe?'

'We believe that Linnet Ridgeway's unexpected marriage put you in a financial quandary. That you came over posthaste to try and find some way out of the mess you were in—that is to say, some way of gaining time. That, with that end in view, you endeavoured to obtain Madame Doyle's signature to certain documents and failed. That on the journey up the Nile, when walking along the cliff top at Abu Simbel, you dislodged a boulder which fell and only very narrowly missed its object——'

'You're crazy.'

'We believe that the same kind of circumstances occurred on the return journey. That is to say, an opportunity presented itself of putting Madame Doyle out of the way at a moment when her death would be almost certainly ascribed to the action of another person. We not only believe, but *know*, that it was your revolver which killed a woman who was about to reveal to us the name of the person who she had reason to believe killed both Linnet Doyle and the maid Louise——'

'Hell!' The forcible ejaculation broke forth and interrupted Poirot's stream of eloquence. 'What are you getting at? Are you crazy? What motive had I to kill Linnet? I wouldn't get her money; that goes to her husband. Why don't you pick on him? *He's* the one to benefit—not me.'

Race said coldly: 'Doyle never left the lounge on the night of the tragedy till he was shot at and wounded in the leg. The impossibility of his walking a step after that is attested to by a doctor and a nurse—both independent and reliable witnesses. Simon Doyle could not have killed his wife. He could not have killed Louise Bourget. He most definitely did not kill Mrs. Otterbourne. You know that as well as we do.'

'I know he didn't kill her.' Pennington sounded a little calmer. 'All I say is, why pick on me when I don't benefit by her death?'

'But, my dear sir,' Poirot's voice came soft as a purring cat, 'that is rather a matter of opinion. Madame Doyle was a keen woman of business, fully conversant with her own affairs and very quick to spot any irregularity. As soon as she took up the control of her property, which she would have done on her return to England, her suspicions were bound to be aroused. But now that she is dead and that her husband, as you have just pointed out, inherits, the whole thing is different. Simon Doyle knows nothing whatever of his wife's affairs except that she was a rich woman. He is of a simple, trusting disposition. You will find it easy to place complicated statements before him, to involve the real issue in a net of figures, and to delay settlement with pleas of legal formalities and the recent depression. I think that it makes a very considerable difference to you whether you deal with the husband or the wife.'

Pennington shrugged his shoulders.

'Your ideas are—fantastic.'

'Time will show.'

'What did you say?'

'I said "Time will show!" This is a matter of three deaths —three murders. The law will demand the most searching investigation into the condition of Madame Doyle's estate.'

He saw the sudden sag in the other's shoulders and knew that he had won. Jim Fanthorp's suspicions were well founded.

Poirot went on: 'You've played—and lost. Useless to go on bluffing.'

'You don't understand,' Pennington muttered. 'It's all square enough really. It's been this damned slump—Wall Street's been crazy. But I'd staged a comeback. With luck everything will be O.K. by the middle of June.'

With shaking hands he took a cigarette, tried to light it, failed.

'I suppose,' mused Poirot, 'that the boulder was a sudden temptation. You thought nobody saw you.'

'That was an accident. I swear it was an accident!' The man leant forward, his face working, his eyes terrified. 'I stumbled and fell against it. I swear it was an accident. . . .'

The two men said nothing.

Pennington suddenly pulled himself together. He was still a wreck of a man, but his fighting spirit had returned in a certain measure. He moved towards the door.

'You can't pin that on me, gentlemen. It was an accident. And it wasn't I who shot her. D'you hear? You can't pin that on me either—and you never will.'

He went out.

Chapter Twenty-seven

As the door closed behind him, Race gave a deep sigh.

'We got more than I thought we should. Admission of fraud. Admission of attempted murder. Further than that it's impossible to go. A man will confess, more or less, to attempted murder, but you won't get him to confess to the real thing.'

'Sometimes it can be done,' said Poirot. His eyes were dreamy —catlike.

Race looked at him curiously.

'Got a plan?'

Poirot nodded. Then he said, ticking off the items on his fingers: 'The garden at Assuan. Mr. Allerton's statement. The two bottles of nail polish. My bottle of wine. The velvet stole. The stained handkerchief. The pistol that was left on the scene of the crime. The death of Louise. The death of Madame Otterbourne. Yes, it's all there. Pennington didn't do it, Race!'

'What?' Race was startled.

'Pennington didn't do it. He had the motive, yes. He had

the *will* to do it, yes. He got as far as *attempting* to do it. *Mais c'est tout.* For this crime, something was wanted that Pennington hadn't got! This is a crime that needed audacity, swift and faultless execution, courage, indifference to danger, and a resourceful, calculating brain. Pennington hasn't got those attributes. He couldn't do a crime unless he knew it to be safe. This crime wasn't safe! It hung on a razor edge. It needed boldness. Pennington isn't bold. He's only astute.'

Race looked at him with the respect one able man gives to another.

'You've got it all well taped,' he said.

'I think so, yes. There are one or two things—that telegram for instance, that Linnet Doyle read. I should like to get that cleared up.'

'By Jove, we forgot to ask Doyle. He was telling us when poor old Ma Otterbourne came along. We'll ask him again.'

'Presently. First, I have someone else to whom I wish to speak.'

'Who's that?'

'Tim Allerton.'

Race raised his eyebrows.

'Allerton? Well, we'll get him here.'

He pressed a bell and sent the steward with a message.

Tim Allerton entered with a questioning look.

'Steward said you wanted to see me?'

'That is right, Monsieur Allerton. Sit down.'

Tim sat. His face was attentive but very slightly bored.

'Anything I can do?' His tone was polite but not enthusiastic.

Poirot said: 'In a sense, perhaps. What I really require is for you to listen.'

Tim's eyebrows rose in polite surprise.

'Certainly. I'm the world's best listener. Can be relied on to say "Oo-er!" at the right moments.'

'That is very satisfactory. "Oo-er!" will be very expressive. *Eh bien,* let us commence. When I met you and your mother at Assuan, Monsieur Allerton, I was attracted to your company very strongly. To begin with, I thought your mother was one of the most charming people I had ever met——'

The weary face flickered for a moment; a shade of expression came into it.

'She is—unique,' he said.

'But the second thing that interested me was your mention of a certain lady.'

'Really?'

'Yes, a Mademoiselle Joanna Southwood. You see, I had recently been hearing that name.'

He paused and went on: 'For the last three years there have been certain jewel robberies that have been worrying Scotland Yard a good deal. They are what may be described as Society robberies. The method is usually the same—the substitution of an imitation piece of jewellery for an original. My friend, Chief Inspector Japp, came to the conclusion that the robberies were not the work of one person, but of two people working in with each other very cleverly. He was convinced, from the considerable inside knowledge displayed, that the robberies were the work of people in a good social position. And finally his attention became riveted on Mademoiselle Joanna Southwood.

'Every one of the victims had been either a friend or acquaintance of hers, and in each case she had either handled or been lent the piece of jewellery in question. Also, her style of living was far in excess of her income. On the other hand it was quite clear that the actual robbery—that is to say the substitution—had *not* been accomplished by her. In some cases she had been out of England during the period when the jewellery must have been replaced.

'So gradually a little picture grew up in Chief Inspector Japp's mind. Mademoiselle Southwood was at one time associated with a Guild of Modern Jewellery. He suspected that she handled the jewels in question, made accurate drawings of them, got them copied by some humble but dishonest working jeweller and that the third part of the operation was the successful substitution by another person—somebody who could have been proved never to have handled the jewels and never to have had anything to do with copies or imitations of precious stones. Of the identity of this other person Japp was ignorant.

'Certain things that fell from you in conversation interested me. A ring that disappeared when you were in Majorca, the fact that you had been in a house-party where one of these fake substitutions had occurred, your close association with Mademoiselle Southwood. There was also the fact that you obviously resented my presence and tried to get your mother to be less friendly towards me. That might, of course, have been just personal dislike, but I thought not. You were too anxious to try and hide your distaste under a genial manner.

'*Eh bien!* after the murder of Linnet Doyle, it is discovered that her pearls are missing. You comprehend, at once I think of you! But I am not quite satisfied. For if you are working, as I suspect, with Mademoiselle Southwood (who was an intimate friend of Madame Doyle's), then substitution would be the method employed—not barefaced theft. But then, the pearls quite unexpectedly are returned, and what do I discover? That they are not genuine, but imitation.

'I know then who the real thief is. It was the imitation string which was stolen and returned—an imitation which you had previously substituted for the real necklace.'

He looked at the young man in front of him. Tim was white under his tan. He was not so good a fighter as Pennington; his stamina was bad. He said, with an effort to sustain his mocking manner: 'Indeed? And if so, what did I do with them?'

'That I know also.'

The young man's face changed—broke up.

Poirot went on slowly: 'There is only one place where they can be. I have reflected, and my reason tells me that that is so. Those pearls, Monsieur Allerton, are concealed in a rosary that hangs in your cabin. The beads of it are very elaborately carved. I think you had it made specially. Those beads unscrew, though you would never think so to look at them. Inside each is a pearl, stuck with Seccotine. Most police searchers respect religious symbols unless there is something obviously queer about them. You counted on that. I endeavoured to find out how Mademoiselle Southwood sent the imitation necklace out to you. She must have done so, since you came here from Majorca on hearing that Madame Doyle would be here for her honeymoon. My theory is that it was sent in a book—a square hole being cut out of the pages in the middle. A book goes with the ends open and is practically never opened in the post.'

There was a pause—a long pause. Then Tim said quietly: 'You win! It's been a good game, but it's over at last. There's nothing for it now, I suppose, but to take my medicine.'

Poirot nodded gently.

'Do you realise that you were seen that night?'

'Seen?' Tim started.

'Yes, on the night that Linnet Doyle died, someone saw you leave her cabin just after one in the morning.'

Tim said: 'Look here—you aren't thinking . . . It wasn't

I who killed her! I'll swear that! I've been in the most awful stew. To have chosen that night of all others . . . God, it's been awful!'

Poirot said: 'Yes, you must have had uneasy moments. But, now that the truth has come out, you may be able to help us. Was Madame Doyle alive or dead when you stole the pearls?'

'I don't know,' Tim said hoarsely. 'Honest to God, Monsieur Poirot, I don't know! I'd found out where she put them at night—on the little table by the bed. I crept in, felt very softly on the table and grabbed 'em, put down the others and crept out again. I assumed, of course, that she was asleep.'

'Did you hear her breathing? Surely you would have listened for that?'

Tim thought earnestly.

'It was very still—very still indeed. No, I can't remember actually hearing her breathe.'

'Was there any smell of smoke lingering in the air, as there would have been if a firearm had been discharged recently?'

'I don't think so. I don't remember it.'

Poirot sighed.

'Then we are no further.'

Tim asked curiously, 'Who was it saw me?'

'Rosalie Otterbourne. She came round from the other side of the boat and saw you leave Linnet Doyle's cabin and go to your own.'

'So it was she who told you.'

Poirot said gently, 'Excuse me; she did not tell me.'

'But then, how do you know?'

'Because I am Hercule Poirot I do not need to be told. When I taxed her with it, do you know what she said? She said: "I saw nobody." And she lied.'

'But why?'

Poirot said in a detached voice: 'Perhaps because she thought the man she saw was the murderer. It looked like that, you know.'

'That seems to me all the more reason for telling you.'

Poirot shrugged his shoulders. 'She did not think so, it seems.'

Tim said, a queer note in his voice: 'She's an extraordinary sort of a girl. She must have been through a pretty rough time with that mother of hers.'

'Yes, life has not been easy for her.'

'Poor kid,' Tim muttered. Then he looked towards Race. 'Well, sir, where do we go from here? I admit taking the pearls from Linnet's cabin and you'll find them just where you say they are. I'm guilty all right. But as far as Miss Southwood is concerned, I'm not admitting anything. You've no evidence whatever against her. How I got hold of the fake necklace is my own business.'

Poirot murmured: 'A very correct attitude.'

Tim said with a flash of humour: 'Always the gentleman!' He added: 'Perhaps you can imagine how annoying it was to me to find my mother cottoning on to you! I'm not a sufficiently hardened criminal to enjoy sitting cheek by jowl with a successful detective just before bringing off a rather risky coup! Some people might get a kick out of it. I didn't. Frankly, it gave me cold feet.'

'But it did not deter you from making your attempt?'

Tim shrugged his shoulders.

'I couldn't funk it to that extent. The exchange had to be made sometime and I'd got a unique opportunity on this boat—a cabin only two doors off, and Linnet herself so preoccupied with her own troubles that she wasn't likely to detect the change.'

'I wonder if that was so——'

Tim looked up sharply. 'What do you mean?'

Poirot pressed the bell. 'I am going to ask Miss Otterbourne if she will come here for a minute.'

Tim frowned but said nothing. A steward came, received the order and went away with the message.

Rosalie came after a few minutes. Her eyes, reddened with recent weeping, widened a little at seeing Tim, but her old attitude of suspicion and defiance seemed entirely absent. She sat down and with a new docility looked from Race to Poirot.

'We're very sorry to bother you, Miss Otterbourne,' said Race gently. He was slightly annoyed with Poirot.

'It doesn't matter,' the girl said in a low voice.

Poirot said: 'It is necessary to clear up one or two points. When I asked you whether you saw anyone on the starboard deck at one-ten this morning, your answer was that you saw nobody. Fortunately I have been able to arrive at the truth without your help. Monsieur Allerton has admitted that he was in Linnet Doyle's cabin last night.'

She flashed a swift glance at Tim. Tim, his face grim and set, gave a curt nod.

'The time is correct, Monsieur Allerton?'

Allerton replied, 'Quite correct.'

Rosalie was staring at him. Her lips trembled—fell apart.
. . .

'But you didn't—you didn't——'

He said quickly: 'No, I didn't kill her. I'm a thief, not a murderer. It's all going to come out, so you might as well know. I was after her pearls.'

Poirot said, 'Mr. Allerton's story is that he went to her cabin last night and exchanged a string of fake pearls for the real ones.'

'Did you?' asked Rosalie. Her eyes, grave, sad, child-like, questioned his.

'Yes,' said Tim.

There was a pause. Colonel Race shifted restlessly.

Poirot said in a curious voice: 'That, as I say, is Monsieur Allerton's story, partially confirmed by your evidence. That is to say, there is evidence that he did visit Linnet Doyle's cabin last night, but there is no evidence to show why he did so.'

Tim stared at him. 'But you know!'

'What do I know?'

'Well—you know I've got the pearls.'

'*Mais oui—mais oui!* I know you have the pearls, but I do not know when you got them. It may have been *before* last night. . . . You said just now that Linnet Doyle would not have noticed the substitution. I am not so sure of that. Supposing she *did* notice it. . . . Supposing, even, she knew who did it. . . . Supposing that last night she threatened to expose the whole business, and that you knew she meant to do so . . . and supposing that you overheard the scene in the saloon between Jacqueline de Bellefort and Simon Doyle and, as soon as the saloon was empty, you slipped in and secured the pistol, and then, an hour later, when the boat had quieted down, you crept along to Linnet Doyle's cabin and made quite sure that no exposure would come. . . .'

'My God!' said Tim. Out of his ashen face, two tortured, agonised eyes gazed dumbly at Hercule Poirot.

The latter went on: 'But somebody else saw you—the girl Louise. The next day she came to you and blackmailed you. You must pay her handsomely or she would tell what she knew. You realised that to submit to blackmail would be the beginning of the end. You pretended to agree, made an appointment to come to her cabin just before lunch with the money. Then, when she was counting the notes, you stabbed her. 'But again luck was against you. Somebody saw you go to her cabin'—he half turned to Rosalie—'your mother. Once again you had to act—dangerously, foolhardily—but it was the only chance. You had heard Pennington talk about his revolver. You rushed into his cabin, got hold of it, listened outside Dr. Bessner's cabin door and shot Madame Otterbourne before she could reveal your name.'

'No-o!' cried Rosalie. 'He didn't! He didn't!'

'After that, you did the only thing you could do—rushed round the stern. And when I rushed after you, you had turned and pretended to be coming in the *opposite* direction. You had handled the revolver in gloves; those gloves were in your pocket when I asked for them. . . .'

Tim said, 'Before God, I swear it isn't true—not a word of it.' But his voice, ill-assured and trembling, failed to convince.

It was then that Rosalie Otterbourne surprised them.

'Of course it isn't true! And Monsieur Poirot knows it isn't! He's saying it for some reason of his own.'

Poirot looked at her. A faint smile came to his lips. He spread out his hands in token surrender.

'Mademoiselle is too clever. . . . But you agree—it was a good case?'

'What the devil——' Tim began with rising anger, but Poirot held up a hand.

'There is a very good case against you, Monsieur Allerton. I wanted you to realise that. Now I will tell you something more pleasant. I have not yet examined that rosary in your cabin. It may be that, when I do, I shall find nothing there. And then, since Mademoiselle Otterbourne sticks to it that she saw no one on the deck last night, *eh bien*! there is no case against you at all. The pearls were taken by a kleptomaniac who has since returned them. They are in a little box on the table by the door, if you would like to examine them with Mademoiselle.'

Tim got up. He stood for a moment unable to speak. When he did, his words seemed inadequate, but it is possible that they satisfied his listeners.

'Thanks!' he said. 'You won't have to give me another chance!'

He held the door open for the girl; she passed out and, picking up the little cardboard box, he followed her.

Side by side they went. Tim opened the box, took out the sham string of pearls and hurled it far from him into the Nile.

'There!' he said. 'That's gone. When I return the box to Poirot the real string will be in it. What a damned fool I've been!'

Rosalie said in a low voice: 'Why did you come to do it in the first place?'

'How did I come to start, do you mean? Oh, I don't know. Boredom—laziness—the fun of the thing. Such a much more attractive way of earning a living than just pegging away at a job. Sounds pretty sordid to you, I expect, but you know there was an attraction about it—mainly the risk, I suppose.'

'I think I understand.'

'Yes, but you wouldn't ever do it.'

Rosalie considered for a moment or two, her grave young head bent.

'No,' she said simply. 'I wouldn't.'

He said: 'Oh, my dear—you're so lovely . . . so utterly lovely. Why wouldn't you say you'd seen me last night?'

'I thought—they might suspect you,' Rosalie said.

'Did you suspect me?'

'No. I couldn't believe that you'd kill anyone.'

'No. I'm not the strong stuff murderers are made of. I'm only a miserable sneak-thief.'

She put out a timid hand and touched his arm.

'Don't say that.'

He caught her hand in his.

'Rosalie, would you—you know what I mean? Or would you always despise me and throw it in my teeth?'

She smiled faintly. 'There are things you could throw in my teeth, too. . . .'

'Rosalie—darling. . . .'

But she held back a minute longer.

'This—Joanna?'

Tim gave a sudden shout.

'Joanna? You're as bad as Mother. I don't care a damn about Joanna. She's got a face like a horse and a predatory eye. A most unattractive female.'

Presently Rosalie said: 'Your mother need never know about you.'

'I'm not sure,' Tim said thoughtfully. 'I think I shall tell her. Mother's got plenty of stuffing, you know. She can stand up to things. Yes, I think I shall shatter her maternal illusions about me. She'll be so relieved to know that my relations with Joanna were purely of a business nature that she'll forgive me everything else.'

They had come to Mrs. Allerton's cabin and Tim knocked firmly on the door. It opened and Mrs. Allerton stood on the threshold.

'Rosalie and I——' began Tim. He paused.

'Oh, my dears,' said Mrs. Allerton. She folded Rosalie in her arms. 'My dear, dear child. I always hoped—but Tim was so tiresome—and pretended he didn't like you. But of course I saw through *that*!'

Rosalie said in a broken voice: 'You've been so sweet to me—always. I used to wish—to wish——'

She broke off and sobbed happily on Mrs. Allerton's shoulder.

Chapter Twenty-eight

As the door closed behind Tim and Rosalie, Poirot looked somewhat apologetically at Colonel Race. The Colonel was looking rather grim.

'You will consent to my little arrangement, yes?' Poirot pleaded. 'It is irregular—I know it is irregular, yes—but I have a high regard for human happiness.'

'You've none for mine,' said Race.

'That *jeune fille*. I have a tenderness towards her, and she loves that young man. It will be an excellent match; she has the stiffening he needs; the mother likes her; everything is thoroughly suitable.'

'In fact the marriage has been arranged by heaven and Hercule Poirot. All I have to do is to compound a felony.'

'But, *mon ami,* I told you, it was all conjecture on my part.'

Race grinned suddenly.

'It's all right by me,' he said. 'I'm not a damned policeman, thank God! I daresay the young fool will go straight enough now. The girl's straight all right. No, what I'm complaining of is your treatment of *me*! I'm a patient man, but there are limits to my patience! *Do* you know who committed the three murders on this boat or *don't* you?'

'I do.'

'Then why all this beating about the bush?'

'You think that I am just amusing myself with side issues? And it annoys you? But it is not that. Once I went professionally to an archæological expedition—and I learnt something there. In the course of an excavation, when something comes up out of the ground, everything is cleared away very carefully all around it. You take away the loose earth, and you scrape here and there with a knife until finally your object is there, all alone, ready to be drawn and photographed with no extraneous matter confusing it. That is what I have been seeking to do—clear away the extraneous matter so that we can see the truth—the naked shining truth.'

'Good,' said Race. 'Let's have this naked shining truth. It wasn't Pennington. It wasn't young Allerton. I presume it wasn't Fleetwood. Let's hear who it was for a change.'

'My friend, I am just about to tell you.'

There was a knock on the door. Race uttered a muffled curse. It was Dr. Bessner and Cornelia. The latter was looking upset.

'Oh, Colonel Race,' she exclaimed, 'Miss Bowers has just told me about Cousin Marie. It's been the most dreadful shock. She said she couldn't bear the responsibility all by herself any longer, and that I'd better know, as I was one of the family. I just couldn't believe it at first, but Dr. Bessner here has been just wonderful.'

'No, no,' protested the doctor modestly.

'He's been so kind, explaining it all, and how people really can't help it. He's had kleptomaniacs in his clinic. And he's explained to me how it's very often due to a deep-seated neurosis.'

Cornelia repeated the words with awe.

'It's planted very deeply in the subconscious; sometimes it's just some little thing that happened when you were a child. And he's cured people by getting them to think back and remember what that little thing was.'

Cornelia paused, drew a deep breath, and started off again.

'But it's worrying me dreadfully in case it all gets out. It would be too, too terrible in New York. Why, all the tabloids would have it. Cousin Marie and Mother and everybody —they'd never hold up their heads again.'

Race sighed. 'That's all right,' he said. 'This is Hush Hush House.'

'I beg your pardon, Colonel Race?'

'What I was endeavouring to say was that anything short of murder is being hushed up.'

'Oh!' Cornelia clasped her hands. 'I'm *so* relieved. I've just been worrying and worrying.'

'You have the heart too tender,' said Dr. Bessner, and patted her benevolently on the shoulder. He said to the others: 'She has a very sensitive and beautiful nature.'

'Oh, I haven't really. You're too kind.'

Poirot murmured, 'Have you seen any more of Mr. Ferguson?'

Cornelia blushed.

'No—but Cousin Marie's been talking about him.'

'It seems the young man is highly born,' said Dr. Bessner. 'I must confess he does not look it. His clothes are terrible. Not for a moment does he appear a well-bred man.'

'And what do you think, Mademoiselle?'

'I think he must be just plain crazy,' said Cornelia.

Poirot turned to the doctor. 'How is your patient?'

'Ach, he is going on splendidly. I have just reassured the Fräulein de Bellefort. Would you believe it, I found her in despair. Just because the fellow had a bit of a temperature this afternoon! But what could be more natural? It is amazing that he is not in a high fever now. But no, he is like some of our peasants; he has a magnificent constitution, the constitution of an ox. I have seen them with deep wounds that they hardly notice. It is the same with Mr. Doyle. His pulse is steady, his temperature only slightly above normal. I was able to pooh-pooh the little lady's fears. All the same, it is ridiculous, *nicht wahr*? One minute you shoot a man; the next you are in hysterics in case he may not be doing well.'

Cornelia said: 'She loves him terribly, you see.'

'Ach! but it is not sensible, that. If *you* loved a man, would you try and shoot him? No, you are sensible.'

'I don't like things that go off with bangs anyway,' said Cornelia.

'Naturally you do not. You are very feminine.'

Race interrupted this scene of heavy approval. 'Since Doyle is all right there's no reason I shouldn't come along and resume our talk of this afternoon. He was just telling me about a telegram.'

Dr. Bessner's bulk moved up and down appreciatively.

'Ho, ho, ho, it was very funny that! Doyle, he tells me

about it. It was a telegram all about vegetables—potatoes, artichokes, leeks—Ach! pardon?'

With a stifled exclamation, Race had sat up in his chair.

'My God,' he said. 'So that's it! Richetti!'

He looked round on three uncomprehending faces.

'A new code—it was used in the South African rebellion. Potatoes mean machine guns, artichokes are high explosives —and so on. Richetti is no more an archæologist than I am! He's a very dangerous agitator, a man who's killed more than once, and I'll swear that he's killed once again. Mrs. Doyle opened that telegram by mistake, you see. If she were ever to repeat what was in it before me, he knew his goose would be cooked!'

He turned to Poirot. 'Am I right?' he asked. 'Is Richetti the man?'

'He is *your* man,' said Poirot. 'I always thought there was something wrong about him. He was almost too word-perfect in his rôle; he was all archæologist, not enough human being.'

He paused and then said: 'But it was not Richetti who killed Linnet Doyle. For some time now I have known what I may express as the "first half" of the murderer. Now I know the "second half" also. The picture is complete. But you understand that, although I know what must have happened, I have no proof that it happened. Intellectually the case is satisfying. Actually it is profoundly unsatisfactory. There is only one hope—a confession from the murderer.'

Dr. Bessner raised his shoulders sceptically. 'Ah! but that —it would be a miracle.'

'I think not. Not under the circumstances.'

Cornelia cried out: 'But who is it? Aren't you going to tell us?'

Poirot's eyes ranged quietly over the three of them. Race, smiling sardonically, Bessner, still looking sceptical, Cornelia, her mouth hanging a little open, gazing at him with eager eyes.

'*Mais oui*,' he said. 'I like an audience, I must confess. I am vain, you see. I am puffed up with conceit. I like to say: "See how clever is Hercule Poirot!"'

Race shifted a little in his chair.

'Well,' he asked gently, 'just how clever *is* Hercule Poirot?'

Shaking his head sadly from side to side Poirot said: 'To begin with I was stupid—incredibly stupid. To me the stumbling block was the pistol—Jacqueline de Bellefort's pistol. Why had that pistol not been left on the scene of the crime? The idea of the murderer was quite plainly to incriminate her. Why then did the murderer take it away? I was so stupid that I thought of all sorts of fantastic reasons. The real one was very simple. The murderer took it away because he *had* to take it away—because he had no choice in the matter.'

Chapter Twenty-nine

'You and I, my friend,' Poirot leaned towards Race, 'started our investigation with a preconceived idea. That idea was that the crime was committed on the spur of the moment, without any preliminary planning. Somebody wished to remove Linnet Doyle and had seized their opportunity to do so at a moment when the crime would almost certainly be attributed to Jacqueline de Bellefort. It therefore followed that the person in question had overheard the scene between Jacqueline and Simon Doyle and had obtained possession of the pistol after the others had left the saloon.

'But, my friends, if that preconceived idea was wrong, the whole aspect of the case altered. And it *was* wrong! This was no spontaneous crime committed on the spur of the moment. It was, on the contrary, very carefully planned and accurately timed, with all the details meticulously worked out beforehand, even to the drugging of Hercule Poirot's bottle of wine on the night in question!

'But yes, that is so! I was put to sleep so that there should be no possibility of my participating in the events of the night. It did just occur to me as a possibility. I drink wine; my two companions at table drink whisky and mineral water respectively. Nothing easier than to slip a dose of harmless narcotic into my bottle of wine—the bottles stand on the tables all day. But I dismissed the thought. It had been a hot day; I had been unusually tired; it was not really extraordinary that I should for once have slept heavily instead of lightly as I usually do.

'You see, I was still in the grip of the preconceived idea. If I had been drugged, that would have implied premeditation, it would mean that before seven-thirty, when dinner is served, the crime had already been decided upon; and that (always from the point of view of the preconceived idea) was absurd.

'The first blow to the preconceived idea was when the pistol was recovered from the Nile. To begin with, if we were right in our assumptions, the pistol ought never to have been thrown overboard at all. . . . And there was more to follow.'

Poirot turned to Dr. Bessner.

'You, Dr. Bessner, examined Linnet Doyle's body. You will remember that the wound showed signs of scorching—that is to say, that the pistol had been placed close against the head before being fired.'

Bessner nodded. 'So. That is exact.'

'But when the pistol was found it was wrapped in a velvet stole, and that velvet showed definite signs that a pistol had been fired through its folds, presumably under the impression that that would deaden the sound of the shot. But if the pistol had been fired through the velvet, there would have been no signs of burning on the victim's skin. Therefore, the shot fired through the stole could not have been the shot that killed Linnet Doyle. Could it have been the other shot—the one fired by Jacqueline de Bellefort at Simon Doyle? Again no, for there had been two witnesses of that shooting, and we knew all about it. It appeared, therefore, as though a *third* shot had been fired—one we knew nothing about. But only two shots had been fired from the pistol, and there was no hint or suggestion of another shot.

'Here we were face to face with a very curious unexplained circumstance. The next interesting point was the fact that in Linnet Doyle's cabin I found two bottles of coloured nail polish. Now ladies very often vary the colour of their nails, but so far Linnet Doyle's nails had always been the shade called Cardinal—a deep dark red. The other bottle was labelled Rose, which is a shade of pale pink, but the few drops remaining in the bottle were not pale pink but a bright red. I was sufficiently curious to take out the stopper and sniff. Instead of the usual strong odour of peardrops, the bottle smelt of vinegar! That is to say, it suggested that the drop or two of fluid in it was red ink. Now there is no reason why Madame Doyle should not have had a bottle of red ink, but it would have been more natural if she had had red ink in a red ink bottle and not in a nail-polish bottle. It suggested a link with the faintly stained handkerchief which had been wrapped round the pistol. Red ink washes out quickly but always leaves a pale pink stain.

'I should perhaps have arrived at the truth with these slender indications, but an event occurred which rendered all doubt superfluous. Louise Bourget was killed in circumstances which pointed unmistakably to the fact that she had been blackmailing the murderer. Not only was a fragment of a *mille* franc note still clasped in her hand, but I remembered some very significant words she had used this morning.

'Listen carefully, for here is the crux of the whole matter. When I asked her if she had seen anything the previous night she gave this very curious answer: "Naturally, if I had been unable to sleep, if I had mounted the stairs, *then* perhaps I might have seen this assassin, this monster enter or leave Madame's cabin. . . ." Now what exactly did that tell us?'

Bessner, his nose wrinkling with intellectual interest, replied promptly: 'It told you that she *had* mounted the stairs.'

'No, no; you fail to see the point. Why should she have said that, to *us*?'

'To convey a hint.'

'But why *hint* to us? If she knows who the murderer is, there are two courses open to her—to tell us the truth, or to hold her tongue and demand money for her silence from the person concerned! But she does neither. She neither says promptly: "I saw nobody. I was asleep." Nor does she say: "Yes, I saw someone, and it was so and so." Why use that significant indeterminate rigmarole of words? *Parbleu,* there can be only one reason! She is hinting to the murderer; therefore the murderer must have been present at the time. But, besides myself and Colonel Race, only two people were present —Simon Doyle and Dr. Bessner.'

The doctor sprang up with a roar.

'Ach! what is that you say? You accuse me? Again? But it is ridiculous—beneath contempt.'

Poirot said sharply: 'Be quiet. I am telling you what I thought at the time. Let us remain impersonal.'

'He doesn't mean he thinks it's you now,' said Cornelia soothingly.

Poirot went on quickly: 'So it lay there—between Simon Doyle and Dr. Bessner. But what reason has Bessner to kill Linnet Doyle? None, so far as I know. Simon Doyle, then? But that was impossible! There were plenty of witnesses who could swear that Doyle never left the saloon that evening until the quarrel broke out. After that he was wounded and it would then have been physically impossible for him to have done so. Had I good evidence on both those points? Yes, I had the evidence of Mademoiselle Robson, of Jim Fanthorp, and of Jacqueline de Bellefort as to the first, and I had the skilled testimony of Dr. Bessner and of Mademoiselle Bowers as to the other. No doubt was possible.

'So Dr. Bessner *must* be the guilty one. In favour of this theory there was the fact that the maid had been stabbed with a surgical knife. On the other hand Bessner had deliberately called attention to this fact.

'And then, my friends, a second perfectly indisputable fact became apparent to me. Louise Bourget's hint could not have been intended for Dr. Bessner, because she could perfectly well have spoken to him in private at any time she liked. There was one person, *and one person only,* who corresponded to her necessity—Simon Doyle! Simon Doyle was wounded, was constantly attended by a doctor, was in that doctor's cabin. It was to him therefore that she risked saying those ambiguous words, in case she might not get another chance. And I remember how she had gone on, turning to him: "Monsieur, I implore you—you see how it is? What can I say?" And this answer: "My good girl, don't be a fool. Nobody thinks you saw or heard anything. You'll be quite all right. I'll look after you. Nobody's accusing you of anything." That was the assurance she wanted, and she got it!'

Bessner uttered a colossal snort.

'Ach! it is foolish, that! Do you think a man with a fractured bone and a splint on his leg could go walking about the boat and stabbing people? I tell you, it was *impossible* for Simon Doyle to leave his cabin.'

Poirot said gently: 'I know. That is quite true. The thing was impossible. It was impossible, but it was also true! There could be only one logical meaning behind Louise Bourget's words.

'So I returned to the beginning and reviewed the crime in the light of this new knowledge. Was it possible that in the period preceding the quarrel Simon Doyle had left the saloon and the others had forgotten or not noticed it? I could not see that that was possible. Could the skilled testimony of Dr. Bessner and Mademoiselle Bowers be disregarded? Again I felt sure it could not. But, I remembered, there was a gap between the two. Simon Doyle had been alone in the saloon for a period of five minutes, and the skilled testimony of Dr. Bessner only applied to the time after that period. For that period we had only the evidence of visual appearance, and, though apparently that was perfectly sound, it was no longer certain. What had actually been *seen*—leaving assumption out of the question?

'Mademoiselle Robson had seen Mademoiselle de Bellefort

fire her pistol, had seen Simon Doyle collapse on to a chair, had seen him clasp a handkerchief to his leg and seen that handkerchief gradually soak through red. What had Monsieur Fanthorp heard and seen? He heard a shot, he found Doyle with a red-stained handkerchief clasped to his leg. What had happened then? Doyle had been very insistent that Mademoiselle de Bellefort should be got away, that she should not be left alone. After that, he suggested that Fanthorp should get hold of the doctor.

'Accordingly Mademoiselle Robson and Monsieur Fanthorp got out with Mademoiselle de Bellefort and for the next five minutes they are busy, on the port side of the deck. Mademoiselle Bowers', Dr. Bessner's and Mademoiselle de Bellefort's cabins are all on the port side. Two minutes are all that Simon Doyle needs. He picks up the pistol from under the sofa, slips out of his shoes, runs like a hare silently along the starboard deck, enters his wife's cabin, creeps up to her as she lies asleep, shoots her through the head, puts the bottle that has contained the red ink on her washstand (it mustn't be found on him), runs back, gets hold of Mademoiselle Van Schuyler's velvet stole, which he has quietly stuffed down the side of a chair in readiness, muffles it round the pistol and fires a bullet into his leg. His chair into which he falls (in genuine agony this time) is by a window. He lifts the window and throws the pistol (wrapped up with the tell-tale handkerchief in the velvet stole) into the Nile.'

'Impossible!' said Race.

'No, my friend, not *impossible*. Remember the evidence of Tim Allerton. He heard a pop—*followed* by a splash. And he heard something else—the footsteps of a man running— a man running past his door. But nobody could have been running along the starboard side of the deck. What he heard was the stockinged feet of Simon Doyle running past his cabin.'

Race said: 'I still say it's impossible. No man could work out the whole caboodle like that in a flash—especially a chap like Doyle who is slow in his mental processes.'

'But very quick and deft in his physical actions!'

'That, yes. But he wouldn't be capable of thinking the whole thing out.'

'But he did not think it out himself, my friend. That is where we were all wrong. It looked like a crime committed on the spur of the moment, but it was *not* a crime committed on the spur of the moment. As I say, it was a very cleverly planned and well thought out piece of work. It could not be *chance* that Simon Doyle had a bottle of red ink in his pocket. No, it must be *design*. It was not *chance* that he had a plain un-marked handkerchief with him. It was not *chance* that Jac-queline de Bellefort's foot kicked the pistol under the settee, where it would be out of sight and unremembered until later.'

'Jacqueline?'

'Certainly. The two halves of the murder. What gave Simon his alibi? The shot fired by Jacqueline. What gave Jacqueline *her* alibi? The insistence of Simon which resulted in a hospital nurse remaining with her all night. There, between the two of them, you get all the qualities you require—the cool, resourceful, planning brain, Jacqueline de Bellefort's brain, and the man of action to carry it out with incredible swiftness and timing.'

'Look at it the right way, and it answers every question. Simon Doyle and Jacqueline had been lovers. Realise that they are still lovers, and it is all clear. Simon does away with his rich wife, inherits her money, and in due course will marry his old love. It was all very ingenious. The persecution of Madame Doyle by Jacqueline, all part of the plan. Simon's pretended rage. . . . And yet—there were lapses. He held forth to me once about possessive women—held forth with real bitterness. It ought to have been clear to me that it was his wife he was thinking about—not Jacqueline. Then his manner to his wife in public. An ordinary, inarticulate Englishman, such as Simon Doyle, is very embarrassed at showing any affection. Simon was not a really good actor. He overdid the devoted manner. That conversation I had with Mademoiselle Jacqueline, too, when she pretended that somebody had over-heard, *I* saw no one. And there *was* no one! But it was to be a useful red herring later. Then one night on this boat I thought I heard Simon and Linnet outside my cabin. He was saying, "We've got to go through with it now." It was Doyle all right, but it was to Jacqueline he was speaking.

'The final drama was perfectly planned and timed. There was a sleeping draught for me, in case I might put an incon-venient finger in the pie. There was the selection of Madem-oiselle Robson as a witness—the working up of the scene, Mademoiselle de Bellefort's exaggerated remorse and hysterics. She made a good deal of noise, in case the shot should be heard. *En vérité,* it was an extraordinarily clever idea. Jacqueline says she has shot Doyle; Mademoiselle Robson says so; Fanthorp says so—and when Simon's leg is examined he *has* been shot. It looks unanswerable! For both of them there is a perfect alibi—at the cost, it is true, of a certain amount of pain and risk to Simon Doyle, but it is necessary that his wound should definitely disable him.

'And then the plan goes wrong. Louise Bourget has been wakeful. She has come up the stairway and she has seen Simon Doyle run along to his wife's cabin and come back. Easy enough to piece together what has happened the following day. And so she makes her greedy bid for hush money, and in so doing signs her death warrant.'

'But Mr. Doyle couldn't have killed *her*?' Cornelia objected.

'No, the other partner did that murder. As soon as he can, Simon Doyle asks to see Jacqueline. He even asks me to leave them alone together. He tells her then of the new danger. They must act at once. He knows where Bessner's scalpels are kept. After the crime the scalpel is wiped and returned, and then, very late and rather out of breath, Jacqueline de Bellefort hurries in to lunch.

'And still all is not well, for Madame Otterbourne has seen Jacqueline go into Louise Bourget's cabin. And she comes hot-foot to tell Simon about it. Jacqueline is the murderess. Do you remember how Simon shouted at the poor woman? Nerves, we thought. But the door was open and he was trying to convey the danger to his accomplice. She heard and she acted—acted like lightning. She remembered Pennington had talked about a revolver. She got hold of it, crept up outside the door, listened and, at the critical moment, fired. She boasted once that she was a good shot, and her boast was not an idle one.

'I remarked after that third crime that there were three ways the murderer could have gone. I meant that he could have gone aft (in which case Tim Allerton was the criminal), he could have gone over the side (very improbable) or he could have gone into a cabin. Jacqueline's cabin was just two away from Dr. Bessner's. She had only to throw down the revolver, bolt into the cabin, ruffle her hair and fling herself down on the bunk. It was risky, but it was the only possible chance.'

There was a silence, then Race asked: 'What happened to the first bullet fired at Doyle by the girl?'.

'I think it went into the table. There is a recently made hole there. I think Doyle had time to dig it out with a penknife and fling it through the window. He had, of course, a spare cartridge, so that it would appear that only two shots had been fired.'

Cornelia sighed. 'They thought of everything,' she said. 'It's—horrible!'

Poirot was silent. But it was not a modest silence. His eyes seemed to be saying: 'You are wrong. They didn't allow for Hercule Poirot.'

Aloud he said, 'And now, Doctor, we will go and have a word with your patient.'

Chapter Thirty

It was very much later that evening that Hercule Poirot came and knocked on the door of a cabin.

A voice said 'Come in' and he entered.

Jacqueline de Bellefort was sitting in a chair. In another chair, close against the wall, sat the big stewardess.

Jacqueline's eyes surveyed Poirot thoughtfully. She made a gesture towards the stewardess.

'Can she go?'

Poirot nodded to the woman and she went out. Poirot drew up her chair and sat down near Jacqueline. Neither of them spoke. Poirot's face was unhappy.

In the end it was the girl who spoke first.

'Well,' she said, 'it is all over! You were too clever for us, Monsieur Poirot.'

Poirot sighed. He spread out his hands. He seemed strangely dumb.

'All the same,' said Jacqueline reflectively, 'I can't really see that you had much proof. You were quite right, of course, but if we'd bluffed you out——'

'In no other way, Mademoiselle, could the thing have happened.'

'That's proof enough for a logical mind, but I don't believe it would have convinced a jury. Oh, well—it can't be helped. You sprang it all on Simon, and he went down like a ninepin. He just lost his head utterly, poor lamb, and admitted everything.' She shook her head. 'He's a bad loser.'

'But you, Mademoiselle, are a good loser.'

She laughed suddenly—a queer, gay, defiant little laugh.

'Oh, yes, I'm a good loser all right.' She looked at him.

She said suddenly and impulsively: 'Don't mind so much, Monsieur Poirot! About me, I mean. You do mind, don't you?'

'Yes, Mademoiselle.'

'But it wouldn't have occurred to you to let me off?'

Hercule Poirot said quietly, 'No.'

She nodded her head in quiet agreement.

'No, it's no use being sentimental. I might do it again. . . . I'm not a safe person any longer. I can feel that myself. . . .' She went on broodingly: 'It's so dreadfully easy—killing people. And you begin to feel that it doesn't matter . . . that it's only *you* that matters! It's dangerous—that.'

She paused, then said with a little smile: 'You did your best for me, you know. That night at Assuan—you told me not to open my heart to evil. . . . Did you realise then what was in my mind?'

He shook his head.

'I only knew that what I said was true.'

'It was true. I could have stopped, then, you know. I nearly did. . . . I could have told Simon that I wouldn't go on with it. . . . But then perhaps——'

She broke off. She said: 'Would you like to hear about it? From the beginning?'

'If you care to tell me, Mademoiselle.'

'I think I want to tell you. It was all very simple really. You see, Simon and I loved each other. . . .'

It was a matter-of-fact statement, yet, underneath the lightness of her tone, there were echoes. . . .

Poirot said simply: 'And for you love would have been enough, but not for him.'

'You might put it that way, perhaps. But you don't quite understand Simon. You see, he's always wanted money so dreadfully. He likes all the things you get with money—horses and yachts and sport—nice things all of them, things a man ought to be keen about. And he'd never been able to have any of them. He's awfully simple, Simon is. He wants things just as a child wants them—you know—terribly.

'All the same he never tried to marry anybody rich and horrid. He wasn't that sort. And then we met—and—and that sort of settled things. Only we didn't see when we'd be able to marry. He'd had rather a decent job, but he'd lost it. In a way it was his own fault. He tried to do something smart over money, and got found out at once. I don't believe

215

he really meant to be dishonest. He just thought it was the sort of thing people did in the City.'

A flicker passed over her listener's face, but he guarded his tongue.

'There we were, up against it; and then I thought of Linnet and her new country house, and I rushed off to her. You know, Monsieur Poirot, I loved Linnet, really I did. She was my best friend, and I never dreamed that anything would ever come between us. I just thought how lucky it was she was rich. It might make all the difference to me and Simon if she'd give him a job. And she was awfully sweet about it and told me to bring Simon down to see her. It was about then you saw us that night at Chez Ma Tante. We were making whoopee, although we couldn't really afford it.'

She paused, sighed, then went on: 'What I'm going to say now is quite true, Monsieur Poirot. Even though Linnet is dead, it doesn't alter the truth. That's why I'm not really sorry about her, even now. She went all out to get Simon away from me. That's the absolute truth! I don't think she even hesitated for more than about a minute. I was her friend, but she didn't care. She just went baldheaded for Simon. . . .

'And Simon didn't care a damn about her! I talked a lot to you about glamour, but of course that wasn't true. He didn't want Linnet. He thought her good-looking but terribly bossy, and he hated bossy women! The whole thing embarrassed him frightfully. But he did like the thought of her money.

'Of course I saw that . . . and at last I suggested to him that it might be a good thing if he—got rid of me and married Linnet. But he scouted the idea. He said, money or no money, it would be hell to be married to her. He said his idea of having money was to have it himself—not to have a rich wife holding the purse strings. "I'd be a kind of damned Prince Consort," he said to me. He said, too, that he didn't want anyone but me. . . .

'I think I know when the idea came into his head. He said one day: "If I'd any luck, I'd marry her and she'd die in about a year and leave me all the boodle." And then a queer startled look came into his eyes. That was when he first thought of it. . . .

'He talked about it a good deal, one way and another—about how convenient it would be if Linnet died. I said it was an awful idea, and then he shut up about it. Then, one day, I found him reading up all about arsenic. I taxed him with it then, and he laughed and said: "Nothing venture, nothing have! It's about the only time in my life I shall be near to touching a fat lot of money."

'After a bit I saw that he'd made up his mind. And I was terrified—simply terrified. Because, you see, I realised that he'd never pull it off. He's so childishly simple. He'd have no kind of subtlety about it—and he's got no imagination. He would probably have just bunged arsenic into her and assumed the doctor would say she'd died of gastritis. He always thought things would go right.

'So I had to come into it, too, to look after him. . . .'

She said it very simply but in complete good faith. Poirot had no doubt whatever that her motive had been exactly what she said it was. She herself had not coveted Linnet Ridgeway's money, but she had loved Simon Doyle, had loved him beyond reason and beyond rectitude and beyond pity.

'I thought and I thought—trying to work out a plan. It seemed to me that the basis of the idea ought to be a kind of two-handed alibi. You know—if Simon and I could somehow or other give evidence against each other, but actually that evidence would clear us of everything. It would be easy enough for me to pretend to hate Simon. It was quite a likely thing to happen under the circumstances. Then, if Linnet was killed, I should probably be suspected, so it would be better if I was suspected right away. We worked out details little by little. I wanted it to be so that, if anything went wrong, they'd get me and not Simon. But Simon was worried about me.

'The only thing I was glad about was that I hadn't got to do *it*. I simply couldn't have! Not go along in cold blood and kill her when she was asleep! You see, I hadn't forgiven her—I think I could have killed her face to face, but not the other way. . . .

'We worked everything out carefully. Even then, Simon went and wrote a J in blood which was a silly melodramatic thing to do. It's just the sort of thing he *would* think of! But it went off all right.'

Poirot nodded.

'Yes. It was not your fault that Louise Bourget could not sleep that night. . . . And afterwards, Mademoiselle?'

She met his eyes squarely.

'Yes,' she said 'it's rather horrible isn't it? I can't believe that I—did that! I know now what you meant by opening your heart to evil. . . . You know pretty well how it hap-

pened. Louise made it clear to Simon that she knew. Simon
got you to bring me to him. As soon as we were alone
together he told me what had happened. He told me what
I'd got to do. I wasn't even horrified. I was so afraid—
so deadly afraid. . . . That's what murder does to you.
Simon and I were safe—quite safe—except for this miserable
blackmailing French girl. I took her all the money we could
get hold of. I pretended to grovel. And then, when she
was counting the money, I—did it! It was quite easy. That's
what's so horribly, horribly frightening about it. . . . It's so
terribly easy. . . .

'And even then we weren't safe. Mrs. Otterbourne had
seen me. She came triumphantly along the deck looking for
you and Colonel Race. I'd no time to think. I just acted like
a flash. It was almost exciting. I knew it was touch or go
that time. That seemed to make it better. . . .'

She stopped again.

'Do you remember when you came into my cabin afterwards? You said you were not sure why you had come. I
was so miserable—so terrified. I thought Simon was going to
die. . . .'

'And I—was hoping it,' said Poirot.

Jacqueline nodded.

'Yes, it would have been better for him that way.'

'That was not my thought.'

Jacqueline looked at the sternness of his face.

She said gently: 'Don't mind so much for me, Monsieur
Poirot. After all, I've lived hard always, you know. If we'd
won out, I'd have been very happy and enjoyed things and
probably should never have regretted anything. As it is—
well, one goes through with it.'

She added: 'I suppose the stewardess is in attendance to
see I don't hang myself or swallow a miraculous capsule of
prussic acid as people always do in books. You needn't be
afraid! I shan't do that. It will be easier for Simon if I'm
standing by.'

Poirot got up. Jacqueline rose also. She said with a sudden
smile: 'Do you remember when I said I must follow my
star? You said it might be a false star. And I said: "That
very bad star, that star fall down."'

He went out on to the deck with her laughter ringing in his
ears.

Chapter Thirty-one

It was early dawn when they came into Shellâl. The rocks came down grimly to the water's edge.

Poirot murmured: '*Quel pays sauvage!*'

Race stood beside him. 'Well,' he said, 'we've done our job. I've arranged for Richetti to be taken ashore first. Glad we've got him. He's been a slippery customer, I can tell you. Given us the slip dozens of times.'

He went on: 'We must get hold of a stretcher for Doyle. Remarkable how he went to pieces.'

'Not really,' said Poirot. 'That boyish type of criminal is usually intensely vain. Once prick the bubble of their self-esteem and it is finished! They go to pieces like children.'

'Deserves to be hanged,' said Race. 'He's a cold-blooded scoundrel. I'm sorry for the girl—but there's nothing to be done about it.'

Poirot shook his head.

'People say love justifies everything, but that is not true. . . . Women who care for men as Jacqueline cares for Simon Doyle are very dangerous. It is what I said when I saw her first. "She cares too much, that little one!" It is true.'

Cornelia Robson came up beside him.

'Oh,' she said, 'we're nearly in.' She paused a minute or two, then added, 'I've been with her.'

'With Mademoiselle de Bellefort?'

'Yes. I felt it was kind of awful for her boxed up with that stewardess. Cousin Marie's very angry, though, I'm afraid.'

Miss Van Schuyler was progressing slowly down the deck towards them. Her eyes were venomous.

'Cornelia,' she snapped, 'you've behaved outrageously. I shall send you straight home.'

Cornelia took a deep breath. 'I'm sorry, Cousin Marie, but I'm not going home. I'm going to get married.'

'So you've seen sense at last,' snapped the old lady.

Ferguson came striding round the corner of the deck. He said: 'Cornelia, what's this I hear? It's not true!'

'It's quite true,' said Cornelia. 'I'm going to marry Dr. Bessner. He asked me last night.'

'And why are you going to marry him?' asked Ferguson furiously. 'Simply because he's rich?'

'No, I'm not,' said Cornelia indignantly. 'I like him. He's kind, and he knows a lot. And I've always been interested in sick folks and clinics, and I shall have just a wonderful life with him.'

'Do you mean to say,' asked Mr. Ferguson incredulously, 'that you'd rather marry that disgusting old man than Me?'

'Yes, I would. You're not reliable! You wouldn't be at all a comfortable sort of person to live with .And he's *not* old. He's not fifty yet.'

'He's got a stomach,' said Mr. Ferguson venomously.

'Well, I've got round shoulders,' retorted Cornelia. 'What one looks like doesn't matter. He says I really could help him in his work, and he's going to teach me all about neurosis.'

She moved away.

Ferguson said to Poirot: 'Do you think she really means that?'

'Certainly.'

'She prefers that pompous old bore to me?'

'Undoubtedly.'

'The girl's mad,' declared Ferguson.

Poirot's eyes twinkled.

'She is a woman of an original mind,' he said. 'It is probably the first time you have met one.'

The boat drew in to the landing-stage. A cordon had been drawn round the passengers. They had been asked to wait before disembarking.

Richetti, dark-faced and sullen, was marched ashore by two engineers.

Then, after a certain amount of delay, a stretcher was brought. Simon Doyle was carried along the deck to the gangway.

He looked a different man—cringing, frightened, all his boyish insouciance vanished.

Jacqueline de Bellefort followed. A stewardess walked beside her. She was pale but otherwise looked much as usual. She came up to the stretcher.

'Hullo, Simon!' she said.

He looked up at her quickly. The old boyish look came back to his face for a moment.

'I messed it up,' he said. 'Lost my head and admitted everything! Sorry, Jackie. I've let you down.'

She smiled at him then. 'It's all right, Simon,' she said. 'A fool's game, and we've lost. That's all.'

She stood aside. The bearers picked up the handles of the stretcher. Jacqueline bent down and tied the lace of her shoe. Then her hand went to her stocking top and she straightened up with something in her hand.

There was a sharp explosive 'pop.'

Simon Doyle gave one convulsed shudder and then lay still.

Jacqueline de Bellefort nodded. She stood for a minute, pistol in hand. She gave a fleeting smile at Poirot.

Then, as Race jumped forward, she turned the little glittering toy against her heart and pressed the trigger.

She sank down in a soft huddled heap.

Race shouted: 'Where the devil did she get that pistol?'

Poirot felt a hand on his arm. Mrs. Allerton said softly, 'You—knew?'

He nodded. 'She had a pair of these pistols. I realised that when I heard that one had been found in Rosalie Otterbourne's handbag the day of the search. Jacqueline sat at the same table as they did. When she realised that there was going to be a search, she slipped it into the other girl's handbag. Later she went to Rosalie's cabin and got it back, after having distracted her attention with a comparison of lipsticks. As both she and her cabin had been searched yesterday, it wasn't thought necessary to do it again.'

Mrs. Allerton said: 'You wanted her to take that way out?'

'Yes. But she would not take it alone. That is why Simon Doyle has died an easier death than he deserved.'

Mrs. Allerton shivered. 'Love can be a very frightening thing.'

'That is why most great love stories are tragedies.'

Mrs. Allerton's eyes rested upon Tim and Rosalie, standing side by side in the sunlight, and she said suddenly and passionately: 'But thank God, there is happiness in the world.'

'As you say, Madame, thank God for it.'

Presently the passengers went ashore.

Later the bodies of Louise Bourget and Mrs. Otterbourne were carried off the *Karnak*.

Lastly the body of Linnet Doyle was brought ashore, and all over the world wires began to hum, telling the public that Linnet Doyle, who had been Linnet Ridgeway, the famous, the beautiful, the wealthy Linnet Doyle was dead.

Sir George Wode read about it in his London club, and Sterndale Rockford in New York, and Joanna Southwood in

Switzerland, and it was discussed in the bar of the Three Crowns in Malton-under-Wode.

And Mr. Burnaby said acutely: 'Well, it doesn't seem to have done her much good, poor lass.'

But after a while they stopped talking about her and discussed instead who was going to win the Grand National. For, as Mr. Ferguson was saying at that minute in Luxor, it is not the past that matters but the future.

THE END

Agatha Christie

The most popular and prolific writer of detective fiction ever known, her intricately plotted whodunits are enjoyed by armchair crime-solvers everywhere.

They Do It With Mirrors
Hercule Poirot's Christmas
Elephants Can Remember
The Hound of Death
The Murder of Roger Ackroyd
Mrs McGinty's Dead
Cards on the Table

After the Funeral
Murder on the Orient Express
The Sittaford Mystery
Endless Night
Nemesis
Passenger to Frankfurt
Hickory Dickory Dock
The Clocks

and many others

Agatha Christie is also the author of novels of romance and suspense under the name

Mary Westmacott

Absent in the Spring

The Burden
Giant's Bread

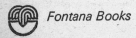 *Fontana Books*

Fontana Books

Fontana is a leading paperback publisher of fiction and non-fiction, with authors ranging from Alistair MacLean, Agatha Christie and Desmond Bagley to Solzhenitsyn and Pasternak, from Gerald Durrell and Joy Adamson to the famous Modern Masters series.

In addition to a wide-ranging collection of internationally popular writers of fiction, Fontana also has an outstanding reputation for history, natural history, military history, psychology, psychiatry, politics, economics, religion and the social sciences.

All Fontana books are available at your bookshop or newsagent; or can be ordered direct. Just fill in the form and list the titles you want.

FONTANA BOOKS, Cash Sales Department, G.P.O. Box 29, Douglas, Isle of Man, British Isles. Please send purchase price, plus 8p per book. Customers outside the U.K. send purchase price, plus 10p per book. Cheque, postal or money order. No currency.

NAME (Block letters)

ADDRESS

While every effort is made to keep prices low, it is sometimes necessary to increase prices on short notice. Fontana Books reserve the right to show new retail prices on covers which may differ from those previously advertised in the text or elsewhere.